ENTICE
EAGLE ELITE BOOK 3

by
Rachel Van Dyken

Entice
Eagle Elite Book 3
by Rachel Van Dyken

This is a work of fiction. Names, places, characters, and events are fictitious in every regard. Any similarities to actual events and persons, living or dead, are purely coincidental. Any trademarks, service marks, product names, or named features are assumed to be the property of their respective owners, and are used only for reference. There is no implied endorsement if any of these terms are used. Except for review purposes, the reproduction of this book in whole or part, electronically or mechanically, constitutes a copyright violation.

ENTICE
Copyright © 2014 RACHEL VAN DYKEN
ISBN 13: 978-1499343069
ISBN: 149934306X
Cover Art Designed by P.S. Cover Design

PROLOGUE

Chase

I'd always wondered what it would be like — to sacrifice yourself so another person could live. It wasn't like I was morbid or anything, but in my line of work it was just a daily reality. You don't work for the mafia and not think about it. Death was at your door constantly. Shit, it practically camped there.

I'd just thought it would come knocking a little bit later in life, you know? Every muscle in my body tensed as the second gunshot rang out.

Funny how at the end of your life you think about the beginning. Even crazier? It was her smile that had first attracted me to her. The way her entire face lit up, the way her eyes said she'd eat me alive if I didn't watch it. Damn, but so many things changed over the course of a few weeks.

I don't even know how it happened, how she'd maneuvered her way into my soul, how she'd made it so that I was overcome with madness for her — a type of obsession that I never wanted to be done with. She had destroyed me, and in my destruction, I'd found my salvation.

I touched my chest and examined my fingers. My blood was wet and sticky. Slowly, I fell to my knees, I heard shouting around me. A foreign grunt came from my lips as my body slumped against the ground. Nixon came running, then Trace, and finally her, my tough as shit, Mil.

My wife.

And now… a widow.

"I'm s-sorry." My breaths were coming in sharp, as if there was too much pressure on my lungs to breathe. Every gasp hurt like the fires of hell. I was being choked by the pressure in my chest, pushing and tearing, just waiting to pull me into the fiery pit.

"Don't talk. You're going to be fine, Chase, you have to be fine!" Mil pressed her hand hard over mine. Tears splashed onto my chest — her tears. "Damn it, Chase! Fight!"

"It's not cold…" I sighed happily as the pain started to dissipate, leaving me in a state of shock. "It's so warm." And it was. Death was warm, not cold as I'd always thought.

Mil slapped me hard across the cheek. "And it's gonna get hotter than hell if you don't listen to me. You have to fight, Chase Winter. I refuse to live without you."

"Okay." I smiled. I would have probably rolled my eyes too, but moving anything more seemed too much of an effort. She would be fine. She was a fighter, after all. "Love you…" And then I succumbed to the blackness of my warm death. At least I knew, in those last few seconds, that for once in my life, I would have done nothing different.

Because every damn road had eventually led me to her, my wife. Going back? Hell no. Not a chance. Because life is about one thing. Love. And Mil? She was mine.

CHAPTER ONE

Entice: *To attract or tempt by offering pleasure or advantage. Origin: Middle English, possibly from set on fire.*

Chase

I looked in the mirror one last time. What the hell was I doing? What deranged lunatic had taken control of my body and said yes to that woman's proposition? The worst part was I couldn't even blame my *yes* on alcohol.

It wasn't as if Mil, the newest mafia boss for the De Lange family had drugged me. Hell, I wish. Instead, she'd simply asked me a question, albeit a stupid question.

But I'd actually answered her in the affirmative. Stupid mistake number one, followed by number two, which was obviously me keeping my word.

Which meant only one thing.

My broken heart had caused me to lose my mind.

"You ready?" Nixon knocked on the door and let himself in. He was dressed in a nice black Armani suit, looking every inch the mafia boss of the Abandonato family, while I just looked petrified and pissed. My reflection in the mirror was pale. Green eyes stared back at me accusingly, as if to say, you're the one who got us into this mess. Yeah, thanks. Got it. Fully aware of my many sins. Just add to the naughty list.

You'd think after all the hell Nixon and I had gone through these last few weeks, he would be the last person I wanted at my wedding. But he was family — my best friend. Even though he was with Trace, the love of my life. Shit, that was some messed-up love triangle. He'd gone so far as to fake his own death all in the name of saving our family and now... now, it seemed, was time for my sacrifice, my death. Pretty sure Mil would castrate me if she knew I was comparing marrying her to getting shot at.

"Shit, no." I pulled a flask out of my pocket and took a shaky swig. "What the hell was I thinking? What's wrong with me?" The one time I should have said no in my life and I'd said yes. I'd even shrugged and then laughed like it wasn't a big freaking deal!

Nixon shrugged, the ass, and then took a swig from my flask. "How am I to know the mind of my best friend, hmm? I thought you were joking."

"Does this look like a joke?" I jerked at my tie and let out a long string of curses that should have gotten me kicked out of the church.

"You can always back out," Nixon suggested, leaning against the door. The only thing he needed was a giant cigar sticking out of his cocky mouth and the look would be complete. His lip ring looked completely out of place with the black and white tux. Tattoos peeked out from under his collared shirt in a way that said F-off to anyone who stole a glance in his direction.

"And get stabbed in my sleep? Or worse yet? Feel like shit because I'm the only thing keeping Mil from marching down to a money lender — or even another family — and asking a favor."

Nixon sighed. "You don't have to sacrifice your own happiness just to keep the peace."

The air was thick with tension as we both fell silent. Because we both knew the ugly truth. The one time I had decided not to sacrifice my own happiness, I had made a gargantuan error, a lapse in judgment. I had allowed Trace, the love of my life, to slip through my fingers and land firmly within Nixon's grasp. Shit, I was still holding onto the idea that it had all been within my control. My fault. It was my fault.

"Nah, man." I shook my head. "I think I'll finally choose someone else over me. Besides, she only needs protection and money for a year. I can do anything for a year." *Inebriated, that is.*

At that exact moment Mil came storming into the room, color high. She wore a short white cocktail dress and threw her bouquet at my face. "You're late, jackass."

I caught the bouquet with a grimace and gently set it on the table next to me, while Mil's eyes sent a seething glare from me to Nixon and back to me. I itched to run in the opposite direction, those eyes, Mil's eyes, they saw too much, she knew too much.

Nixon choked out, "Famous last words."

I was doing the right thing? Wasn't I?

Not how I pictured my life going.

It was always Trace I'd seen at the end of the aisle — not a sworn enemy — and not the first girl I'd slept with in my entire life. Not my dead best friend's stepsister.

Not the future I had planned.

Not at all.

Hell.

I had to hand it to her though, she looked really pretty, the type of pretty that guys like to stare at but are afraid to touch. She was scary pretty, terrifyingly so.

Her pitch-black hair was curled in loose waves around

her face, her naturally tan skin brought out her bright blue eyes, and her sharp cheekbones were decorated with something pink and shimmery.

So maybe looking at her wouldn't be that awful.

But talking to her was a completely different issue. I'd probably end up chopping off my own ears by the time the marriage was annulled. Either that or begging Nixon to shoot me, not that it would be the first time I'd stared down the barrel of a gun with him smiling on the other end.

"Well?" I slowly held out my arm. "I hate to keep my future bride waiting."

Mil rolled her eyes and took my arm.

"Did you just hiss?"

"Depends." Her bright blue eyes met mine. "Did you just call me your future bride?"

"Um, yeah?" What else was I supposed to call her? Satan?

"Then I hissed," she said, nodding. "It's a business arrangement, Sleeping Beauty."

"Am I ever going to live that down?"

"Getting drunk and passing out on your own bed just because a girl rejected you? Probably not. Think of me as the yin to your yang, the ointment to your cut, the—"

"I think I get the picture." I held up my hand. "Let's just get this over with."

Mil gripped my arm. "Ready for the honeymoon, eh?" She slowly licked her lips and winked.

Holy hell, I was going to end up on Dateline. I was going to end up strangling my bride — in bed, and not Fifty Shades-style.

Shit.

CHAPTER TWO

Mil

I tried to keep the shaking at a minimum. After all, I was a mafia boss now, and a female one at that. The suits, as I liked to call them, could smell fear from a mile away, and I had a few hundred of them witnessing my death march toward matrimony.

It was the only way.

Chase knew it, I knew it. I would be the first woman to take hold of the De Lange family. One of the only two female bosses, and I was only twenty. Funny, I'd never thought life would end up this way.

My brother, my last remaining family, was dead. All that was left were a few aunts and uncles, who were either in prison or in hiding, and some cousins I hadn't spoken to in years. It was me. I was left to pick up the pieces of our heritage and I had exactly no money to do it. Which left me with one option.

Chase.

He probably hated me as much as I hated him, but

marriages could be based on a lot worse, and at least I respected him. I'd known it wouldn't end well when I'd seen the way he looked at Tracey, Nixon's girlfriend. But you can't help who you love, right? Years ago, I thought I loved Chase, but I'd also been sporting a side ponytail and thought Twinkies were one of the four basic food groups.

"You sure about this?" Chase whispered in my ear. My grip on his hand tightened. His breath caught against my face, making my knees feel weak. "You can just say no. You don't have to break off my hand in the process."

"Sorry." I cleared my throat and repeated, "Sorry." Only in a stronger voice the second time. That scared little fourteen-year-old was gone, and in her place, a woman who had been forced to grow up way faster than should have been necessary. A woman who single-handedly had been given the responsibility of redeeming her family name — the same family name she'd helped destroy.

CHAPTER THREE

Chase

I waited for Mil to say something, but it was like she was in another place. I snapped my fingers in front of her face as she shook her head and then licked her lips.

"I'm fine."

"Well, as long as you're fine," I said dryly.

She turned very slowly to face me. It was one of those moments guys have where you know you've pissed the girl off but the damage has already been done, so all you can really do is stand and wait for the damn bomb to go off and pray that the shrapnel doesn't imbed so deep into your man parts that you can't produce children later in life.

"Look." She released my hand and took a step forward. She was only a few inches shorter than me and hot as hell when she was pissed, not that I was going to actually say that out loud, lest she castrate me with one of her razor-sharp nails. "I said I'm fine, and I'm fine. Don't make this situation worse by being yourself, Chase."

"Myself?" I asked, momentarily thrown off by the way

her lips moved when covered with pale lip gloss.

"She means an ass," Nixon said, coming up from behind me and slapping me on the back. "So basically, just don't talk."

"Noted." I glared after Nixon and then turned back toward Mil. "And I'm sorry for teasing you. Clearly this isn't the right sort of…" I searched for a word. "Atmosphere?"

Nixon winced ahead of me and shook his head, a smirk forming on his lips. Yeah, jackass, laugh it up.

"For, uh…" I cleared my throat and tried to fix it, tried to make her feel better. "That sort of… banter."

"Banter?" Nixon mouthed in disbelief.

I flipped him the bird behind Mil's back so she wouldn't see. Didn't he realize how freaking hard this was for me? Not helping. Nothing he was doing was helping.

"It's fine," she said for the third or fourth time. By then I'd lost count.

Why was I always the guy that had to give the tough love? Was that my lot in life? To constantly be the bad guy who told someone to buck up, come hell or high water.

I held up my hand to Nixon. "Five minutes."

He nodded.

Mil's nostrils flared as I grabbed her forcefully by the elbow and led her toward the closest door, the bathroom to be exact.

When I locked the door and turned, I half-expected her to assault me with toothbrushes and toilet paper, but all she did was back away and sit on the floor, holding her hands to her chest while she took in deep breaths.

I sat down on the cold tile next to her and offered my hand.

She took it without reservation. Her skin was smooth but clammy. She shivered, her grip tightening in my hand each time her body gave an involuntary shudder.

We sat like that for a few minutes, neither of us really saying anything.

A knock came at the door. "You guys ready?" It was Nixon. He sounded anxious. It wasn't as if he was the one getting married.

"Honest." I licked my lips and gripped Mil's hand harder. "I won't let you down. I may be a lot of things, and I may be a terrible husband, since I'm still nursing a broken heart and all that, but I'll be loyal. I'll help you. I'll protect you. That's what family does. Broken heart or no broken heart."

"I don't need your heart," Mil whispered. "Just your gun, maybe some of your millions, and your balls — preferably both of them."

"Well, it may just be your lucky day!" I slapped my thighs with my hands and winked. "I'm in full possession of two."

"Lucky me." She laughed.

And suddenly, whatever humor had invaded my body left me to be replaced with absolute obsession at the way her laugh echoed across the bathroom. It was like hearing a symphony for the first time, all the moving parts of the instruments playing together yet separate to create such a haunting melody that a person was left speechless. Mil's laugh reminded me of that. It was deep, throaty, and when she let go, her face erupted from a pinched look to a dazzling smile that had me staring at her damn mouth like I'd never seen one before. I swallowed the dryness in my throat and kept watching — hell, as long as she didn't catch me staring, I'd stare all morning.

"Let's go." She stood and held her hand out to me. I took it, and tried not to look affected. It was probably all the whiskey I had snuck in before the ceremony. Sure, I had two balls, but really that was all I could offer.

The whole heart issue?

Well, let's just say, my heart had broken into a million pieces a few weeks ago, and I was still trying to decide if it was worth finding them again. After all, some things are better left broken.

CHAPTER FOUR

Nixon

"You look pale." I touched my girlfriend's face and noticed that she had dark circles under her eyes. I knew that she hadn't been sleeping for the past few weeks, ever since I'd miraculously come back to life. Things hadn't been easy for her.

Losing Chase.

Gaining Mil.

Losing Phoenix.

Damn, but there had been a lot of loss, and now Chase and Mil getting married was just one more thing causing her stress. She'd never come out and said it — but when you're in crazy, obsessive, I-will-die-for-you love, you know those things.

I noticed everything.

Like the way she tapped her foot when she was annoyed with me, or the soft moans that escaped her lips when I kissed her just below her neck, or the way she'd roll her eyes when she thought I wasn't looking — or even just the way her breathing would change depending on her mood.

"It's just weird."

Thank God, at least she was talking.

"What is?" I played dumb. Hell, I knew exactly what was going on in that pretty little head of hers, damn it, and I didn't like it. Freaking hated it.

Her eyes darted to her hands, and she shrugged and said, "Chase."

Hearing his name on her lips still made me want to commit murder. I hated to admit how many times I'd imagined his face on the other side of my gun in the past few weeks. He still longed for her. I'd even told him to cut it out with the puppy dog eyes. I knew it wasn't on purpose, but it was still irritating as hell. Up until Mil asked him for a favor, he'd been planning on leaving. Things were just easier without him being part of our weird triangle. And it wasn't as if he was leaving the family, just moving to the other side of town so he didn't have to see me and Trace go into the same bedroom at night, or eat breakfast across from us when her face was flush with pleasure.

If the positions had been switched, I probably would have run myself over with my car by now.

Either that or sailed to Europe and drowned my sorrows in enough wine to kill anyone who wasn't Sicilian.

"What about him?" I kept my voice from sounding angry, though it came out as more of a hoarse whisper than anything. I fought like hell to keep my hand from squeezing the life out of hers — I was a great actor when it came to the job, but when it came to Trace? I struggled. I was weak. Her love made me both weak and strong.

"He's getting married." The way Tracey said *married* made my entire body tense, as if she was going to be that one psycho who stood up in the middle of the ceremony and yelled, "I object!"

"Right." I nodded. I'd like to think I'd come a long way

with the whole anger-management thing. At least now I could be decent and ask questions without pulling out my gun first. "Does that upset you?" Wow, I was borderline channeling a therapist with that deep-as-shit question. I inwardly groaned.

"Do you know anything?" Trace's eyes pooled with tears. I lifted my hands in surrender.

"Trace, I—"

"I love you!" She all but shouted, causing people to look in our direction. I know I shouldn't have laughed, but I couldn't help it; her expression was so confused.

"I love you too," I said slowly, my smile fading as her eyes laced with more sadness. "So what is this about?"

Her nostrils flared just a bit as she lifted up her left hand.

I narrowed my eyes.

She pointed at her hand.

I kept staring. Did she cut herself or something? Hell, did she know I was packing and was pissed that I had a gun a few feet away from the priest? Or had Chase's nuptials caused her to lose her mind?

She pointed at her ring finger.

And then, I felt like an absolute idiot. "Oh!"

"Shh!" Tex nudged me then kicked me in the calf. We were all standing side by side waiting to go in to the ceremony, but Chase and Mil had yet to return.

"You mean you're..." I couldn't find the words. When had that ever happened? I was born to talk my way out of any and every situation. If the President of the United States needed me to sweet-talk a terrorist, I wouldn't even blink, but now? Nothing. Game over.

"She's not pregnant, you idiot." Mo hissed from behind me. "What I think she's trying to say, you know, without actually saying it—"

"Thanks, Mo," Trace grumbled.

"—is that she wants to get married." Mo grinned triumphantly. "So... grow a pair and put a ring on it."

Tex snickered behind me.

I lifted the back of my jacket to reveal both of my pistols.

The snickering stopped.

"Still the boss," I said.

"Still an ass," Mo sang.

"Or the devil," Tex added. "However you want to put it."

Trace gave me a sassy smile. "I was trying to be suggestive."

"Suggestive, huh?" I licked my lips and looked at her chest. "You sure that's what you meant?"

"I had a plan." She grinned. "Suggestive first, seduction next—"

"Unplanned pregnancy to trap mob boss, third." Tex coughed.

"I'm sorry." Mo released his arm. "I can't walk down the aisle with this ass hat. Change partners? Anyone? Anyone?" she called.

"Get in line." I nudged my sister and looked behind her just in time to see Chase and Mil walk hand in hand toward the front of the line.

"I love you, baby." I kissed Trace's cheek. "We'll talk later, alright?"

She nodded and let me go while I took my position with Chase at the front of the church. I was his best man. Thank God it wasn't for his wedding with Trace. I would have had to be three sheets to the wind to stay good on that particular promise.

CHAPTER FIVE

Mil

I watched each of the couples slowly walk down the aisle. The entire church was lit with candles. It was meant to be beautiful — special, but all I felt was sick to my stomach and trapped — as if I was screaming and drowning, yet no one was able to offer help. No life raft. No savior. Just... nothingness.

"Ready?" Luca Nicolasi held out his elbow. I wanted to shake my head. I wanted to yell no and run screaming out of the church — but I couldn't be that girl. That choice was made for me. My dreams of a normal life? Stolen, just like my childhood. I pushed back the dark memories and regained control of my emotions. I was going to be okay. Everything was going to be fine.

"I'm ready," I said, more confident than I felt, taking Luca's arm with mine. Never would I have imagined that I'd be getting married at twenty, or that Luca, basically the most hated boss known to all the American mafia families, would be walking me down the aisle.

Well, at least I had evil on my side; that had to be good, right? Nobody would try to shoot me as I made my way toward Chase.

I took one step then another. People stood. Everyone was wearing black. Funny, because it really fit my mood. Forced smiles, undying loyalty, suspicion, riches — this was my life.

Every girl imagined marrying someone she loved — a prince or a knight in shining armor. Not the villain who has an A-plus in torturing information out of people, and not the one person who was the equivalent to the final nail-in-the-coffin called life. By marrying him, I was solidifying myself within the family. The only escape for me would be death — and I had a choking feeling it would be sooner rather than later. After all, it was only a matter of time before the truth about my family was discovered.

In that moment, I realized I wasn't a bride on her wedding day — I was a prisoner on death row, and they'd just unlocked my cell. By saying *yes* I was securing my fate. The way I saw it, marrying Chase just prolonged the inevitable. Funny, because death wasn't something brides usually contemplated while taking those final steps to the altar — but hell if I didn't reek of it.

I stopped directly in front of Chase and licked my lips. His clear green eyes looked about two seconds away from bursting into flames. Either he was really pissed or — nah, I couldn't even entertain the thought of him being attracted to me. At least I knew with Chase my heart was safe — because his had been spoken for a long time ago, and I knew it would take a lot more than a desperate girl in a wedding dress to put the mess that was Chase Winter back together again.

"Who gives this woman?" the priest asked.

"I do," Luca said with a menacing grin. "I give her." As he bent over to kiss my cheek, he whispered in my ear. "I give, I take, I steal, I destroy — never forget who truly pulls the strings, my dear. I will be watching." He pulled back and sighed as if he hadn't just threatened my life, and took a seat in the front row. I couldn't shaking as I put my hand in Chase's grasp.

His eyes darted down to our hands. Quickly, he pulled me closer to his side and whispered so his lips were touching my ear. "I've got this. I've got you, Mil."

It was the first time in months I'd actually felt safe.

CHAPTER SIX

Chase

She was shaking like a damn leaf. Had it really been necessary for Luca to scare her half to death on her wedding day? Didn't she, of all people, deserve a break? I tried to focus on keeping myself calm as we recited our vows. What seemed like seconds passed, and then the announcement was made.

"I present to you Mr. And Mrs. Chase Abandonato." They had to use my legal name, rather than Winter. Damn, if it didn't feel weird hearing it out loud.

The audience, mostly filled with family who weren't currently serving prison time — and those who visited from Sicily — clapped and stood.

I raised Mil's hand into the air and forced a smile, just as my gaze fell on Trace. And just like that, I was done. No longer was I the one comforting Mil. I needed comfort. Damn, I needed something, because I was ready to put a gun to my head. Breathing suddenly became overrated as I watched Trace's teary smile.

Her. I'd always wanted it to be her.

Life wasn't merely unfair; it was unjust, uncontrollably bleak, and dark — because the only thing I'd ever wanted had been her, and I'd lost her, lost everything dear to me and gained another full responsibility. How shitty of a husband could I be? I mean, less than two minutes after saying I'd love and protect Mil with my life, and I wanted to end it — all because Trace had smiled at me.

"Let's go." Mil tugged my hand, pulling my gaze away from Trace's and back to all the smiling faces around me. No one knew the reason Mil and I were getting married. Nixon had fabricated such a ridiculously good story that even I would have believed it, had I not been living my own personal hell these past few months.

According to every person present at the wedding, Mil and I had reconnected at Phoenix's funeral, and the rest was history. Love at first sight and all that.

We walked arm-in-arm down the aisle, wordlessly gripping one another as if each of us was waiting for the other to be the first to crack. To hell with that. I wasn't going to show weakness — I couldn't. I'd messed up too much in the past few months. It was time to do my job regardless of my personal feelings in the matter. I had been slacking — I'd allowed a girl to get so deep under my skin that I'd forgotten what I was. A born killer, a made man, son of a very dead mafia boss — and husband to one of the De Lange leaders.

As far as Mil was concerned, I was it. I just needed to prove to her that I could take it — that I could push past my sorry-ass heartbreak and be the man she needed me to be, because after seeing the look of sheer terror on her face as she walked down the aisle, I had come to one conclusion. She was hiding something big. The pit of my stomach dipped — whatever that something was — it could very well get us all killed.

****

"Ten bucks says the only person not packing is Mil's grandma by marriage," Mo said once we'd all finished eating our dinner, which had basically been a painful process of chewing, swallowing, drinking unhealthy amounts of wine, and trying to stare at my plate to keep from looking at Trace, while my wife sat next to me. Hell had officially risen to earth, and I was smack-dab in the middle of it, trying my damnedest to remember how to swallow without choking — without dying a little bit inside each time I saw him touch her face. And trying not to feel like an ass when Mil caught me staring — again. I'd resolved about an hour ago to actually be the man she needed me to be, and I was already failing. Horribly. The second time I looked, Mo kicked at me under the table but accidently hit Tex instead, causing everyone to look up, which was probably why Mo had said what she had.

We all turned heads to look at the hundred-year-old woman. She was currently on her fourth glass of wine and looked to be about two seconds away from falling into her chicken cacciatore.

"Nope." Nixon shook his head. "It's always the ones you don't suspect. My money's on Grandma."

"I'll take that bet." Tex rose. "Seems like someone needs to fall on their own knife and all that. This has to be the most depressing wedding I've ever gone to, and that includes the fake one Mo made for her kittens when she was four."

"They lived happily ever after." Mo tilted her head into the air and narrowed her eyes.

Tex leaned down and tapped her on the nose. "Yes, if happily means they lived for five damn minutes before marching directly into oncoming traffic."

"I think the wedding reception just hit its low point," Mil muttered. "Save us, Tex. I beg you. Find the gun, and I'll give you a prize."

"Prize?" Tex's eyes lit up. "As in—"

"As in her new husband won't punch you in the face.

You're welcome. Hooray for prizes!" I did a fake punch into the air. "Now go create some excitement before Nixon starts picking people off with his semi-automatic."

Nixon rolled his eyes. "Right, like I'd even bring—"

"It's in the SUV," Trace answered, sounding bored. "Saw it when I took out my dress."

"Damn." He looked away.

Just then a very drunk-looking cousin, Vinnie, got up and took the microphone from the band. "Look here! I have a toast to the bride and groom!" Shrill feedback from the microphone pierced the air, and Vinnie staggered, seemed to struggle, but finally found his footing. The microphone stand wobbled and then fell onto the stage with a loud clang. In a rush to grab it, Vinnie tripped over the cord and landed flat on his ass with a loud "Oomph."

"For the love of God, save us all," I grumbled, pushing Tex toward Grandma. Hopefully that would provide us some entertainment even if it was just watching them talk. Right, that's how bad things had gotten.

We all sat at the table, the very depressing bridal party table, and watched as Tex slowly made his way toward the elderly woman.

"This won't end well," Trace said under her breath. "The man has the subtleness of a bomb."

"Exactly." Mo grinned from ear to ear. "I did say we needed entertainment, didn't I?"

"Mo..." Nixon warned.

"He cheated on me, Nixon. Let me have my fun," she said smoothly.

"He what?" Nixon roared, jumping to his feet. Curious stares pinned in our direction as Mo grabbed his hand and pulled him back to his seat.

I let out a low whistle. Dysfunctional didn't even begin to cover it.

"I've got this. You aren't the only one who knows how to

use his powers for evil, brother. Revenge is a bitch. Isn't that what they say, Trace?"

She looked guiltily down at her hands. Yeah, double meanings I could really do without. Hopefully, Mo wasn't going to get Tex shot at our wedding, not that I'd be against it. This was the first I'd heard of him cheating. Granted, Mo hadn't really been all that for sharing recently. She'd been as secretive as ever. Something told me it was for a reason, but I'd been too wrapped up in my own drama to even ask. How bad did I suck as a half-brother? Bad, real bad. On a scale of one to ten in the suckiness department, I'd be around an eleven.

Tex finally reached his unlucky target and sat down in the chair next to Grandma, his smile wide. I couldn't tell what he was saying, but his hands were all over the place, and then he set one hand on the old lady and winked.

"Oh, this isn't going to end well." Mo chuckled. "She hates being touched."

"It *is* Tex," I pointed out. "She could do a lot worse."

"Doubtful." Mo snorted, crossing her arms.

Holy shit, what the hell? I really had been living under my own personal rock somewhere. What had gone down? And how didn't I know about it?

I winced when Tex moved his other hand next to Grandma's leg. Probably wouldn't be a good time to tell him that she'd seen her fair share of murder. I almost closed my eyes when she looked down at his hand.

"Aw, shit." Nixon shook his head. "You had to challenge him, Mo."

Mo's face twisted into a murderous smile as she pointed and exclaimed, "Game. Set. Match!"

Grandma had Tex by the balls.

"Ouch!" This from Mil.

"Look, I know it's not me." I cringed when Tex's face twisted in pain. "But I can literally feel my sperm dying."

"That's too bad." Nixon smirked in my direction. "Because I was hoping to see little Chases running around now that you're married."

I didn't laugh.

Neither did anyone else.

Nixon immediately looked apologetic, but it didn't matter. It was done, he'd released those idiotic words out into the atmosphere. No take backs.

And it had officially gotten more awkward — didn't think that was possible, but there it was. The only sounds were those of Vinnie still trying to make his toast, and Tex's screams coupled with Mo's laughter. I was officially ready to call it a night.

I stood. "Let's go, Mil."

Wordless, she put her hand in mine as we said our goodbyes and walked out the door. Not once did I look at Trace or Nixon. It was as if the door was my only salvation. In walking out, I was leaving them and starting my own life. Hell, even if it ended in death, it would still be better than sitting on the sidelines while my best friend screwed the girl I loved.

Past tense.

My feet crossed the threshold. I paused. I hated that hesitation was becoming my new thing, but I had to know. Was she watching, or did she even freaking care?

I glanced over my shoulder.

They were gone.

And my answer was again made clear. So I walked forward and gripped Mil's hand a little tighter, damning my family to hell the entire freaking way.

CHAPTER SEVEN

Mil

If you asked me, rejection sucked worse than getting shot at, and I'd been shot at a lot. Chase's muscles tensed as we walked to the waiting SUV. Because of the seriousness of the situation, I'd turned down the opportunity for a vacation. Right. That was the last thing I needed, but Chase wouldn't have any of that, so we were stuck together for four days in the last place I wanted to be.

Vegas.

To be fair, it was close to fly to, and the cabin we were supposed to rent for the extended weekend had fallen through.

Our flight left tomorrow.

I had seven hours alone with the man before I was able to drink myself into a stupor on the plane. God help us all.

I stole a glance at Chase. It would be easier if he were ugly — unfortunately, he was a god masquerading as a mortal. He was so sexy that I swear it strained my eyes to look in his direction for periods longer than five seconds. Dark hair fell just below his ears, meeting a strong jaw line that was just as muscular as the rest of him. When he was pissed, that same muscle twitched like crazy. His teeth were a perfect white and almost looked predatory when he smiled. A large warm arm wrapped around my waist, and I was reminded all over again why I'd wanted him in the first place. Chase was anything but safe. In fact, he was damn hazardous to my health. But he was also loyal. And I needed loyal more than anything.

I knew whatever he learned from me — he'd take to his grave.

If he hadn't totally ruined my first sexual experience when I was fifteen, it's possible I'd like him — well, that and the whole fact that his heart wasn't even in his possession anymore. But maybe that was a good thing; it made what we both had to do easier. He killed, bribed, worked — and I stood by and let him.

"You okay?" Chase asked after he'd gotten into the car and buckled his seatbelt.

"Peachy."

"Don't say *peachy*, Mil. It doesn't suit you. Kinda scares the hell out of me."

"What do you want me to say, Chase?" I played with the radio, trying to fill the car with any kind of distracting noise. I'd even take classical music over the erratic beating of my own heart.

"That's just it, Mil." Chase pushed my hand away from the controls, pushed a few buttons, and turned to me as music began to filter throughout the car. "I'd rather you offend the shit out of me than ask me what the hell I want you to do. Don't ask, Mil. Be who you are. Be a bitch. Yell, scream, just don't be..." A muscle ticked in his jaw as he ground his teeth together. "Don't be submissive, okay?" He turned the ignition over and the SUV growled to life.

I burst out laughing.

"What?" He scowled, rolling his eyes.

"Thought guys liked that sorta thing," I said in a throaty voice, then gave him a once-over.

"Only the ones who got something to prove, and sweetheart, I'm pretty sure I've proved over and over and over and over—"

"Stop saying *over* or I swear I'll jump out of a moving vehicle."

"—and over…" he ignored me. "…again."

He pulled out of the church parking lot and drove toward the hotel, which rhymed with hell. Perfect.

"Pretty sure that last time you tried to rock my world, it went very badly," I pointed out just to spite him.

The car slammed to a stop.

"Are you trying to kill us?" I yelled, slamming my hand against the dashboard while my seatbelt nearly choked me to death.

"Let's get one thing straight, Mil." The light was green, but Chase was staring at me as if he had all the time in the world; a slow burn invaded his eyes as he met my gaze. "I didn't know what the hell I was doing then, but now…" His voice trailed off.

"Now?" I challenged in the most confident voice I could manage. "What? You've been practicing? Is that it, Chase?"

With his violent twist of the steering wheel, the SUV turned so abruptly I would have hit my head against the dashboard had my seatbelt not been on. We came to a sudden stop in the middle of an empty gravel parking lot. Dust burst into the air all around us. Chase rammed the gearshift up and grabbed me by the back of my head before I even realized he was moving. All I could do was gasp as our lips collided.

And then his tongue was in my mouth.

And I was dying.

Little bits and pieces of my soul, my heart, my defenses crumbled at each coax, at each touch of his tongue, his lips. His hands moved into my hair and tugged, not hard but enough to hurt. A moan escaped from the back of my throat, and I leaned into the kiss, moving my lips beneath his. It was like his mouth was coaxing the life out of me, beckoning my soul, and I was powerless to stop the flood of emotion he demanded I give. But how could I forget? That's how it had always been with Chase.

He was like an addiction, a very very bad one. I'd always been told that if you feed something it grows. With Chase, I'd done nothing of the sort, but it hadn't mattered, because after one taste... my body had remembered. It had kept Chase in the most secret parts of my subconscious and hidden him until it was time. The clock had struck midnight. I. Was. Screwed.

All too soon his mouth left mine. He released his hold on me and stared into my eyes. "Practice makes perfect."

"R-right." I couldn't find my voice. Who was that weak-minded female speaking? Me? Really? Where the hell was my gun when I needed it?

"Oh, and Mil?" He tugged my hair again, gentler this time, and winked. "Didn't take you for a moaner."

"Ass." I jerked back and crossed my arms.

"Hey!" He lifted his hands into the air. "Anytime you wanna moan while I pull your hair, fine with me. Just don't forget my name."

"Huh?" I really should learn to stop responding to the man.

"My name," he said just above a whisper. "I want you to say it."

"Because I might forget?" Not wanting to show him that he affected me with his dangerous words, I slumped even lower in my seat. I hated that he was winning again and that I felt like the weak one.

"Nah." He put the car back in drive. "Because it sounds so damn good coming from those swollen lips."

For the first time in twenty years, I was absolutely speechless for more than ten minutes. Every time I tried to open my mouth to speak no words would come — maybe I was in deeper than I'd realized. Maybe I wasn't as prepared for what had to be done. Those were my last thoughts as Chase turned off the SUV. The last words in my head as I touched my lips with my hand and memorized the burn of what it had felt like to have his mouth on mine.

Such a good burn. I craved the burn. I'd always been attracted to danger. And Chase? His very name was the definition of the word.

"Ready, wife?" Chase nudged me with his elbow in the most unromantic way known to humanity.

"Ready," I croaked. But I wasn't. I wouldn't ever be. Because I hadn't predicted this. In every possible outcome, the answer had been the same.

Marry Chase — fix family.

Never had the odds turned against me.

But I felt the twist. I felt the turn in my gut. Hell, I felt it in my chest as I watched him hop out of the car and grab his bags.

He could possibly own me — and I'd let him. Because as we walked wordlessly into the hotel lobby, as the lights burned my eyes and caused me to squint, I'd never felt so alive.

And it was all because Chase Winter had not only scolded me, but kissed me, put me in my place, and caused me to forget my own address.

I blinked a few times then squeezed my eyes shut.

"Mil? You wanna room upgrade?" came Chase's voice.

I shook my head no.

He upgraded anyway.

The ding of the elevator came too soon. The sliding of the key card too fast. And suddenly the room was too hot.

And I was alone with my husband.

Never had I imagined I'd be so attracted.

Let that be a reminder to any woman out there — math

can fail you, logic will lead you in the opposite direction. Numbers? Not always solid. But your heart? That's the biggest failure of all, because just when you've told yourself it's safely in your keeping, it gets freaking stolen by a guy with green eyes and dark hair.

The sound of the door clicking shut almost had me bolting for the window. And then every ounce of air was sucked out of the suite. Chase turned. His eyes met mine, demanding, craving, lusting. I clenched my fists, letting my nails bite into my flesh.

My heartbeat pounded hard against my neck, making me dizzy. And it had only been a few hours.

Hell.

CHAPTER EIGHT

Chase

I'd just redefined the meaning of coming on too strong. Hell, that woman made me want to react. Every single word that came out of her mouth caused a gut instinct reaction. I hadn't planned on kissing her; it had just happened. I wasn't aware that I no longer controlled my body or my thoughts where she was concerned. But I wasn't going to apologize. It had been a damn good kiss. She'd tasted warm, like a hot dessert that just came out of the oven. And I was a sucker for chocolate cake.

That mouth of hers was perfection. Clearly my mind had done me a favor by allowing me to forget just how soft her lips were. A man should never forget the way a woman tastes — and somehow I'd done it.

Never again.

I had planned on our kiss to feel frigid, cold, lifeless. Instead my body had responded with such heat that the entire drive to the hotel I'd gripped the steering wheel hard enough to pry it from the dash.

Thank God, she'd been kissed into silence, especially if that was how I reacted when she challenged me.

The only reason I even upgraded the room was to give us more space — being too close to her made me feel like a caged animal just waiting for the zookeeper to unlock the cage. I ran my hands through my hair in frustration and dropped our bags onto the ground.

"I, uh, I'm going to go get some ice." Small talk of epic proportions.

"Fine." Mil shrugged and grabbed the TV remote.

My eyes narrowed as she lay down on the bed, her entire demeanor screamed calm; whereas, I was contemplating how many ways I could dump ice in my pants without looking like I'd just had an accident.

"Whatever," I grumbled under my breath, grabbing the bucket and making my way down the hall. Call me paranoid, but even though we were staying at the Waldorf Astoria, I wasn't taking any chances. I kept my gun tucked into my pants and muttered curses under my breath the entire length of the hall toward the ice machine. I needed time to cool off, time to think, time to form a game plan.

Did we have to have sex? And what guy actually asked that on his wedding night? But that mouth, her mouth, I groaned as my mind tortured me with the memories of what she'd tasted like, what her mouth had felt like pressed against mine. How was it possible to be so intrigued by someone else when I knew that no one would ever captivate me the way Trace had? My body clearly didn't have trouble with it. That much I was painfully aware of.

Shit.

I wiped my forehead with the back of my hand. I needed a solid minute or several of them before going back into that room. The last thing Mil needed was for me to go back in there so damn turned on I had trouble walking. May as well wave a flag or something. It was beyond obvious, not to mention irritating.

By the time I reached the ice machine, I wanted to shoot so many holes through it that I was already regretting the fact that I'd brought my gun. Pretty sure destroying hotel property would land me in jail.

Groaning, I leaned my forehead against the machine and took a few deep breaths.

Just as I was about to press the button, the hair on the back of my neck stood on edge. It was quiet, too quiet. The elevator dinged, and then I heard some shuffling, footsteps. The normal hotel guest would be talking, or at least purposefully walking. Quietly, I ducked into the corner and looked down the hall. Two men in suits were quietly walking and talking. Nothing out of the ordinary. But that's the problem. It's never the creepers I worry about. But normal people? Men in suits? People who looked like they belong — those are the real threats. They're the moms and dads taking their kids to school in the sick SUV. The clean cut ones were a pain in my ass. I watched, I waited. They stopped in front of my room.

Shit.

The tall one on the right seemed to be in charge. He motioned for the other to step aside as he pulled out his gun and moved to the front of the door. Wow, a silencer. How predictable. The taller one knocked on the door and said in a low baritone, "Security."

I rolled my eyes. Security, my ass.

They weren't my men. They sure as hell weren't familiar. I reached for my Glock and held it behind me, making my way casually down the hall. As I approached, they both looked up and offered easy smiles, which meant one thing.

They weren't there for me. They didn't even know who I was.

They were there for Mil.

I gave them a cocky grin, counting the seconds until I

could punch in their shit-eating faces. On the plus side, I could take out all my pent-up frustration on them, poor bastards.

The door handle twisted, gaining their attention. With a swift thrust of my gun, I knocked the first one out and then used my elbow to get the other guy in the face. He shook it off as if I'd barely touched him.

Of course, tonight of all nights, when all I really wanted was peace and quiet and possibly to let out some sexual frustration — I'd be stuck with someone who, by the feel and looks of it, clearly had had his fair share of training in the ring.

With a grunt he pushed me against the hallway wall, ramming his fist into the side of my face. After three hits, I was able to finally duck on the fourth, so his hand hit the wall. And just like that, I knew the boxer's choreography. His dance, if you will. Right hook, uppercut, right hook, left. I landed a double jab to his stomach and then kneed him a few times before he toppled over, compliments of Muay Thai, bitch. With a grunt, his hand clamped around my wrist, knocking my gun to the floor. I kicked him again then slammed down my arms on his grasp around my waist, momentarily giving me enough time to scramble to my pant leg so I could grab my knife.

We danced around one another. He smirked, throwing his gun and pulling out his own knife. So it was going to be like that, cocky piece of work. He lunged first. I let the blade get within inches of my face before moving to the right and using his momentum to throw him over my shoulder and onto the carpet. I got on top of him and punched him repeatedly in the face until blood covered his smirk. A tooth went flying as he spat blood from his mouth.

"You're going to have to kill me." He spit out some more blood as he knocked his head against mine.

Groaning, I fell to the side as we switched positions. But I still had my knife. When he came down a second time, I held up the blade so it went into his palm. He howled in pain and fell back, giving me enough time to grab the knife he'd dropped and thrust it into his chest as the weight of his body fell back on top of me.

I had a love and hate relationship with knives.

I loved the control they gave me.

But I hated that, as gravity caused his body to slide to the handle of the knife, I could see the life leave his eyes, his soul finally finding rest. With a grunt, I pushed him off of me just in time to see the other guy wake up and scramble for the extra gun.

I moved as fast as I could and jumped on top of him, but his gun wasn't trained on me. It was trained on himself.

I held up my hands. "I don't think we've met. I'm Chase Abandonato, and you are?" I asked in a calm voice slowly leaning away from him. His hand shook as he held the gun to his chin. Why wasn't he putting up a fight? I looked down, and that's when I saw, somehow in the fight his leg had twisted. No way could he win against me. Even with a gun, he would most likely die trying.

Blood poured from the guy's face as he looked up at me and answered, "A dead man."

One gun shot.

His body slumped to the floor in a bloody heap as blood splattered all over the wall behind him. It was a complete mess. Blood began to pool at my feet.

"Son of a bitch." I wiped my hands on my pants and gazed back at the door, hoping Mil hadn't witnessed the entire thing.

Her face was pale, her lower lip trembled as she leaned against the door. Shit, she needed to sit down before she passed out.

"I'm fine." She waved me off once I reached her. "I'm fine. I mean…" She swallowed. "I'm good."

"Stop saying you're fine and good before I take you to the damn hospital." I held out my hand. "Cell phone. Now."

Eyes still trained on the dead bodies in the hall, she handed me the phone from the nearby desk and crossed her arms, huddling into her own body.

I dialed Nixon; he answered on the first ring. "Well, that was fast."

"Not the time, Nixon," I said in a low voice. "Look, we've got a situation."

"Alright." His voice took on a business tone. "How many?"

"Two dead."

"By you?"

"One by me, the other... self inflicted."

"Identification?" I could hear the car roaring to life as Nixon yelled orders to men in the background.

"Never seen them before. Let me ask Mil." I lowered the phone. "Mil." I didn't have time to be gentle with her, to coax her out of shock. I needed answers and I needed them fast. "You know them?" I pointed down at the bodies. "I need to know if you can ID them."

Her eyes watered with tears. She nodded her head and looked away. "My cousins." Her voice was barely a whisper. "Those are my cousins. I saw them a few years ago during Christmas break."

"Shit," I mumbled into the phone. Adrenaline was starting to leave my body. Every position I stood in caused a growing ache to radiate down my spine. "Nixon, it was the De Langes."

"Of course," he said in clipped tones. "They have such a nasty habit of trying to kill off their own blood — no respect, no—"

"Not the time, Nixon. Just get your ass down here. Now."

"I'll call Sergio." The phone went dead.

We only called in Sergio when things went above our heads. Shit, above our heads? I looked down the hall. Cameras. Not good. Hell yeah, we needed Sergio, because if this security footage got out, we were going to be front-page news, and I'd be spending my honeymoon in prison.

Thankfully we were in one of the penthouse suites. Only four rooms were on our level and none of the doors budged. I kept the door open so I could monitor the hall for any movement, praying the rooms were empty. If they weren't… there would be more bodies, and they would be innocent.

CHAPTER NINE

Mil

Yeah, I was fooling nobody. I tried to keep my teeth from chattering, but it was impossible. I'd killed before. I wasn't a stranger to death, but I'd never witnessed someone killing himself. It was… it was desperate, horror-inspiring. There was blood everywhere, on the walls, on Chase, on the floor. It was such a violent act. My brain couldn't wrap around or fathom why the same cousin who'd teased me about my crush on Justin Timberlake when I was sixteen would not only turn his gun on me, but on himself.

As a family, we'd never been close. We were the De Langes for crying out loud; we ate nails for breakfast and sold out to the highest bidder in order to keep the family in power and make money.

We were the ugly of the mafia, the desperate joke — never did it occur to me that my own family would be out for blood. That the very people I'd sworn to protect — had ordered a hit on me.

"Mil, sit down before I lose my damn mind." I felt

Chase's body wrap around mine. I took the comfort like a homeless person takes shelter in a storm. I shuddered as he pulled me against his chest. "Are you okay?"

"I've had better nights."

Chase's body shook with laughter. "Right, I mean, I knew our wedding night would be epic, but mainly because I figured the minute I got naked you'd pull a gun on me or something."

I smiled against his torn and bloody shirt. Pieces of muscled skin were visible through the holes; heat invaded my palms when I placed them on his chest and pulled back to look at him. "Thank you."

"Wow, you haven't shot me yet, and you've said thank you? Where's my wife and what have you done with her?"

My grin grew so wide I almost forgot how scared I was. "Yeah well, don't get used to it."

"Wouldn't dream of it," he whispered, his eyes trained on my mouth.

I leaned in first.

He met me halfway.

Our lips were an inch apart, and then a knock sounded on the door. Chase motioned for me to be quiet and went to look through the peephole. With a muttered curse, he opened the door. "Sergio, worst timing ever."

"Says the guy with two dead bodies outside his door." A deep male voice said. A hint of an accent was audible, but hardly. Soon, the owner of the voice stepped into the room and held out his hand. "Sergio. And you must be the bride? Or the assassin?"

"Assassin." I pointed at Chase. "Bride." I pointed at myself.

"Pity." Sergio winked, his dark hair was pulled back into a low ponytail, pieces of it grazed his chin. He looked like he belonged in a medieval novel.

"Pardon?"

He shrugged. "I was hoping you were the assassin. It would make it so much easier on my conscience to steal you that way. But being already married..." He shook his head. "Really complicates things in my book."

"Why? Because you're such a rule follower?" I asked sarcastically.

"Damn you, Abandonato men." Sergio looked back at Chase. "Always stealing the women before I even get a chance to get in the fight."

"I'll make it easy on you," I said. "You would have lost. It's probably better for your ego that you weren't even in the ring."

"Ouch." Sergio laughed. "Lucky bastard." He pulled out his cell phone and pulled up a picture on his screen. "Is this the way the hall looked when you arrived?"

"Are you asking me?" I squinted at the picture.

"Women tend to pay more attention to detail." Sergio shrugged. "If I asked Chase what color the flowers were, he'd probably shrug and say, *there were flowers?*"

"Right." I nodded. "And yes, this is how it looked, though I think the flowers were poinsettias."

"Of course." Sergio slid the phone back into his pocket. "This particular hotel changes flowers depending on the season. I'll get my men on it." He walked toward the door. "I'll destroy the evidence on the cameras."

"Try not to kill anyone in the process," Chase added. "We have enough dead bodies."

"Haven't killed anyone in years. I may have forgotten how," Sergio joked. With another wink in my direction, he opened the door and left.

"He's—"

"A ghost." Chase finished. "According to you, he doesn't exist."

"Fine." I shivered and licked my lips. I think my body was still in shock because I suddenly felt exhausted, like I needed to sit down or lose complete control over my body.

Another knock.

This time the person identified himself. "It's Nixon."

Chase still checked the peephole to make sure and then opened the door wide. Nixon and Tex walked in with a few other men I didn't recognize. Nixon quickly instructed them in a low voice to help Sergio with anything he needed, the door soon clicked shut, the last vision I had was of a body getting put into something black.

This shit was real. I knew, because every time I blinked I imagined it would go away. But it didn't… If anything, it just made me even sicker to my stomach.

The door was closed. I was trapped in a room with the three remaining members of The Elect. My stepbrother had been part of their inner circle once — and he'd paid with his life. Though that was partially his fault. My father had gotten to him like he got to everyone. Now they were both dead, and I was left to pick up the pieces.

And now I'd been given no choice. I'd known I had a giant target on my back. I just wasn't aware my number would be up so soon.

"Mil." Nixon paced in front of me. His crystal blue eyes were like laser beams, making me want to shift in my seat. Light reflected off his lip ring with each tilt of his head. Finally, he pulled a chair from the desk and took a seat. He leaned forward, stretching his white t-shirt across his muscled and tattooed body. "I need to know."

"Know what?"

He chuckled once and then pulled out his gun, aiming it for my head. Shit.

"What the hell, man!" Chase took a step toward Nixon just as Tex's arms came around him, rendering him useless. Besides, the poor guy was probably ready to crumple after what he'd just been through.

"No games. No lies. We both know I'd shoot you without

hesitation. I've done it once. I'd do it again."

"Don't remind me." My voice shook. I swore I could still feel the pain of him shooting me in the leg last year when he'd thought I'd been double-crossing everyone. "What's the question again?"

Nixon smirked. "I've always liked you, Mil."

"Funny, I've always hated you." I smiled sweetly.

"Lies." Nixon waved the gun in the air and licked his lips. "Your own family wants you dead. That tells me one thing."

"They're pissed?" I offered.

"The De Langes are always pissed." This from Tex.

I nodded in agreement.

Nixon pulled the chamber back on his pistol. It was still aimed at my head. "They're afraid."

"Well, that makes two of us." I nodded to the gun. "Why do you think I asked for Chase to marry me?"

All eyes fell to Chase; he was still unable to move, since Tex had pinned his arms behind his back, but he managed a shrug. "And here I thought it was my good looks and sexual prowess."

"Don't forget cooking skills," Tex added.

"Helpful." Chase groaned. "Thanks."

"No problem." Tex kept his firm grip.

Nixon laughed and returned his attention back to our conversation. "You needed his protection. I get that. Chase gets that. But what I don't get is how you knew you needed his protection, his help. We can do this the easy way or the hard way. I don't care if you're the last woman alive. I don't give a flying rat's ass if your heart is pure gold, your intentions totally selfless. I will freaking put a bullet in your head if you put my family in jeopardy. So I'm going to ask again. What. Do. You. Know?"

I had to close my eyes. If I kept them open, I'd see the look of betrayal on everyone's faces — the absolute shock and disgust that my family were spawns of the devil himself. "Everything." My voice was hoarse. "I know every damn thing."

CHAPTER TEN

Chase

My body relaxed when Nixon lowered the gun. Did I think he'd really shoot her? Yeah. He would. Because I knew it wasn't just about his family but Trace as well. Hell, he'd kill me if it would keep her safe. And I wouldn't blame him. I'd probably just look up at him with smiling eyes and tell him he'd done the right thing. Damn, we were a messed up-bunch.

"Everything," Nixon repeated, nodding his head as he put the safety back on his gun. "What is *everything*?"

Mil looked at me. Why me, of all people? I tried to give her a reassuring nod.

Her voice was quiet. I hated when she acted docile and compliant; it was so against her character that it pissed me off, making me want to get in a fight with her just so she'd get some of that spark back.

"Sex trafficking." She swallowed. "My dad was desperate for money. He had a… um, a bit of a drug problem."

"What drug?" Nixon squinted.

She looked down at her hands. "I think the better

question would be what drugs didn't he have an interest in?"

"So that's how," Nixon muttered. "So the family ran out of money really fast, and without our support, it just got worse, I imagine… so he dabbled in prostitution?"

He made it sound like he had it all figured out, but I knew it was just the tip of the iceberg. Mil would never tell him everything all at once; she didn't work that way. None of us did.

"What we're dealing with," she continued. "It's bigger than just our family, it's—"

"It's what?" Nixon asked.

When she didn't answer, he leveled the gun on her and thumbed off the safety. She rolled her eyes in frustration.

"It's what?"

"Phoenix tried to protect me," Mil whispered. "I didn't know that by taking his protection, by going to school, I was damning him to hell. He was too deep in to see his way out. He found out too much — he discovered the connections my father had made — and by then it was too late."

"What connections?"

"I can't say." Tears formed in her eyes as she looked at each of us in turn. "Please don't make me say it. Please."

"Mil." Nixon's voice was cold as death. "Please don't make me force you in front of Chase. Don't turn me into the villain."

"Don't think I've ever heard him say please," Tex muttered.

I think he was trying to lighten the dark-as-hell mood, but it wasn't working. I debated on whether or not to try to punch him in the throat or just wait until Mil was done confessing, not that I could do anything with my arms pinned, but still.

"Nixon." Her voice shook. "My family has broken every single one of the rules for the Sicilian Mafia. Every last one. They've stomped on them. They've spat at them. But worst of all, they've decided the only way to get even with everyone is to do the worst possible thing a member can do."

"Look at another man's wife?" Tex said under his breath.

"Tex," we said in unison, all of us clearly annoyed.

"Exposure." Nixon cursed a blue streak and stood. "Tell me you don't mean exposure. Tell me your family isn't hell-bent on flushing every last member of our families out of the country. Tell me they haven't made a deal."

Mil lifted her head, tilting her chin in defiance. "That's just the thing. I can't."

Tex gripped me harder. I tried to get free, cursing in the process, nobody moved.

It was their worst fear. It was mine.

Our lifestyle, our legacy, our money — property of the US government, compliments of one of our own families.

That's where jealousy got you. A shiny seat in prison next to every last family member you used to joke around with at family dinner. Only the De Langes would come out smelling like roses while everyone else burned in hell.

CHAPTER ELEVEN

Nixon

She wasn't telling the whole truth. Every time I questioned her, she bit down on her lip, her eyes always focusing on the floor to the left, and then her body language would change. She'd tap her foot or turn her knees away from me toward Chase.

He was the key to everything.

Because if he could get Mil to trust him with her heart, with her life, with her secrets, then it would be possible to save everyone before the shitstorm hit our family.

He'd hate me for it.

But Mil never had to know, and as far as I was concerned, it was good relationship therapy. Pretend to be in love — hadn't he done that a few months ago? Only, it wasn't fake — it was as real as death.

"Okay." My knees popped as I got up from my seat and tucked the gun back in my pants. "Let's just say I believe you. Your family's in some deep shit. You know everything there is to know — the dirty secrets, the lies, and whatever else they have up their sleeve this year. What exactly," I paused my face pinching in irritation and hatred, hopefully scaring her and getting my point across in dramatic fashion, "is your brilliant plan?"

A rosy blush spread across Mil's face. "I hadn't exactly gotten that far yet."

"Oh?" I raised my eyebrows and gave her a mocking look. "And why's that? Wedding plans trump life and death situations?"

"Ass," Chase muttered under his breath. I shot him a glare. He shook his head. Fine, I knew I was pouring salt on a wound, I knew I was making it worse, and it was working like a charm. "Tell me, Mil, were you so focused on yourself — your own worries, your own fears, your own damn plans to have the happily-ever-after — that you forgot all about the lives hanging in the balance?"

Her eyes darted between Chase and me. Then she closed them as a tear trailed down her cheek.

"Pathetic," I muttered under my breath. "Are you crying because I'm right or because you've finally realized you are the last person on earth who should be a mafia boss? After all, you are a woman." Yeah, had Trace been there, she would have slapped me.

"Go to hell!" Chase shouted. "Leave her alone, Nixon! Damn it." He fought against Tex, finally freeing himself and then pulled the gun from Tex's pants, all before Tex knew what the hell was going on. Within seconds, I was staring down the barrel of a gun, Chase's finger tense on the trigger, his face filled with rage. "It's been a long night. I suggest you leave."

"Or what?" I leveled him with a menacing glare, baring my teeth. "You going to shoot me? Threaten me? Kill everyone in this damn room, because I hurt her feelings?" I pointed at Mil and laughed.

Chase's eyes narrowed. Shit, he was catching on.

I ignored the gun pointed at my face and turned toward Mil. "They will break you. They will find you. And when they do, they'll pull every last finger from your hand. They'll waterlog you until you beg for death, and when you finally see the light of heaven calling you home, they'll damn your soul to hell before you can seek forgiveness." I paused. "Maybe those are the things you should be thinking about. Forget pretty dresses. Forget the happily ever after—"

"I will shoot you," Chase said in a cold voice. "If you ever speak to her like that again, I won't just put one bullet through your head, *friend*. I'll put two, just to make sure you're dead."

"Not such a good shot anymore, eh, Chase?" I teased then motioned for Tex to follow me out the door. "Seems like you both have a lot to think about. You know, they say the first year of marriage is the hardest." With that, Tex and I walked out of their room, the door clicking shut behind us. I snapped my fingers; the men already had the mess cleaned up and bodies removed.

Once we were in the elevator, Tex muttered, "Mind telling me what that was all about?"

I waited for the elevator to stop and for our two men to walk out into the lobby before turning and answering. "She needs a family. Someone to trust. It can't be you, and it sure as hell can't be me."

Tex's eyes widened an inch. "You're breaking her on purpose."

"Of course," I said smoothly as we made our way through the lobby, classical music played in the background. "And we'll stand by and watch as Chase puts Humpty Dumpty back together again, hopefully saving everyone's lives in the process."

The doors opened; the crisp night air was a welcome change from the emotionally-charged hotel room.

"How do you figure?" Tex asked.

"Because in the end, every girl wants a hero, and I just

made Chase hers."

****

For the last few weeks, ever since I'd miraculously come back from the dead — Trace stayed up until I got home. I'd told her I wouldn't leave her again, but it didn't matter. I wouldn't put it past her to sew a damn tracking device in every piece of clothing I owned.

It was close to eleven by the time we got back to my house. The lights were on in the kitchen. I walked in and found Trace drinking wine and playing cards with Mo.

"Who's dead?" Mo asked without looking up from her card game. "Rummy!"

"Shoot!" Trace took another swig of wine.

They seemed normal, we seemed normal, but we weren't. Who asked that?

I walked over to Trace and kissed the top of her head. "Nobody important."

"Says the guy who's aged ten years in the past two hours," Mo muttered.

Trace looked up, her eyes squinting as she gazed at my face. "What really happened?"

"Death." I shrugged and took a seat next to her. "Lots and lots of death. Hey, you going to finish that?" I stole her wine and drank the rest of it.

"I'm heading to bed." Tex took off his jacket and stared awkwardly at Mo.

"Okay," Trace answered her eyes darting between Tex and Mo. The silence was deafening.

"Like right now." Tex was still staring at Mo, while she studied her cards as if they held the cure for cancer. "As in, I'm going to bed, to sleep, by myself."

I groaned.

Could they not bring their drama into the house?

"Sleep tight," Mo said through clenched teeth, slapping her cards hard against the table. "Oh, and be sure to lock your doors. Wouldn't want any more skanks accidently falling into your bed like last time."

"Mo—"

"Goodnight, Tex," I interrupted him and shook my head once. He threw his hands up in the air and stomped off down the hall.

"Well, that wasn't awkward," Trace sang.

"Sorry." Mo slumped in her seat and leaned back, crossing her arms. "I swear I don't mean to be dramatic, but if that man looks at me one more time, I'm pulling a knife on him."

"Him or his parts?" I inquired, raising an eyebrow. "We both know you're a fan of torture… wonder what you'd go with."

Mo seemed to think about that. "Both. Definitely both."

"Damn. Mind filling me in?" I reached for the wine bottle and poured another glass. It wasn't as if I was going to go to sleep any time soon, not after all that adrenaline pumping through my system.

Trace leaned against me while Mo started talking.

"As you know, we broke up."

I nodded.

"And then got back together again."

"Wait, did he know you were back together?" I asked.

Mo rolled her eyes. "Yes, you ass. Do you want to hear the story or not?"

Was that a trick question? I held up my hands in surrender. "Fine, continue."

"Anyway…" Mo leaned forward, playing with the edge of the table cloth. "We decided to take things slow."

"So what's the problem?"

"Stop interrupting me, Nixon, or I swear it won't just be Tex at the opposite end of my knife."

What the hell? I glanced to Trace for help but she seemed to be just as shocked as I was. Mo rarely threatened me — she had to be pretty freaked out to actually be serious about her threats. Either that or pissed.

Mo's eyes filled with tears. "I heard them first."

"Aw, hell." I reached for my gun. Trace put her hand on mine and shook her head.

"I thought Tex was talking on the phone or something, and then I heard laughter. I was curious, so I knocked on the door. When he didn't answer, I let myself in."

"Mo—" I groaned.

"What?" She shrugged. "I figured it was my right. I mean, we'd been dating for almost a year on and off."

"So he was with a girl?"

Mo rolled her eyes dramatically as if I was just as bad as Tex.

Trace winced.

"What am I missing?" I asked. "I don't speak girl."

"You don't speak guy either, but we still love you," Trace joked, jabbing me with her elbow.

"You speak scary mafia mojo." Mo rolled her eyes. "And he wasn't with one girl."

"He was with a guy?" I asked, confused.

"I swear, sometimes I wonder how you're the leader of our family." Mo groaned into her hands. "No jackass, he was with two girls. As in two slutty girls, both in barely any clothing, in his room. Alone. With Tex."

"Was he—"

"You don't need to finish that sentence." Mo took a deep breath and leaned her elbows on the table. "He was. They were. And I may have assaulted both of them."

"The girls?"

"And Tex." Mo shrugged.

Trace snorted. "He's lucky you didn't shoot him in the—"

"Trace." I nudged her.

"Sorry." She blushed and sighed against my chest. "But it's true."

"So now you've heard it all." Mo ground her teeth together. "You know what sucks though?"

The room was silent except for the droning rhythm of the dripping faucet. Each drop that landed in the stainless steel sink may as well have been a bomb going off in that room. Mo flinched; her eyes darted to the table as if she was confused about her own emotions.

"I could have loved him," Mo said quietly. "I could have married him. He could have been my future, instead of my past."

"Do you want me to talk to him?" I reached across the table and grabbed her hand. "Maybe if he says he's sorry…"

"Tex can ride up on a giant white horse, spouting Shakespeare, and I'll still want to pull a gun on him. Thanks but no thanks, brother. I'll deal with it on my own, in my own way."

"Which doesn't include going to prison, right?"

"Please." Mo rose from her seat. "Like you'd ever allow me to get caught." She waved goodnight and walked down the hall.

"Well, that was a reassuring conversation." I took another sip of wine. "Any other confessions before I take you to bed?"

Trace kissed me hard on the mouth. "Just one."

"Oh yeah?" My heart froze in my chest.

"Yeah." Trace's tongue trailed across my lower lips. "I love you."

"I like that confession."

"Figured that."

"Bed?"

"But I'm not tired…" Trace's voice trailed off.

I helped her to her feet, slapped her ass, and bit her ear as I whispered, "Good, 'cause I'm sure as hell ready to stay up all night."

That's all it took and she was running toward the bedroom.

I'd tell her about Chase and Mil later, when I wasn't ready to physically hurt every one of my friends for different reasons. Damn Tex and Chase.

I slammed the door behind me and pulled Trace into my arms, attacking her mouth with ferocity as she wrapped her legs around my waist. Tonight wasn't about thinking — I'd done enough of that. There was always room to make war, but tonight? It was time to make love; it was time to remember why I did what I did. Why I woke up every freaking day with blood on my hands. Trace moaned as I pulled her shirt over her head and snapped off her bra, weighing her breasts in my hands. For her, I did this all to keep her safe.

CHAPTER TWELVE

Chase

It was officially the worst wedding night in the history of wedding nights. Mil stared at the door after Nixon had slammed it shut. It pissed me off that he'd treat her that way. I swear, I almost shot him, but then again, Nixon never did anything just to do it. I was just too blinded by rage to care about the why or how. I wanted to fix things — I wanted Mil to be okay. I needed her to stop looking like I'd just run over her puppy — repeatedly.

"You should take a shower," I whispered, trying to sound gentle when really all I was able to do was sound arrogant and controlling.

"Why?" Mil glanced down at herself and snickered. "Am I dirty?"

"You're lucky I'm tired as hell, otherwise I would have used that opportunity to piss you off even more by making some sort of wise-ass sexual comment."

"Counting my stars." Mil licked her lips, her eyes still trained on the door.

Everyone knew how much it infuriated me when people went into shock. Call me crazy, fine. But I hated inaction. I hated when people didn't fight, when they were passive as hell. When they didn't march toward doom and thrust their fists into the air. So what if it made me weird? That's how I survived. I ran head first into battle, not caring that I was David and the world was my Goliath. So watching Mil stare at the door as if just waiting for someone else to come back in the room and try to... kill her — pissed. Me. Off. Didn't she trust me to protect her? To protect us?

"Get up." I grabbed her elbow and helped her to her feet.

She stood, her eyes narrowing in on me. There's that spark. Well, I was either going to get shot or make everything better.

I was banking on getting shot — I rarely made things better.

There went nothing. I cupped her chin firmly between my fingers. "Look at me."

"I am, you ass." Her eyes blazed with fury.

"You know you can always call me *sir* if you get tired of calling me *ass*. I respond to both."

"Tell you what. Every time I curse, just imagine I'm referring to you. That way you won't get confused, I know how you meatheads can be."

"Aw, now you're just trying to butter me up." I released her chin and pulled her body against mine. The contact was hot — soothing to my very core. She tried to push against me, but I had her body locked with my arms. "You're not going anywhere."

"What? Now that Nixon's gone, are you going to threaten me too?"

"No," I said quietly. "Just the opposite."

"Opposite? So you plan on showering me with compliments?"

"Hell, yeah." My lips grazed her ear. "I plan on

showering you with lots of things. Compliments, gifts, affection, a kick-ass gun—"

She relaxed against my chest, but only slightly. One exhale. She gave me one exhale.

"But most of all… I plan on giving you something you need more than air right now."

"How would you know what I need?" Her voice pleaded; it was the type of tone you hear people use when they hate admitting weakness but secretly hope to God you'll agree to be their strength.

"Reassurance." I nipped her ear and moved my lips down her neck, twirling pieces of dark hair with my left hand while my right held her tight against me. "Mil…"

She stiffened, then relaxed, then stiffened again. Taming her was like trying to steal a cheetah from the wild and expecting it not to eat you.

"You. Are. Safe." I couldn't stop kissing her neck. It was like a drug. Shit, I felt like one of those crazy vampires that stare at people's veins. I watched blood pulse at the base of her neck, and I wanted to touch it with my tongue. I wanted to see what it would feel like — to taste what made her heart beat, to touch the location that gave her life.

I kissed her again.

Her body slumped against mine.

My hands shook as I pulled back and cupped her face so that her mouth was inches from mine. What the hell was wrong with me?

Her eyes hooded as she locked her gaze on my lips.

"Tell me what you want," I whispered, hoping, praying, begging it would align with what I wanted. For the first time in weeks, I wasn't conjuring up images of Trace. Mil's body trembled beneath my touch.

"I think," she whispered. "That a shower would be a good idea."

"Alright." I didn't release her.

Mil didn't move either.

A knock at the door jolted us apart from one another like we were teenagers just about to do the deed under the watchful eyes of a parent.

I held my finger to my lips as I grabbed my gun, took off the safety, and bent down to look through the peephole.

Breathing a sigh of relief, I opened the door.

Sergio handed me a bottle of whiskey. "Figured you might need this tonight. Everything's been taken care of, enjoy your... festivities."

"Wow, worse choice of words a person could come up with."

"Yeah, well." He tried to peer past me, but I moved so he couldn't see Mil. "You're no fun."

"I'm married. Fun and me don't really fit in the same sentence anymore. Now go bother someone else."

With a salute, Sergio turned on his heel and thrust his hands in his pockets, whistling the entire way to the elevator.

I shut the door and leaned against it.

"Who was it?" Mil asked.

"No one."

"Oh." Her voice was quiet. "I'll just take a shower then."

"Fine."

"Fine!" she half yelled.

Why the hell did she sound so dejected and upset? I turned around just in time to see her half-naked form as she walked into the bathroom and slammed the door behind her.

CHAPTER THIRTEEN

Mil

I gripped the countertop, allowing each finger to push into the porcelain sink as I got my breathing under control.

What the hell had I been thinking?

One moment of weakness. That was all it had taken. Actually, that was a lie. It had been a moment of weakness paired with Chase's green eyes, his maddening touch, and his ability to both make me feel comforted and wanted all in the same mind-numbing breath.

A moment of pure insanity had washed over me. I'd taken off my shirt. I hadn't been thinking — all I'd wanted was for him to see all of me, accept all of me, push our past behind us, and power through toward whatever the hell my family had planned for me.

I'd panicked when he didn't turn around.

He had to have seen me. There was a mirror near the door. He'd looked up, directly at me, or at least it looked like he had. And his face, God, I wasn't sure I'd ever get over the look on his face.

It hadn't been lust.

Or love.

It had been absolute torture. The lines around his eyes had suddenly seemed so much more pronounced than I'd realized. He'd looked old. He hadn't looked carefree — he'd just looked, pissed.

And he'd been looking right at me.

Angry, I'd run back into the bathroom. He could yell my name until his voice went hoarse; no way was I coming back out until I was fully clothed and ready to face him.

"Mil!" Chase pounded on the door. "Open the damn door!"

"I'm just going to take a shower," I said in a detached voice. "Like you said."

"Mil…" He growled then pounded against the door again. "I need to talk to you."

"So talk." I shivered as I started the water in the shower and waited for his apology.

It didn't come.

The water was already starting to get hot. Steam began to fill the room, causing the mirror to turn a whitish gray.

"Chase?" I called out.

Sighing impatiently, I cracked open the door. Which is apparently all the bastard needed to stick his boot in the small space and push it the rest of the way open.

"You always were too curious for your own good." He smirked, letting himself in the bathroom and closing the door behind him.

I backed away from him until the backs of my calves touched the cool tub. I was trapped. Heck, I could be in Russia, and I'd still feel trapped by his magnetism.

"Mil." Chase's eyes zeroed in on my face, quite impressive, considering I was, at that point, still clad in only my bra and underwear.

"Chase, did you need something? I'm kind of busy." I

shrugged him off, trying to appear unaffected as his tattered shirt clung to his muscled chest.

"Yeah." He smirked. "I did. *I do.*"

"Well?" I wish I could say that my voice didn't sound breathless — expectant, turned on. Crap.

"You don't run out on me."

My eyes widened. "You're upset because I—"

"Threw a damn temper tantrum," Chase finished. "I don't have time for it. I don't have time to placate your delicate feminine sensibilities. I think we should establish some rules in this relationship."

I was about five seconds from attacking him with my bare hands.

"Rules?" I licked my lips. "What kind of rules? Play fair? Don't lie? Don't cheat? Don't go to bed angry? Those types of things?"

"Nah." Chase shortened the distance between us. I could smell his cologne as it mixed with the heavy steam in the bathroom. My knees weakened.

His hands braced my arms as he held me in front of him. "Rules, Mil."

"Rules," I repeated, trying to sound totally unaffected — which should seriously earn me points. Chase Winter was a god. Sweat began to trickle down his temple, and I swear all I wanted to do was smack the crap out of his gorgeous face and then catch the sweat with my tongue. I shivered.

"Cold?" His eyes mocked as they crinkled at the edges in smug humor.

"Nah, just irritated," I fired back.

"Well, that makes two of us." He didn't remove his hands. I shivered again. Damn, treacherous body.

"You're not allowed to feel," Chase whispered. "Neither of us can afford that luxury for now. We have people most likely coming after not only you, but me. You can't throw a shit fit every minute you're upset or every time something doesn't go your way—"

"I did not—"

"You did," Chase confirmed. "No running away."

"I would never run."

"You want to run so damn bad you can't even think straight," he whispered. "And I can't be worried about you running when I'm supposed to be protecting you."

I laughed bitterly.

"That funny?" He breathed so close to my lips I could taste him.

"You, being worried? Yeah, hilarious as hell."

His eyes narrowed into slits. "One more rule..."

"Oh yeah?"

"You're mine."

"P-pardon?" My brain wasn't expecting that. I wasn't able to form words. My body, however, arched toward him, having ideas of its own.

"Mine. You're... mine." He said it simply, slowly, as if I had English comprehension issues. "What's mine is mine. Nobody lays a hand on you. Until this whole fiasco is over — it's you and me. I'll kill anyone who touches you, and if I see you look at a another man in a way I deem less than respectful toward me, your husband, I will not only end his life where he stands, but hold you personally responsible for doing so."

I just lost my ability to breathe.

"That's it." He stepped back while I collapsed onto the side of the tub, nearly falling into the shower spray. Pretty sure those two words, *that's it,* held new meaning. He made it sound so easy.

"Fine," I whispered. "I think I can handle that."

He gave a jerky nod and walked back to the door. His hand hovered over the handle. *Dear Lord, please just leave!*

"One more thing." He turned. "How many?"

"Uh, three?" I shrugged. "Fourteen? What the hell are you asking? I don't read minds."

"Guys." A muscle flexed across Chase's jaw as his green eyes bore into me. "How many since you and I were together?"

"Two."

He swore and let himself out of the bathroom. I charged toward the door and locked it as fast as I could. With a jerky sigh, I slid down the door and collapsed onto the cool tile.

I'd lied.

It hadn't been two.

It hadn't even been one.

I hadn't been with anyone since Chase — because nobody would ever compare to the boy who'd stole my innocence, my heart, and refused to give it back. I'd tucked that little secret deep into myself, because as Chase had said, *I don't get to feel*. My father had made sure of that. He'd made sure that Phoenix and I hadn't felt anything when it came to the ugliness of the world. And in the end, it had been my saving grace. My bastard of a father had saved my life — and all because he'd taught me how to close into myself.

I looked down at the scar on my arm, my battle wound, my trophy. Four years ago, I'd been afraid.

Now all I felt was numb.

Chase had my heart, but he would never get my soul; it had been taken from me the same day I'd earned my scar, never to be returned.

He'd been right about one thing. I'd refused to feel because I'd refused to go down without a fight. I was going to finish what the De Langes started, and they were all going to die.

CHAPTER FOURTEEN

Chase

I half-expected the word *jackass* to be written across my forehead when I woke up the next morning and looked into the mirror. I wouldn't put it past Mil. I wouldn't put anything past that woman — after all, I had seduced her when she was a teen. Not that I'd done it well, by any stretch of the imagination. I winced at the memory...

"What are you doing?" Mil asked as I kissed her mouth long and hard.

"Kissing a pretty girl."

"You really think I'm pretty?" She blushed and looked down.

No. She was freaking beautiful. Her eyes were so blue that it almost hurt to look at her, silky black hair slid through my fingers each time I gripped her head with my hands. Every touch, every sensation felt like heaven, and I wanted to go to heaven so damn bad — that's what happened when you lived in hell — you wanted what you couldn't have. And I wanted her.

"Is this okay?" I reached for her shirt and slowly undid the buttons. She blushed, but still nodded, so I continued, hands shaking.

I didn't know what the hell I was doing. All I knew was that she called out to me; she was my siren song, and I was lost at sea.

"Chase." Mil's hands shook as they pressed against my chest. "I've never done this before."

"Me either." I laughed. "Do you still want to?"

She nodded shyly and tucked her hair behind her ears, looking more innocent than ever.

"Good." Because I wasn't sure my body knew the word stop at that point. I finished unbuttoning her shirt and let it drop to the floor. With a shudder, she straightened her shoulders and undid her bra, letting it too, fall to the floor.

Blood roared in my ears as I stared.

I couldn't do anything but that.

I stared like a lunatic, like a man who'd never seen breasts before — I had — but never on a woman so perfect. With a groan, I threw her onto the bed. Her hands moved to my jeans. Cursing my own inexperience, I pushed away from her to strip off the rest of my clothes.

And then it hit me.

I really, seriously, had no idea what to do next.

She must have read the panic in my eyes, because she tried to push me away.

"No, no." I kissed her mouth. "It's not you."

"But you, you—"

I silenced her with my lips again. "Mil, look at me. It's not you, I'm just… you make me nervous."

"Oh." She fell back onto the bed and smiled. "Well, you make me nervous too, but I still want my first to be with you."

"Why's that? You barely know me," I joked. We'd met at breakfast. I'd assumed she was one of the cousins. We vacationed big in our business, never went anywhere without all the family, always. Besides, there had been some big deal our dads were involved in that had luckily made it so that all of us friends could go to Vegas with them and the women.

Between Nixon, Tex, and me, we had enough cousins to

probably fill at least two towers at Caesar's Palace.

"I know enough." Mil's eyes glistened. "I know you'll keep me safe."

"Oh yeah?" My brows furrowed. "And what gives you that idea."

She grabbed the necklace I always wore around my neck and gave it a little tug. It was a silver cross with a giant letter A across it. "Because you're an Abandonato. She said you'd be safe."

"She?"

"Are we doing this or not?" Mil wrapped the necklace around her fingers, tugging my face closer to hers.

"We're doing it." I kissed her hard. "And you're right. I'm safe."

"I know you are." She sighed against my mouth. "It's why I picked you."

Five horrifyingly short minutes later, and we were both laughing our asses off.

"It's okay!" Mil told me for the third time. "Really, I knew it wouldn't be that great at first."

"Wow, thanks." I swore.

"You know what I mean!" She wrapped her arms around me. "We'll keep practicing."

"Practicing?"

"Yeah, silly." She pushed against my chest. "I mean, I imagine we've skipped past the whole dating thing and slipped to sleeping together. But, after today—"

"Wait." Panicking, I pushed away from her and told myself to stop freaking out. "Mil, I mean, don't get me wrong. You're hot as hell, but I thought this was just a one-time thing, you know? For fun." I gave her a really big smile, hoping she'd smile back and shrug.

No smile. No shrug. But I did see tears begin to well.

"Aw, shit." I pinched the bridge of my nose. "Mil, we can talk about it, I mean, if you wanted a boyfriend you should have—"

"I never said I wanted a boyfriend." Mil looked down at her

hands. "I said I wanted to feel safe. You promised you were safe. You promised."

"I know and I am. Why? Did I hurt you?"

"You're hurting me now!" She threw a pillow at my face and jumped out of her bed. "Where the hell is my bra?"

"Mil, stop freaking out."

"I'm not freaking out. I just can't believe how stupid I am. You know what? It's not even worth it. At least I'm not a virgin anymore. At least he can't hurt me." Tears were streaming down her cheeks; she wiped them away and laughed. 'Try not to feel, Mil.' What a pathetic joke. Because I feel every damn thing."

"Mil!" I grasped her shoulders and shook her. "Look at me."

She raised her eyes, but they were empty. What the hell was going on?

"Mil?" A knock came on the door. Phoenix? What the hell was Phoenix doing there? I went to open it, but Mil punched me in the jaw before I was able to do anything.

"What the hell!" I yelled from the floor.

"Don't open the door!" Tears mixed with rage made her face like a mask of turmoil. I pushed her away, still gripping my jaw, and jerked open the door.

"Not a good time, man." I rubbed my jaw. Phoenix's eyes took in my state of undress, then he pushed me out of the way and stomped toward Mil.

"What the hell do you think you're doing? Dad's going to go ape-shit if he finds you in here!"

"Dad?" I croaked.

Mil didn't look apologetic.

"Let him," Mil said in a numb voice. "What's done is done."

"Mil—" Phoenix closed his eyes and leaned against the wall. "Please tell me you didn't... not with Chase."

"Like I said, what's done is done. Now he can't hurt me."

Confusion went off like a freaking atom bomb in my system. Now I couldn't hurt her? Or was she talking about someone else? And who the hell was she?

Phoenix threw a shirt at Mil and stalked toward me. "If you touch her again, I'll gut you from head to toe."

"I didn't know, man, I promise. I had no idea." I held up my hands. "Swear."

Mil cursed and pushed her way into our conversation. "Let's go, Phoenix."

Phoenix gave me one last look and led the way out the door.

"Why me?" I whispered as Mil stepped by.

"Because I knew you wouldn't hurt me," she answered.

"But I did."

"Not in the way I was worried about." She sighed and grabbed Phoenix's hand. They walked like that all the way to the elevators, leaving me empty.

It was the last time I saw Mil. And the beginning of the end of my relationship with Phoenix...

"You awake?" Mil elbowed me in the ribs. "Come on, sunshine."

"Everything hurts," I grumbled, not recognizing my own lust-filled voice. Oh great. How was I going to explain that away? *Sorry Mil, but I'm a male, and you're a female, and sometimes when males get...* shit. If I couldn't say *aroused* in my head, I sure as hell couldn't say it out loud.

"Seriously, Chase." Mil smothered me with her pillow. "I know you're sore."

Damn, her choice of words needed help. I wasn't sore. I was dying. Every part of my anatomy that made me a man was slowly going to shrink away into my body if I couldn't get my head out of my ass and focus on anything except the fact that about two seconds ago I'd felt her breast graze my arm.

Married.

We were married.

So breasts? Totally okay. Fine. Not a problem.

"Alright, well if you're not going to go shower first, then I am. We have a plane to catch."

"You can't be serious!" That snapped me out of it. "You

want us to go on our honeymoon after everything that went down last night?"

"It was never a honeymoon." Mil stopped halfway toward the bathroom and turned. "Vegas is close — but it's also where my mom lives, one of the reasons I didn't want to go."

"Wait." I shook my head. "Back up. Your mom's alive?"

"A ghost," Mil corrected. "Just like Sergio, only she may have the keys we need to fix this whole mess."

"How do you figure?"

Mil was silent for a minute before answering in a quiet voice. "She has the ear of the Capo di Capi."

I squeezed my eyes shut and tried to swallow as my body shook — not with anger — no this was pure raw fear. This was something unlike I'd ever experienced in my life.

"Tell me you didn't just say Capo di Capi. Tell me we aren't meeting with Vito Campisi."

"We aren't," Mil answered.

I exhaled.

"We're meeting with his wife."

CHAPTER FIFTEEN

Mil

It had to be a bad sign that I was spending over half our wedding night and morning in the bathroom like a complete coward. Chase's curses filled the otherwise peaceful morning air as I slammed the door shut and locked it.

Wouldn't be the first time we'd woken up in the same bed angry at one another.

I'd chosen Chase because he was safe — I just didn't know that he'd also be tempting as hell. There was something so attractive about his protectiveness — damn. I sounded like every other mafia wife out there. They loved the money, they loved the lifestyle, but mainly — they loved that their husbands were fiercely protective, fiercely loyal.

I closed my eyes and tried to focus. So many scenarios swam around my head that I felt dizzy. Balancing Chase and my family was going to be difficult. Balancing my feelings? Near impossible.

At least I could trust him. He would never betray me. That thought alone got me through the morning as I washed my face and put on fresh clothes. Vegas wasn't for the faint of heart, and I was officially walking into the lions' den. I wasn't sure if we'd make it out alive.

I hadn't planned past the meeting in Vegas, because I wasn't sure how it would go. I'd tried to sleep but sleep wouldn't come, so I planned. I went over and over all the connections I had, went through every scenario that would have us coming out of this alive. And all I was able to come up with was my mom.

Marrying Chase had bought me time as well as protection. And I needed both if I was going to be meeting with Tanya.

My hands trembled as I unlocked the bathroom door. I'd always wondered what it would be like, to know you only had twenty-four hours to live. Would I change anything? Would I be acting any different than I was in that moment? I pushed the door open and gasped.

Chase was texting someone, completely ignoring everything else going on in the universe, which of course gave me adequate time to take in his state of undress. Standing in nothing but a pair of ripped jeans, he looked like every girl's fantasy. Thick, corded muscles lined his flat stomach, leading all the way up to cut shoulders. His tan back had more muscles than I was aware even existed on the human body.

Yes. I gulped. I would do something different.

If I knew I had twenty-four hours to live.

I'd spend every last one staring at him.

Even if it was staring and nothing more — I'd do it. My heart did a little flip in my chest as Chase lifted his eyes and grinned. "You look good, Mil."

I gave a weak nod, using every ounce of strength I had to avert my eyes and appear disinterested.

"I'll just put on a shirt then," Chase mumbled.

Yes, do that. For the love of God, put on some clothes!

I sat on the bed and pretended to be looking at my cell

phone, when I heard the zipper to his suitcase close.

"Let's go."

"Okay." I shoved my phone in my jeans pocket and snatched my purse from the table. Chase carried our two suitcases into the elevator.

That damn elevator music was the only noise as we descended to the lobby. I wasn't sure if I was making it awkward, or if it really was just awkward as hell. Neither of us moved when the elevator doors first opened, and then both of us moved at the same time. As his arm brushed mine, I groaned. Chase cursed and then said, "After you."

I was like a scared rabbit getting chased by a fox. I practically ran to the front desk and waited for Chase.

"Checking out?" the guy asked without looking up.

"Yup," Chase said from behind me, his hands braced my hips. What the—? I trembled and flashed a tight smile to the man, even though he still refused to look up.

"What room?" He cleared his throat.

"Presidential Suite," Chase answered slowly, his lips almost grazing my ear.

"Ah, Mr. Abandonato." The man's hand shook as he typed on his computer. A bead of sweat ran down the side of his face. "And how was your stay?"

"Noisy," Chase said. "A bit messy."

I felt my cheeks heat.

The man finally looked up. His eyes darted between the two of us. "My apologies, if there is anything I can do to—"

"Actually..." Chase leaned forward using my body as a shield as I felt a gun slide from my back to my side, peeking out from my leather jacket. "I think there is something you can do."

"Anything." The man's answer was too fast. He swallowed convulsively, his Adam's apple bobbing up and down as his beady eyes blinked nervously.

"Next time someone offers you a ridiculous amount of

money to give them access to the suites, just say no."

"I'm not sure I know what you're talking about." The man's deep timbre trembled slightly as he wiped his forehead.

"Life lesson number one." I heard the hammer pull back. Shit. Was Chase really going to kill someone?

"I'm listening." The man's eyes pleaded with mine. I looked away.

"Big money always equals big messes that you'll eventually be blamed for. They offer you a lot of money because what idiot says no to something like fifty grand? But trust me, it's rare for a new associate to be able to spend all that money — especially when he's dead. You'll be collateral damage. And I *hate* collateral damage."

I stole a peek at the guy's face through the hair that had fallen across my face.

His eyes continued to dart from Chase to the rest of the lobby.

"Ask me." Chase growled.

"Ask you?" the man repeated.

"Ask me why I hate collateral damage."

"Why…" The man swore as a tiny bead of sweat slipped down his cheek and onto the countertop. "Why do you hate collateral damage?"

"Why, I'm glad you asked." The gun was pushed further through my side so that it was visible to the guy. His eyes never left Chase's. "You see, I hate getting my hands dirty, I hate cleaning up messes, but what I hate the most?" He paused. "When my poor wife has to be involved."

The gun was aimed directly for the guy's chest. I was pushed further into the counter, Chase still leaning heavily into my back. "Apologize."

"I'm sorry, Mr. Aban—"

"Not to me, you jackass. To her," he ordered. "My wife."

The man stumbled over his words. "Miss, my utmost and sincere apologies for putting you in such a dangerous situation. If you ever do decide to stay with us again, know that this will be the last time anything of this — nature will take place."

"Oh, I know." I smiled and leaned back into Chase. "Because if it does, my husband will kill you."

"Shit," the guy muttered under his breath, his hands gripping the counter until his knuckles turned white. He eyed the gun and started whimpering.

"Thanks for the lovely stay." Chase laughed as the gun was removed from under my clothing and placed wherever the hell he had kept it in the first place.

Chase wrapped his arm around me and paused. "Oh and we ate some things from the mini-bar."

"Consider them taken care of, Mr. Abandonato." The man looked ready to pass out, still steadying himself on the counter.

"How nice. Thank you." Chase smirked and pulled me close to him. "Such a fancy establishment, don't you think, Mil?"

The doorman tipped his hat at us.

Yeah, our marriage was so not going to be the typical white picket fence with two-point-five children.

CHAPTER SIXTEEN

Nixon

"Get dressed," I barked and walked back into the bedroom where Trace was sleeping.

I heard the cocking of a gun, my old pistol. Shit, not again. I turned around to see it pointed at my face and Trace looking angry as hell. "I'm not one of your associates, I'm not part of your family, and I'm sure as hell not Tex or Chase. Ask me again… nicely."

"Sorry, Trace." Apologies always sounded so foreign on my tongue. It felt like I'd just swallowed a bitter-tasting pill as I choked down my pride and tried again. "Will you please get off your very nice ass, find something to cover your delectable body, and do it at a speed that doesn't make me want to murder someone for breakfast?"

She put the gun back on the nightstand and yawned. "Not a total apology but a bit better than yelling."

"I didn't—"

"You did."

Glaring, I walked into her closet and pulled out the

smaller of her suitcases. "Pack for warm weather."

"Are we going somewhere?"

"Vegas."

"Nixon!" Trace jumped out of bed and wrapped her body around mine like a koala. "I can't believe it! We're eloping! Oh my gosh, you're the best—"

I shouldn't have winced or tensed when she said *elope*.

"Not exactly." I cleared my throat as she peeled her body away from mine. "It's more of a business dealing."

Trace's eyes narrowed until they were tiny slits.

"Shit, are you going to get the gun again?" I scratched the back of my head and eyed the pistol.

"Spill." Trace sat cross-legged on the bed. "Or I'm not changing into clothes, and I'm not packing."

"Chase needs us."

Her anger disappeared. Just like that. I say his name, and all of a sudden she was ready to run head first into anything? How was that fair? Pissed, I almost said something but thought better of it since she had just pointed a gun at my face.

"Are we all going?" Trace got up from the bed and walked into her closet. "Or is it just us?"

"Everyone." I peered around the closet door and watched her pull her shirt off. It came flying at my face along with a few Sicilian swear words I know she probably learned from Tex, damn him.

"Is Chase already in trouble? By the way, you never told me where you went last night, not that I don't trust you — well, actually..." She paused. "I'm still working on trusting you, you know, after the whole fake death episode."

I winced again. "I deserved that."

"And more." Trace peeked around the door. "You do realize putting Tex and Mo on the same plane may start an all-out war?"

"Too late for that," I murmured.

Trace's face fell. She stepped around the door and pulled

me into a hug. "What's going on?"

I answered her question with a question. "What's the worst possible thing that could happen to us?"

"Other than death?" Her arms tightened round my neck.

"Yeah."

"Going to prison? Being ratted out—"

I licked my lips.

"But we've done nothing wrong. Our dealings are legal, damn it!" Trace stomped her cute little foot and pulled away. "No way can anyone pin anything illegal on us."

Silence was probably my best bet, considering I couldn't lie to her face.

"Nixon." Her voice had a pleading edge. "Tell me your family doesn't do anything illegal."

"Okay." I nodded. "Our family doesn't do anything illegal." It was different when she was asking me to lie, right?

"Jackass."

I grinned at that and smacked her backside. "Just get ready and don't worry about things that you can't fix… oh and don't look too slutty. Your grandpa's coming."

She laughed and threw another shirt at my face. "Grandpa, huh? Three mafia bosses in one plane? Better hope it doesn't go down."

"We'd just parachute out or have Tex fly it," I teased.

"Stop being so calm about everything."

"My job," I said seriously. "Now hurry up."

Trace's nostril flared.

"Hurry up, *please*."

She blew me a kiss and walked back into her closet. I was still smiling when I walked into Tex's room — that is, until I saw a chick there, with him in bed, sprawled across him with lipstick smeared across her cheeks. Classy.

I grabbed her by the hair and jerked her away from Tex. "Out."

"Hey!" The girl tried to lunge for me. Oh, hell no. That

wouldn't end well for her.

"Just leave," Tex said in a muffled voice. "I'll call you."

With a huff, the girl grabbed her things and stomped off down the hall.

"I swear I won't hesitate to put a bullet to your head if you keep bringing skanks into my house." I kicked Tex's bed. He turned over and glared; two hickeys mocked me from his neck.

I really had no other choice — I punched him in the jaw. He cut loose with a string of curses and almost fell off the other side of the bed.

"Pack your shit. We're going to Vegas."

"Really?" He perked up.

"Tex..." I warned.

He scowled, his reddish brown hair fell across his face. He pushed it out of the way and turned. *Damn it to hell.*

"And cover that shit up." I pointed at the two hickeys glaring from his neck.

"Like Mo cares," he grumbled.

"I care. Me. Your boss. Your best friend." I walked over to the bed and slapped his cheek twice in jest. "Now stop feeling so damn sorry for yourself and get your shit together or I will send you to Sicily."

"You'd ship me to my enemies?" Tex had the audacity to look offended.

"To keep myself from shooting you? Or worse, from Mo poisoning your Captain Crunch? Yeah, I would. Now don't make me tell you twice. Better yet, don't make me any more pissed than I already am. My shit's about to blow if you keep this up."

"Fine, fine." He rubbed his jaw and crawled out of bed. I slammed the door behind me and went on to the next room. Why have kids when I already had Tex?

"Mo." I knocked softly on her door then opened it.

"You've got to be shitting me," I muttered. She was

sleeping with noise-canceling headphones on. Her makeup was streaked black down her face.

"Mo." I said it louder, this time sitting on her bed and giving her shake. Her eyes snapped open, and then a gun was pointed in my face. I pushed it away and swore. "What the hell is it with you women?"

"Sorry." She pulled off her headphones. "Thought you were Tex."

"Glad you took the time to make sure before you shot."

She grinned, though her eyes looked swollen from crying.

"Mo... you want me to talk to him? Order a hit? Force him to spend some time with the Alferos? Just tell me how I can make it better."

"You can't." She shrugged. "I'll be fine. Let me handle it in my own way."

"Right." I pointed at the gun. "Your way involves way more blood than mine."

"*Hmph*. That's a first," she said sourly.

Ignoring her, I walked over to the closet and pulled out her favorite Louis Vuitton travel bag. "Pack up. We're going to Vegas."

"No way!" Mo pushed away from the bed and threw her arms around me. "You're going to marry Trace! Finally. Oh no! Does she even have a dress?" She squealed and clapped her hands. "And she has to bring her grandma's shoes, and, oh no, does Frank know? You know how he hates surprises and—" Her face fell as she focused on my lack of smile. "You're not getting married?"

"Are you sure you and Trace weren't separated at birth?"

"I find it uncomfortable that you'd say that about the girl you're in love with." She crossed her arms. "Why Vegas?"

"That isn't information you need to know." I flashed a grin. "Now pack up. And for the love of God, leave your gun at home."

"How can I protect myself if my gun's at home?" she called after me as I reached the door.

"That's what I'm for." I turned back. "Hurry up, Mo."

Satisfied that everyone was on track, I made my way to the kitchen to grab some food. A couple of the guys were sitting around drinking coffee. I'd need all but two to stay at the house. "Vino." I poured myself a cup of coffee. "You and Marco are going with me — the plane leaves in five hours. Pack for the desert and bring cash."

He took a long swig of coffee and nodded. "Yes sir."

The rest of the men waited expectantly. "Nothing to worry about," I lied. "Just keep the house safe and answer your phones."

CHAPTER SEVENTEEN

Nixon

To say that the ride to the airport was awkward would be a gross understatement. To start things off, Tex was wearing a scarf — to Vegas of all places. The fact that his jaw was starting to bruise yellow wasn't helping matters or that he had on sunglasses to hide his terrible hangover.

Every few minutes, Mo would glare in his direction and play with a knife, tossing it into the air and catching it, only to glare at him again.

At least Trace was acting semi-normal.

Until she asked about Chase. Again.

"Was last night — I mean, did he and Mil…" She stopped talking and frowned. "Are they okay?"

Tex snickered.

I sent him a warning glare and wrapped my arm around Trace's shoulders. "He's fantastic. He just got married. Happiest day of a person's life." My smile was forced.

"I wouldn't know," Trace answered evenly then looked out the window.

I needed a drink.

The SUV stopped in front of the airport. I was ready to beat my way out of the car, using my teeth to rip the seatbelts if necessary, when the door finally opened.

"Thank God," Mo whispered under her breath.

We grabbed our bags and made our way toward the Virgin Airways Kiosk, my favorite airline — best seats, always comfortable, and always able to find us a flight, even if it didn't technically exist.

"So, uh." Trace tugged on my arm. "How do we do this?"

"Do what?" I looked around in confusion.

"How do we *fly*?" She whispered *fly* as if she'd said kill or assassinate.

I tried to keep myself from laughing. "Well, we get our tickets over there. Then we go through security and hop on an airplane."

She smacked me on the chest.

"No, I mean, people like us, how do we fly?"

I stared blankly at her face. She muttered a curse then whispered in my ear, "The mafia."

I couldn't hold it in any longer. I threw my head back and laughed. I laughed so loud that people were starting to stare. "Wow, Trace, thanks for that."

"I'm serious!" Her fists clenched.

"I know, baby. That's why it's so damn adorable."

"Hey, what's the holdup?" Mo called from the ticket counter. "Our flight leaves in ninety minutes!"

With one last chuckle, I kissed Trace on the forehead and grabbed her arm. "Everyone flies the same way, sweetheart."

"But—"

"Trust me." I winked and pulled out my ID.

My cell phone lit up with a text from Chase.

Chase: *Already through security, see you on the other side, man.*

Me: *Going through now.*

Chase: *Okay.*
Me: *Trace asked how we fly. As in our Family.*
Chase: *Uh, was she serious?*
Me: *Extremely.*
Chase: *That made my day.*
Me: *Mine too.*

"Where do I put my hands? What if they suspect me of something? Do I lie?" Trace whisper-yelled next to me. I sighed and put my phone away.

She was alternating between pacing and picking at her fingernails. Remind me never to tell her sensitive information. The woman would crack on a dime.

"Trace." I braced her shoulders. "You're fine. Just act normal."

Tex chuckled behind us. "Trace and normal? In the same sentence?"

Trace glared. "I won't hesitate to pull a—"

I covered her mouth with my hand and smiled tightly. "A middle finger, we know, sweetheart, but that's not very ladylike."

She stomped on my foot. Hard.

Mo laughed and took off her sunglasses. "It's a great day."

"Shit." Tex went pale.

"What?" All of us had successfully made it past with our IDs and were now standing in line to put all our earthly possessions into the bins.

"My scarf, man." Tex tugged at it. "If I pull it off…"

"She knows." I grabbed a bin and threw in my ring, my wallet, ticket, and shoes. "Trust me, you made sure of that last night."

Tex's face fell. "What if I told you we didn't actually—"

I held up my hands to stop him. "None of my business. Now hurry up. You're holding up the line."

Tex unwrapped his scarf, swearing the whole time, and

stomped through the security. No beeps went off.

I was the last to go through. I always was.

The minute I stepped in, the red light went off.

I stepped back out, showed them I had empty pockets, and stepped back through again.

"Sir." Security held up his hand. "We're going to need to pat you down."

"Fine," I said through clenched teeth.

A man about half my size walked up to me, put on some plastic gloves and began patting all the way down my pant leg. I glanced at Trace, her face was ashen white. Did she really think I was stupid enough to bring a weapon through security?

"Any fake limbs? Metal plates from surgical procedures—"

"Whoops." I shook my head in annoyance. "Yeah, I actually have a metal plate in my head, right here." I pointed to my temple. "Sorry, I haven't flown in a while, and I always forget."

Sure enough, he lifted the wand to the side of my head, and it went off. With a sigh, he peeled off his gloves. "Next time step through the full body scanner, alright, son?"

Son? Huh, I wondered if he'd still call me that if he knew I possessed at least three hundred different ways to render him without his next breath?

"Sorry." I shrugged.

He waved me off.

Trace ran into my arms, causing my breath to hitch when her body came into contact with my chest. "A metal plate?" she whispered so only I could hear.

"It was a long time ago."

"Nixon—"

"Drop it." I forced a smile. "Everyone ready? Let's go to our gate. Chase and Mil are waiting." Not a chance in hell I wanted to have that talk with her in the middle of an airport.

Sorry, Trace. You see, after my dad locked me in a box, he'd use me as his personal punching bag until I couldn't see straight. Right. Not necessary information. Trace would just want to talk about my feelings, and talking was the last thing I needed to be doing.

CHAPTER EIGHTEEN

Chase

We sat in the far corner at our gate, away from the crowds and against the wall. I didn't want to have to worry about people behind me. It was easier just to keep a look out toward the front, not that anyone would be stupid enough to try anything at an airport.

"You shouldn't have involved them."

"I didn't." I cursed. "You did. The minute you married into the Abandonato family, you invited them into this mess, this drama—"

"I hate Nixon." Mil looked down at her hands. "He's threatened me, shot me, threatened me again, and pointed a gun at my head twice. I want to rip the ring directly from his lip."

"Care to give it a try?" came a confident voice on my right. Great timing.

Mil's eyes narrowed. "You man enough to let me?"

"Cute." Nixon smirked, tilting his head. "Little sister wants to play."

"Guys!" I stood separating them from each other. I wasn't sure what the hell Nixon was playing at, but it was exhausting. Why all his anger was directed at my wife, I had no idea, but I didn't have to stand for it. "Just leave her alone."

"Then tell her," Nixon and I were chest to chest, "to stop being a damn baby and act like the boss."

"You want me to act like the boss, tough guy?" Mil's nails dug into my back as she tried to get at Nixon.

I rolled my eyes and looked up at the ceiling.

Trace pushed Nixon to the side. "Mil, stop. Please."

"Says the boss's whore, or wait, weren't you Chase's? Memory's a little fuzzy. I can't seem to remember—"

Trace lunged for Mil, but my body was blocking her from getting any action. Unfortunately, my face was in the way of Trace's slap.

Her hand came into contact with my face, making me stumble to the side.

Mil stepped back and covered her mouth with her hands.

Trace's eyes widened and welled with tears.

"Damn." I rubbed my face. "Dysfunctional Sicilians!"

Tex chuckled and tugged at the brim of his hat. "That's some messed-up love-triangle shit going on."

"Tex!" everyone yelled in unison.

Great. So much for keeping a low profile; people were openly gaping. I was surprised security hadn't already been called.

With a wave of his hand, Nixon said loud enough for everyone to hear. "Actors, so temperamental."

Trace did a little curtsy. I bowed, still holding my face, and Mil rolled her eyes while Tex gave one solitary clap.

Groaning, I walked over to my seat and grabbed a bottle of water to hold against my cheek. At least the burning was going away.

"Chase, I'm sorry, I—" Trace swallowed and bit down on her lower lip. She always did that when she was thinking, just like she always jumped to conclusions, choosing action before asking questions. Just like her favorite ice cream was strawberry, and her favorite books all had creepy vampires and zombies. Shit, shit, shit. I pushed the feelings down. It wasn't the romance I missed with Trace — it was just her. I missed her. I missed what we'd had. She had been one of my best friends. Let that be a lesson to every guy out there: don't fall for your best friend, not unless you're willing to lose everything in order to have her. Falling in love with someone who has that much power over your entire being — it's dangerous as hell, but if you win? Worth it, just ask Nixon

I reached for her hand.

A smile teased her lips.

Mil had gone over to the counter to pout. Nixon had followed and by the looks of his gestures and all-around pissed off look was most likely telling her what was expected of her as a boss — again. Leaving Mo and Tex to sitting on opposite ends of the gate. And me and Trace.

An eternity separated that hand and mine.

A lifetime.

She grasped my hand and gripped tight as hell.

"I miss you," I whispered, not looking down at our hands, yet still memorizing the warmth radiating from every fingertip. I felt it in my soul, in my bones: we were meant to be together, just not how I'd originally thought.

Trace squeezed tighter. "I miss you too, Chase."

"I'm sorry," we said in unison, finally looking into one another's eyes. I reached across the seat and pulled her in for a hug. Her smell was so familiar, but this time, I didn't react in the same way. There was no desire to do anything except hold on to one of my best friends. Regardless of how things ended between us. I'd give my life for hers. Still.

"Not as sorry as I am," Trace said in a small voice. "Chase, you promised me you'd never leave, but you did."

"Trace — I got married. I had to—"

Her head shook against my shoulder. She pulled back and reached for my hand again, our fingers locked with each other, "Getting married is one thing, but you promised you'd never leave. When I thought Nixon—" Her throat cleared. "When I thought he died, you made me a promise. Please keep it."

"I promise." I licked my lips and squeezed her hand tight within mine. "I won't leave you. I mean it when I say I miss you. I miss your laugh. I miss your smart-ass comments and your stupid cow keychain. I miss it, not because I still want it for myself — I think, well... I think I'm finally over that hurdle or at least I'm trying to be. I just miss our friendship."

"Threatening people on my behalf and buying me ice cream isn't just friendship, Chase."

"It isn't?" I laughed. "Then what is it?"

"It's friendship on fire."

"So we're burning up again?" I released her hand and smirked.

"Always."

We both exhaled and leaned back in our seats, happy in the silence of the moment.

Mil was still talking to Nixon. Correction, Nixon was talking to her, and she was trying her best not to punch him. At least that's what I was getting from their freaky body language.

"She hates me, you know," I said aloud.

Trace followed the direction of my gaze and snorted. "You're an idiot."

"Huh?" I flipped around in my chair. "Didn't we just have this really special talk? Nice moment? Water under the bridge?"

"Right." Trace smacked me on the shoulder. "Doesn't mean you're not still an idiot. That girl," Trace pointed, "is head over heels in love with you. She's just afraid."

"And you get that? What? From her predatory glance in

my direction every few seconds?"

"Kiss her."

"I have," I said defensively.

"Not like that, Chase."

"I don't know what you—"

"Not out of anger." Trace sighed optimistically. "Kiss her because you want to."

"And if she punches me in the face?"

Trace pulled out a magazine and shrugged. "Then make sure she gets the left side so your bruises match."

"Wow. In another life you could have been a marriage counselor."

Trace laughed just as Nixon walked up. "You guys good? Because if you aren't, I'm going to freaking lose my head."

"We're good." I nodded, still a little pissed at Nixon's attitude toward Mil. I got it. He was trying to make her strong by tearing her down, making her weakness nonexistent. But still, she was my wife. I didn't have to like his methods.

"Mil needs you, Chase." Nixon gave a curt nod and plopped down next to Trace.

"Does Chase need a shield or body armor before he goes into enemy territory?" This from Trace.

"Nah, just protect your balls. You should be fine." Nixon chuckled and planted a kiss on Trace's lips.

"Bastard." I walked off toward Mil and cringed when she directed her glare at me. I chanted Trace's words in my head, *just kiss her, kiss her, kiss her like* — I stopped in my tracks. A few guys were trying to get her attention. Oh, hell no.

I lunged for Mil's arm, pulled her against my body, and crashed my mouth onto hers, all before she could even gasp for breath.

She sucked in my every exhale — like I was her lifeline. My mouth worked against hers, tenderly nipping at her lips. My hands dove into her silky hair. I'd always loved that hair, but it was like my mouth was jealous of my hands and vice versa. I broke the kiss and moved my lips to her neck. A curtain of hair fell across my face; it may as well have been velvet.

"Chase—"

"Stop talking." My mouth found hers again, and I was lost. Damn it. Trace had been right. I allowed myself the small opportunity to forget about everything around me and memorize her.

"Chase—"

"Not now, Mil." I growled against her mouth.

"I think," Nixon's irritating voice sounded behind me, "what your wife is trying to tell you is that it's time to board the plane."

I broke away from her, my body trembling from adrenaline.

"Good show." Nixon laughed and walked off.

I, however, could not walk.

I stared at Mil. She stared right back.

"Why'd you kiss me?"

It took me a few seconds to find my voice. "You're my wife."

"Not good enough." She crossed her arms. "I refuse to be kissed, even by my husband, when it's out of jealousy." She nodded to the guys still checking her out.

If only I had my gun… "Is that what you think?"

"I don't think, I know." Mil rolled her eyes and tried to walk past me.

I grabbed her by the elbow and pushed her against the wall for a second time. "Let's get one thing straight." I nipped her lower lip. "I'll kiss you as often and as much as I please. Not because I'm jealous, not because I'm a jackass who gets off by showing my manhood as much as possible…" I released her arm and kissed her nose and inhaled her scent, "…because let's be honest, I don't need to show off when I'm sure as shit that I'll win."

"Oh yeah?" she whispered. "Then why go to all the trouble?"

I cupped her face with my hands. "Because I *wanted* to."

"Guys!" Tex called. "Let's go."

I released her and held out my hand. She squinted at it but took it anyway. We didn't speak to one another the entire time we waited to get our tickets scanned.

But we also didn't stop holding hands.

I counted it a victory.

CHAPTER NINETEEN

Mil

My lips were still buzzing from Chase's mouth. His kisses weren't the same. I hadn't noticed that yesterday. Maybe it was because his first kiss was so damn forceful I wanted to smack him across his perfectly chiseled face or erase his tattoos with a sharp knife.

His kisses used to be — exactly how you'd expect a horny young teenager to kiss. All mouth, all tongue, no tenderness, just plain raw sexuality.

Now? His mouth was crippling in the way it pulled down all my defenses. His tongue coaxing — everything about him was warm and inviting and, Lord help me, but so irresistible that had we not been in a public place I would have made a big giant fool out of myself.

I was playing with fire.

Chase was the flame.

And I had a sinking sensation that I was the solitary leaf in the hot sun just waiting to get scorched alive.

He was beginning to shield his emotions really well

around Trace. I knew it must still be difficult, and I promised myself that my heart wasn't involved, but every time they looked at one another I wanted to scream. She'd taken what wasn't hers to take and had left me with the unwanted pieces.

I wanted to hate her.

But she was basically unhateable. It was like hating Tex. As much as you wanted to smack him around, every time he gave you that goofy grin, all was forgiven.

Collateral damage. Those two words echoed in my head over and over again. Chase had directed them toward the employee at the hotel, yet I couldn't help but wonder if it fit for me too. Because I didn't want to end up like that. The person who was destroyed by the real battle. The battle for Chase's heart.

Hell. I didn't even know how to fight for it.

I just knew that deep down, a part of me wanted to win.

****

"Is this seat taken?" a dark voice said to my right. I looked up and grinned.

"That depends. Who's asking?"

"A striking old man with two knee replacements and a heart of gold," Frank Alfero answered, taking the seat on my right. Frank was Trace's grandfather and an all-around scary individual. He looked like the old guy on the Dos Equis commercials. Up until last year I'd never even seen the man, only heard of his bad blood with the Abandonato family.

Chase chuckled on the left and reached around me to shake Frank's hand.

"It's been awhile."

"It's been three weeks, Chase." Frank gripped his hand. Funny, because a few months ago the families weren't even talking, and now we were all going to Vegas together. Right. What's wrong with that picture?

"How's Luca?" Chase released Frank's hand but was still peering around me.

"Luca," came a heavily accented voice, "is just fine. Thanks for your inquisition, Mr. Winter."

"Ah, speak of the devil." Chase swore.

"Funny, I thought he spoke of me," Luca joked. Though all of us, Nixon mainly, knew it wasn't funny. The man didn't even have fingerprints, and I bet a million dollars no dental files would be found on him either. He had salt and pepper hair that was slicked back at all times. He only wore Italian-made clothing — that fit him to perfection. If I had to guess I'd say he was around forty-nine or fifty, but he was aging extremely well, you know especially considering he was one of the most hated bosses in America.

I shifted in my seat and pretended to look at my magazine as Luca took the seat behind us next to Tex and Mo. The last thing I wanted was to gain his attention again. He'd already threatened me. As if I needed more reminding of what my job was and what would happen to me if I failed to perform.

Well, at least he'd be in his own version of hell during the flight. If anyone deserved to sit between those two for a few hours, it was Luca. Maybe he'd do us all a favor and fix whatever freaky fight they were going through.

"So…"

I jumped in my seat as Luca leaned over and began talking to Chase and Frank like I was nonexistent. "How is the happy couple?"

Chase gripped my hand, scaring the crap out of me. I winced as he squeezed harder and harder. "Just perfect. Right, Mil?"

"In a state of utter and complete bliss unmatched by any other moment or day in my life." I gave him a wide, mocking grin.

"Too far," Chase mumbled under his breath.

"Good." Luca nodded. "So there is nothing for me to be concerned about?"

Nobody said anything. Screw that. Nixon wanted me to take my place alongside these guys? Fine.

"Actually..." I unbuckled my seatbelt so I could turn to face Luca. "There is one problem."

"There is?" Luca and Chase asked in unison while Frank laughed.

"Well, it is a problem, Chase."

"What is?"

Poor guy. He did have it coming though. "Your little problem." I pointed down.

"What?" he roared.

Luca's eyes widened in surprise, taking on an entirely shocked look I'd actually never seen on him before. "Uh, well, uh."

"Luca..." I batted my lashes. "You've been so helpful with every other aspect of this arrangement I thought you could take your help a little further. You see, Chase and I are having problems in the bedroom. Know anything about that? It's so clear how knowledgeable you are about everyone and everything. So why not help with this? After all, you love sticking your nose where it doesn't have any right to be."

Luca sputtered. "Well, I..." He looked helplessly to Frank who lifted his hands in the air and looked away.

"Oh wait. You don't work that way." I tapped my chin. "You work with threats and violence... so how about this. Chase's gun—"

"Oh, dear Lord." Chase swore. "Nixon, get your ass over here!"

Luca's brows furrowed as he held up his hand for Nixon to stay in place. "Do continue, Emiliana."

I cleared my throat. "As I was saying, his gun..." It was as if everyone in the airplane took a deep breath in anticipation. "It keeps getting in the way. And you know how

I hate being the nagging wife, but could you please tell him to put it away? Especially when it's time for bed."

I smiled triumphantly as everyone exhaled.

Luca's right eye twitched as he glared at Chase. "Son, the bedroom is never a place for guns."

"Speak for yourself." This from Nixon. I heard the crack of skin hitting skin. Pretty sure he was going to pay for that many times over.

"Wow, good talk. Thanks." I said thanks with such force there was no guessing at how pissed I was that he kept sticking his nose where it didn't belong. He wanted me to take my place? Fine, cut off the damn apron strings and stop patronizing me and looking over my shoulder.

Chase's eyes narrowed on mine.

"I think," Luca said in low tones, "I underestimated you, Emiliana."

"People always do," I said loudly. "And, Luca?"

"Yes?"

"Until you see me joining in with the De Langes — I'm innocent. I'm in charge of what happens to them. I'm their leader. And they are my responsibility. You've helped put me in this position, now let me do my job. I'm not a puppet, and I don't work well when people are looking over my shoulder every damn minute. I'm a De Lange. I've got venom in my veins, and I'll spit you out like poison if I have to. Now, can everyone please stay out of my business?"

"Yes," Luca said.

Frank blinked as surprise washed over his weathered face.

I smirked and turned my attention to Luca. "Yes, what?"

Luca's smile reached his eyes in amusement. "Yes, ma'am."

I sighed in relief and turned back around just in time to see Nixon silently clap twice and nod his head in my direction.

I didn't want to look at Chase. I expected him to be

pissed that I'd gone and thrown him under the bus or even teased him. My cell phone went off.

Crap, I needed to turn it off before I got in trouble. I quickly glanced at the screen and saw three texts from Chase.

Chase: *I'm so turned on right now.*

Chase: *Oh and I'm proud of you. In that order. Turned on first, proud comes second… always second.*

Chase: *Three words. Mile. High. Club.*

Me: *Three words. I. Don't. Think. So.*

Chase: *That was four words.*

Me: *Just making sure you were still the smart one.*

Chase: *I'm still holding your hand.*

Me: *Okay.*

I turned off my phone and looked at Chase out of the corner of my eye. His grin was so big he looked like he'd just gotten lucky instead of sending a few silly text messages. He was proud of me. And he wanted me.

I could live with that, for now.

CHAPTER TWENTY

Nixon

"Damn," I muttered under my breath. Even I wasn't insane enough to publicly humiliate Luca like that. The girl either had a death wish or balls of steel.

"Nixon." Trace gripped my hand as the plane started its taxi.

"Hmm?" I kept my eyes trained in Luca. He closed his eyes and leaned back against the seat, looking cool as a cucumber. What was his play? His reason for helping us when all signs pointed to him going back to Sicily and letting me handle what he kept referring to as *the situation.*

"Are you okay?"

"Of course," I said gruffly, my eyes darting between Frank and Luca until I got dizzy from blinking so damn much.

"Leave it," Trace grabbed my chin and forced me to look away so my gaze fell onto her perfect face, "and kiss me."

"Trace, you know I love you, but I can't just ignore the fact that—"

Her mouth crushed mine. Hands reached to my seatbelt,

unbuckling it as she tugged me to my feet.

"Uh, Trace?" People weren't necessarily staring, but it was totally possible I'd just moaned out loud — maybe said a few choice words as I'd tasted the mint on her tongue.

Like an idiot, I followed her down the first-class cabin to the bathroom. When I looked back, Tex was giving me a giant thumbs up. He seemed to be the only one really paying attention. And then Frank's head snapped up. No chance in hell I'd make a play for his granddaughter right in front of him.

I smiled confidently just as Trace pulled me around the corner, away from the bathroom, and to the little kitchenette where the flight attendants were getting things ready.

"Five minutes," Trace said in a low voice to the guy making coffee.

He shook his head. "I don't make the rules. The airline does. You kids need to return to your seats."

Did I seriously resemble a child? I was twenty-two — almost twenty-three. I bit the inside of my cheek to keep from saying something that would get us all kicked off the flight.

"It's the baby..." Trace sniffled. "It's yours!"

"What!" I roared, grabbing her arms.

"Never mind, take your time." The guy gave a low whistle and pulled the curtain so we had privacy.

My hands shook as I gripped her arms.

"Gotcha." She winked.

"Not laughing."

"Who said I wanted you to laugh?" Trace gave me a coy smile and snaked her arms around my neck. "I kinda had my heart set on a few moans, some biting—"

My mouth, colliding with hers, stopped whatever else she was going to say. How long had it been since we'd made out? Kissed? Last night I'd gone to bed only to find Trace already sleeping. With a moan, I threw my head back and lifted her legs around my waist.

"I need you."

"I need you too." Her lips moved to my neck, driving me crazy with her little nips as her teeth tugged my skin, only to be replaced by her tongue as it swirled around afterward.

The plane could be crashing, and I'd still stay exactly where I was.

"This is your captain speaking. We'll be pushing off in about two minutes. Flight attendants, please ready the cabin."

"Shit," I mumbled, dropping Trace to her feet.

"Tell me the truth." Trace's piercing eyes held my gaze.

"Which truth? That I love you? That I'd die for you? That if you cut me open with a knife and told me to bleed out, I'd do it in a heartbeat?"

She blushed and looked away. "No, not that, though it's nice to hear I can stab you and you'd just stand there — remind me next time you piss me off."

"I'll remind you tonight," I teased, hoping it was enough to change the subject.

Trace grabbed my hand and squeezed. "About this trip to Vegas. About what's going on with Mil. Are we in danger again?"

Hesitantly, I stroked her lower lip with my thumb. "Sweetheart, it's always going to be dangerous. Getting eggs from the market? Dangerous. Going down the street? Dangerous. Life is dangerous, but just because we do what we do doesn't mean we're to live our lives in constant fear that something's going to happen. So when you start to feel that way, like your heart's going to explode from the intensity of the situation — use that adrenaline, channel it toward adventure. Life's too short — and ours? Even shorter."

A few seconds went by as I watched the information soak into Trace's consciousness. Her eyebrows drew together, and then she gave me one solid nod. "An adventure you say?"

"Yeah." I kissed her hand. "It's exciting."

"Killing equals excitement?" she squeaked.

"Absolutely not," I said quickly. "Killing's the shitty part — but family? Family is life. It's mine and it's yours. Those people sitting in that cabin, they rely on me for everything, and I wouldn't give that up for the world — not even for you."

"Whoa." Trace stepped back. "So if I asked you to abandon this life, your entire family, and become a ghost, what would you say?"

My heart thundered against my chest as the metallic taste of blood filled my mouth. I must have bit my tongue in shock. Honesty. Damn, I hated that part of my personality. "I wouldn't say anything, Trace. I'd let you go. I'd take care of you from afar, but we'd part ways. I'd grow up to be a really crabby and bitter old mafia boss — so basically I'd turn into Luca… and I'd dream about you every night. I'd want you every day. But I'd stay. Our love is strong. But family? What's been bred into me? It will always win, regardless of my feelings for you."

The curtain pulled back. "What are you doing back here?" The female flight attendant looked anything but pleased. With her tight bun and stern smile, she could almost pass for my Aunt B before she went on a killing spree.

"Talking," Trace choked out.

"Well, you can talk in your seats. Out." She shooed us out of the little alcove.

I grabbed Trace's hand on the way to our seats, but she jerked it away. I wasn't sure if it was because she was pissed, or if it was because we'd walked right by her grandfather.

His eyes narrowed as we took our seats, and then they moved to Trace and squinted into pinpoints. I followed his gaze and cursed.

A few tears slid down her perfect cheek.

I stole a glance at Frank. Yeah, pissed. He was definitely pissed; his expression reminded me of the time he'd shot at my feet and had threatened my life.

Shrugging in his direction, I reached for Trace's hand

again, this time not allowing her to jerk it free, and whispered in her ear. "I love you. Never doubt my love, sweetheart." Her hand relaxed. "Oh, and if you ever pull away from me again, there will be consequences."

At that her head snapped up, her eyes saturated with hostility.

Unable to help it, I smirked.

Which earned me a middle finger from her free hand as well as a really uncomfortable situation where I suddenly felt so turned on I wanted to throw her against the floor.

Her nostrils flared, and then she looked down. At my lap.

When she met my gaze again, I winked.

"Are you seriously that turned on by violence, you sick bastard?"

Damn, she wasn't helping; I could feel my body respond with excitement. Shit, I'd take down the whole plane with me — cheerfully.

"Nope," I whispered, my tongue licking the outside of her ear as I spoke. "I just love pissing you off — seems my entire body responds to your anger in an unusual way — I'm not complaining, and you weren't either a few nights ago."

"I complained," she snapped.

"Because I made you go to sleep. It was four a.m., Trace, people have to sleep."

Her eyes narrowed as she jerked her head away from mine and crossed her arms, but I didn't miss the ghost of a smile on her lips as she pretended to still be pissed.

"Slap me later?" I teased.

"Ass." She breathed, her chest heaving slightly.

"Gotcha." I pressed my palm flat against her chest and laughed as I leaned over and kissed her on the neck again. "Admit it. You love fighting with me almost as much as you love what comes after."

"And what comes after?" her voice begged.

"Punishment?"

"Or rewards?" She grinned.

"Either way," I admitted.

"Flight attendants, please take your seats for takeoff."

"Well," I made sure my seatbelt was buckled, "this is going to be the most painfully long plane ride of my life."

Trace giggled. "I'm guessing it's going to be the same for him too."

I looked back where Luca was sitting, and Mo and Tex were fighting on either side of him.

"Now that's punishment," I agreed.

"So is this." Trace moved her hand underneath my shirt and began slowly caressing my back, then my stomach, then moved lower to my jeans. My hips jerked involuntarily.

"Not funny."

"Am I laughing?"

"Damn, I wish you were."

"Nixon..." her hand teased right above the line of my jeans, "...threaten me again, and I'm going to move this little conversation to Sunday Mass."

"You wouldn't!" My head fell back against the seat as my body screamed with pent-up frustration.

"I would."

"Damn you."

"Nixon!" Trace removed her hand. "I don't make the rules. I just follow them."

"Rules? What?" I looked around. "What rules?" Damn the woman had me so wound up I was ready to freaking take her right there and risk getting arrested.

"No PDA. Have a nice flight!" She pulled the magazine from the seatback pocket in front of her and started reading.

While I recited the Rosary.

CHAPTER TWENTY-ONE

Chase

"Nixon looks pissed," I said to no one in particular, halfway into the flight.

"Why are his eyes closed?" Mil asked. "And his lips still moving?"

"Hmm." I shrugged. "Not sure, but Trace seems to be pretty amused with herself."

Mil fell silent.

Probably not the time to have that conversation. Then again, Frank was sleeping, Luca had ear plugs in, and Tex and Mo were pouting. Leaving Trace with her magazine across the aisle and Nixon doing something that looked a lot like praying.

"You can still love her, you know," Mil said in a low voice, her eyes darting between me and Trace. "I don't expect you to get over it that fast, I mean you were in rough shape that night."

"Hilarious." I groaned into my hands and leaned back in my seat. I'd been drunk out of my mind. "I'm not sure I ever fully thanked you for all that."

Mil's blue gaze met mine. My heartbeat sped up a bit, like I'd just taken a hit of something and was feeling the effects of it spread through my bloodstream. "Are you thanking me for slapping you out of your drunken stupor or keeping you from drowning in the shower?"

"Well, when you put it like that..." I said dryly.

"You're welcome." Her smile made me dizzy. It spread wide, showing me her gleaming teeth and pretty dimples. Shit. It was like a light that had finally turned on in that damn airplane. I stared — like an absolute dumbass.

"Chase?" She blinked a few times, her dark eyelashes fanning against her cheekbones like a freaking caress. "Chase, you're not breathing."

I sucked in air and started choking wildly.

Mil patted my back, her touch literally setting my skin on fire. I choked again, looked out the window, and watched my manhood fall into the sky along with my pride.

"Sorry, uh... bug." I pounded my chest a few times to prove my ridiculously lame lie.

"In an airplane?" she asked, her voice dripping with skepticism.

"It happens!" I snapped.

"Okay." She lifted her hands into the air and, thank God, removed her hand from my person. I stared at her hand midair and noticed a scar on her arm. It wasn't a typical scar — it was like a burn of some sort.

"What's this?" I grabbed her wrist and leaned in to examine the mark; it reminded me of a cigarette burn, but it was too big to be a cigarette and on closer inspection it had definite lines, like it was drawn on her. Like it was burned against that perfect skin with a hot knife or something.

Mil clenched her fist and tried to pull away, but I pulled tighter, making it impossible for her to do anything. "It's nothing."

"It's something," I half-snarled. Holy shit, who the hell would mark what was mine? I focused in on the burn; it was an old scar, not recent, but it didn't matter. Not a shot in hell that it mattered. Her skin, her body, everything I touched was mine, not anyone else's to tarnish. Rage like nothing I'd ever known poured through me. My heart slammed against my chest as my jaw clenched and flexed, causing my teeth to grind.

"Another bug?" Mil whispered, a smile appearing on her expressive face.

"Tell me—" My chest heaved. "Who did this?"

"Chase." Mil's voice was pleading. "Let's not do this here, not now."

"But—"

"Leave it, or I swear I'll knife you in your sleep."

I released her hand, a bit ashamed about how attached I clearly was to my anatomy, and looked out the window, refusing to talk to her, like a little child throwing a pity party.

Who the hell would touch her?

My first thought was Phoenix.

My second thought was how I'd find time to go to hell, raise his lifeless corpse, and kill him all over again.

And then a fuzzy memory surfaced.

That night, the night Mil and I had been together, Phoenix had been protective, so protective that it was a bit ridiculous. I mean, I was his best friend and he was still pissed. He hadn't talked to me for weeks...

"Dude!" I slapped my hand onto the table. "You're like a freaking dog with a bone!"

"Poor word choice, Chase."

"Phoenix." I dropped into the chair beside him. "It's been a month. I said I was sorry, I offered to let you shoot me in the foot, I even wrote her an apology, by hand!"

"Not enough." Phoenix leaned his elbows on his knees, both legs shaking with irritation. "You don't understand."

"Then make me understand."

His head shook. "Can't. Don't want to, and it's none of your damn business."

"At least tell me she's okay. You owe me that."

Within seconds, Phoenix was on his feet, gripping my shirt with his hands as he used his body weight to slam me against the wall, still in my chair, I could only gape as his chest heaved, his eyes wild with fury. "I owe you nothing, you sorry piece of shit! You took the only thing she had! The only—" His lips trembled. "—the only thing that was keeping her close. And now? She's going to have to go away. She already is."

"What?" I shook my head. "What the hell are you talking about?"

"Boarding school." Phoenix released me and stepped back, exhaling a curse. "Don't ask me again."

"Ask you what?"

"About Mil." He refused to look at me. "As far as you're concerned, she doesn't exist. You better cherish the one night you had, because it won't ever happen again."

"Dude." I lifted my hands in the air. "I know!"

"No. You don't." Phoenix met my gaze. "Because if you did, you wouldn't have done what you did. You would have known the cost of your actions. Because now... I have no one, but I can thank you for one thing." His smile was tense.

"Yeah, what?" I grumbled.

"She's free." Pain etched in every plane of Phoenix's face. His mouth relaxed as he nodded his head. "She's finally free."

"Huh?"

"Beer?" Phoenix didn't wait for me to answer, just walked into the kitchen, leaving me confused as hell...

"Mil?" I whispered.

Somehow, in my daydreaming, she'd found a way to lean against my shoulder without being too irritated that the shoulder was attached to the person she had just snapped at. Her head was heavy, her breathing shallow. Damn, my questions could wait until we landed.

    After all, we had a year of marital bliss.

    That is, if we lived that long.

    Damn mafia.

CHAPTER TWENTY-TWO

Mil

The smell of cigarettes burned my nose. I waited as the voices quieted and then something stung my face. My vision cleared for a brief second. Though I was still seeing double, it was better than nothing.

"Wake up, baby girl."

I blinked a few more times, relieved to see it was my dad standing in front of me, not some crazy kidnapper. Though, why was it so dark?

A few rough men stood around my father, each of them looking worse than the next. They weren't from our family — most of them were faces I'd never seen before.

"She looks young," *a hoarse voice said from behind me.* "What is the price for this one?"

"Ah, this one." *My dad laughed.* "She will be a special price."

"How much are we talking about?" *a second man asked.* "The last woman I bought was tarnished, practically starved to death."

"I said special," *Dad repeated.* "Because attached to her is one thing you all want — and desperately crave."

The room fell silent as my father's eyes roamed around the room, stopping at each individual before finally settling on me. "Part of the family. Marry her, take her, and you will be welcomed into the De Lange family, no questions asked."

"How do you figure?" someone brave asked.

"She's my daughter." My father chuckled. "Marry her, and you'll be second only to my son."

"But... that's impossible. One has to be born into the family. Even some made men are never fully respected and—"

"Silence," my father snapped. "So we lie, say you're a cousin of a cousin, nobody has to know, and in the end nobody will care. We are the De Langes, after all. Each of you has been chosen for what you can offer."

Silence followed.

My father cleared his throat. "Let the bidding begin at one point five."

"One point five?" The man with the gruff voice asked.

"Million," Father answered. "Do I hear two?"

I gasped for breath, nearly jolting out of my seat as the plane hit the runway.

"Are you okay?" Chase whispered to my left.

"Uh, yeah." I cleared my throat and looked down at my hands. "Flying always makes me have weird dreams."

"You were able to dream, all within twenty minutes?"

I leaned back against the seat. "What can I say? I'm special." I flashed him a quick side grin and licked my lips nervously.

"Yeah." Chase's eyes penetrated mine. "You really are."

Wow, could I wake up like this after every nightmare? My breathing picked up. I was annoyed that all it had taken were a few words of praise, and I was ready to jump his bones in front of everyone.

"Mil." Chase's smile grew. "You hot or something? You're completely flushed."

"Hot," I repeated. "Yeah, really hot." Holy crap. Someone

punch me in the face ASAP. I laughed nervously and tightened my seatbelt.

The next fifteen minutes of landing almost killed me. Every time I wanted to turn and say something to Chase, he was looking directly at me. And not just one of those looks that says *Hey weirdo, what the hell are you staring at?*

No. Because if it was that type of stare, I'd simply flip him off and be on my merry way.

He was staring at me like he was a dying man... a man who'd just gotten out of solitary confinement and had been given a Christmas dinner. Me, being the dinner *and* a freaking Christmas tree.

"Mil." Chase's smooth voice invaded my peace and already-frayed nerves. I could have sworn his tongue just touched my ear.

"Hmm?" I pretended to be unaffected. Let it be known here and now, I'm a terrible actress.

"It's time to get up." As his words hit home, I looked around. People were filing out while I'd been daydreaming. Great. That's just what we needed, my savior to be my distraction.

"Right." I laughed and waved him away, then tried to get up, only to be held down by my seatbelt. With a groan I reached for the buckle — but was beat by Chase's massive hand. Smirking, he reached around where it connected and lifted the buckle. I felt that effing lift all the way down my toes. Mother. Loving. Dying. Damn. Shit. Hell. Storm.

I repeated those words over and over in my head as his hand grazed my thigh. The seatbelt fell and I was frozen, paralyzed by his touch, and fighting a losing battle with actually hating the fact that I still felt the buzz from his fingertips.

"Up." Chase motioned for me to stand. "Things to do, people to see, lives to ruin."

"Wow, you should be a motivational speaker," I

mumbled under my breath.

"Nah." Chase gripped my shoulders and whispered behind me. "I think I'm perfectly happy with being your husband instead."

What the hell? I whipped around so fast I almost fell over. But he was grabbing his bag so I couldn't see his face, meaning I was left to wonder if he'd actually meant what he'd said or if he'd been joking. A large part of my heart begged for him to be joking, because if he wasn't, that other part of my heart, the ten percent, was so heavily invested I knew it was only a matter of time before it spread to one hundred. And I wasn't sure I'd survive that type of transformation.

CHAPTER TWENTY-THREE

Chase

We checked into our hotel without any sort of issues. Frank and Luca decided to go gamble before the big meeting. Something else Mil had failed to mention. We were meeting the day we arrived. What the hell kind of bright idea was that? Exhaustion did not bode well for negotiation or for getting information, and I still wasn't totally convinced we should be talking to the wife of the freaking Godfather of everyone.

Okay, so maybe he wasn't an actual Godfather, but it felt like it. Especially when you knew the facts. He was a Sicilian-born immortal with loads of money and the ability to survive not one, but seven bullets to the head — all on different occasions, but still. In my book, that made him either a freaking vampire or so damn evil that even Satan didn't want him in hell yet.

I let out a sigh and pressed the button for the twenty-first floor.

"You sound frustrated," Nixon said with such a smug know-it-all inflection that I had to count to five before I answered with a voice that sounded cool and reflective.

"Yeah well, not having sex does that to people." Okay, so it was a low blow, but I didn't care.

Mil gasped next to me while Trace's eyes darted to the floor. I'd officially made it so awkward even I wouldn't have minded if the elevator plummeted to the ground.

"Blame it on the alcohol," Tex mumbled behind us while Mo pushed against him in disgust. He grinned. *"Blame it on the al-al-al—"*

"I'll genuinely shoot you in the ass if you keep singing," Nixon growled.

"Whoa." Tex held up his hands. "Since when do both of you have sticks up your asses? Seriously, lighten up."

"Says the guy with two hickeys," Mo grumbled.

Tex stepped back and angled his body almost like he was about to protect himself from a blow. His mask slipped for a brief instant, face twisting in agony, as he begged. "I already told you it was—"

"We know what a hickey is," Mil said impatiently as the elevator dinged and then stopped at the eighteenth floor.

The doors opened. A man with sunglasses walked in. Immediately I was on red alert, not because of the sunglasses, but because when he pressed the button it was for the floor above ours. And because the tattoo on his hand said *Familia*.

"You've been staying here a while?" I asked, trying some small talk.

Nixon's eyes narrowed in on the guy as he stood in-between all of us.

"A few days."

"How's it been?"

"What?" the guy asked.

"The stay," I said slowly. "How has your stay been?"

He looked down at the floor, his hands slowly moving to his back. Nixon and I made eye contact, but Tex was already on it. He snatched the guy's hands and pushed him against the doors, searching his body.

"Aw, only one gun?" With a bark of laughter, Tex dropped it. The gun landed on the red carpeting with a dull thud, bounced and then stayed put. "No knives?" He shook his head, his lip curling in disgust. "And only one gun? Are you ten?"

"Tex…" Nixon warned.

"One gun," Tex repeated as if he couldn't believe it. "He's not ours. Ours have at least three — and he isn't De Lange."

"How do you know?" Mil asked.

"Um, because there aren't any shots fired, and you're still standing," Tex answered. "And because he's too small."

The guy cursed. Apparently he didn't like being called small.

"My bet's on…" Tex pulled out the guy's wallet, still pushing him against the doors. "Bingo. Not Italian, not anything. Just a punk wanting to be a made man. Isn't that right, William Herald? Hmm? What type of name is that anyway? You may as well be John Smith. A nobody," Tex released him and sneered, "Got a pretty little piece waiting for you back home? I bet she tastes good…" He closed his eyes. "Guess what I'm doing? Imagining a little Mrs. Herald on my mouth, damn is that—"

William roared and fought against Tex, but Tex was a pro. He merely pushed the guy against the wall and sighed. "I'm already bored with you. Oh damn, I hope I didn't just quote the missus. She tell you that just this morning before she put her mouth on your best friend's co—"

"—Tex." Nixon rolled his eyes. "Enough." He pressed the stop button on the elevator and turned all his rage towards William. The thing about Nixon? When he was pissed? Or itching for information? You could actually feel the air charged with his frustration. It was like sitting outside just before a thunderstorm. He rose to his full height and narrowed his eyes on William, tilting his head in a predatory stance. "You work for Campisi?"

I grinned in amusement and pulled Mil to my side as the guy stuttered.

"I do not recall that name." A bead of sweat fell from William's temple as his eyes darted to the buttons on the elevator, most likely seeing if he could hit the emergency button to get the thing moving again.

"Cute. He's scared shitless." I tilted my head. "This your first assignment? Scope the elevators for the big bad Abandonatos and get some info?"

William swallowed convulsively, not answering.

"He's quiet," Tex murmured. "I'll give him that."

Nixon pressed the stop button again, and the elevator moved. "You, shit for brains." He snickered. "You're coming with us."

Nixon quickly threw his head back and laughed then pointed to the camera in the corner and made a drinking motion as if the guy had had a few too many and laughed again.

Herald paled, his lips trembled. "But, but—"

I punched him in the jaw. He slumped to the floor.

"Violent." Mil nodded.

"Always," Trace agreed. "Like kids at a playground. Want some wine? This could take a while."

"Don't forget about me!" Mo shouted from behind everyone. The minute the doors opened, the girls made their way toward Nixon's suite.

Nixon pulled out his phone and growled into it, "Sergio, we're at the Hard Rock, elevators, security, yeah it's a mess, deal with it why don't you?"

He pressed end, his eyes bright as they focused expectantly on mine.

"So, I take it we're interrogating in my honeymoon suite?" I grunted, pulling the bastard to his feet.

"First year of marriage — interrogation. Yeah, sounds about right." Tex laughed.

I rolled my eyes and helped the guy to his feet, trying my damnedest not to stare at Mil's ass as she walked away.

"Interesting." Nixon swiped his card.

"What?" For being so small, William Herald was heavier than hell.

"You lusting after a girl that isn't mine."

"What? You like it?"

He smirked, his lip ring pushing against his teeth. "I find it freaking hilarious and, just so you know, I'm glad I won't have to kill you."

"Love you too, brother."

"Brother?" the guy asked, his words jumbled.

Tex punched him again. His fist crushed against the guy's jaw so hard I heard bone crack.

"Thanks, man."

He smiled wide, his eyes crazy with excitement. Ah, he loved the kill. "What are friends for?"

We dragged William the rest of the way into the room and turned on the lights. Bonus: the Hard Rock Hotel had crazy-dark lighting as well as red carpeting. Blood? No problem. Clearly they were used to rock stars trashing the place.

Nixon put William in a chair and started tying him.

"Allow me." I popped my knuckles.

"Because?" Nixon's eyebrows shot up.

"Because I'm serious about the sex, and if that damn woman bites her lip one more time I'm jumping out of my hotel room window."

Nixon nodded, his laugh echoing throughout the empty void. "Have at it, rock star."

CHAPTER TWENTY-FOUR

Mil

On account of there being a bloody interrogation going on in my hotel suite — the girls and I unloaded everything in Nixon and Trace's room.

It was spacious, with red and black carpet and floor-to-ceiling windows facing the strip. In the early afternoon light everything looked kind of boring, not at all like I remembered Vegas looking like. Then again, I'd been young, stupid and, of course, an innocent girl in love with a green-eyed boy, who I'd thought would save me from my crap life.

Amazing how history repeats itself.

"Wine?" Trace called.

I turned around and nodded. She held the bottle in the air and grinned.

"I say we eat every damn thing in that mini-fridge and charge it to Tex's card," Mo said bitterly, though she did seem to at least be smiling.

"We could do that," I agreed. "Then again, it's not like it would make a huge dent in his bank account."

Both girls stared at me like I'd just said I was the voice of Shrek and hailed from Scotland.

"Uh, Mil?" Trace's eyebrows drew together in concern. "Tex—"

"Leave it," Mo snapped.

"What?" I uncrossed my arms and walked over to the bed. "Tex is what?"

Trace's eyes darted between me and Mo as if she was trying to get permission from Mo to give me Tex's entire life story.

"Fine!" Mo threw her hands into the air. "He's not like us."

"Like he's an alien?" I said jokingly.

Trace giggled as she twisted the wine cork out and began pouring into small glasses. "Right. He's an alien. Let's just leave it at that."

Mo took her wine from Trace and swore. "It was such a big deal, me and Tex. Us being together. My own father was against it from the beginning, then again he wasn't really my father, but still. I was so excited when—" Her lower lip trembled, and she looked into her wine glass.

The room was thick with tension. I wasn't sure if I should say something to make it better or let her get it out. I eyed Trace. She shook her head slightly and handed me my own glass. I took a sip and waited.

Mo sighed. "We used to play together."

"You and Tex?" I sipped more wine. Damn, I envied the boys. At least they weren't witnessing an emotional breakdown. I didn't know what to say to make it better because the truth was, I didn't know Mo well enough to pull the best-friend card and put my arm around her. And I didn't know Tex at all; therefore, I couldn't trash talk him and put his face on the wall for target practice.

It left me in that awkward position that girls face, when you know you're the third wheel but to leave means you'd be aimlessly roaming by yourself and damning yourself to a forever where you're always on the outside looking in. And honestly, for the first time in my life, I needed friends, craved them. I needed in. I needed in bad.

"Yeah. We used to play hide and seek all the time. I know it's silly, but I loved the feeling that he was searching for me, made me feel important, you know? Like, I was the treasure he was just waiting to discover. The best part was I always knew he'd eventually be there for me. In the end, it was me and Tex. We grew up like that. I was lost — he'd find me. It didn't take long for us to start developing feelings. Even then I had no idea how much of my soul he already owned, not until it was too late."

I gulped. The stories were too similar. She and Tex, me and Chase. It was petrifying to know that another human being held the keys to your heart and soul. Helpless. It left you defenseless, because the control shifted into another person's hands, and you had to decide just how trustworthy those hands were. Only it didn't matter, because in the end, if the hands dropped the key, if they messed up — even once — your heart was already lost, never to be unlocked again.

That's how I felt about Chase. How Mo felt about Tex, and I'm assuming how Trace felt about Nixon.

They had so many damn pieces of us that losing them would be like losing yourself. How did a person ever recover from that?

"Mo?" Trace cleared her throat. "He'll come around, I promise. Tex is just — different. He needs time to adjust."

"He's had five damn years to adjust, Trace."

"Adjust?" I whispered out loud. Crap. I totally meant to ask that question in my head.

Both Trace and Mo turned with blank stares.

"You really don't know who Tex is? After everything that's gone on? You're not playing dumb?" Mo asked, her face unbelieving.

"No." I shook my head. "Guys, I was at a boarding school for like half of my life. I was tort—" My voice fell. They didn't need to know my past, my reasons for doing what I was doing, for being what I was.

Mo nodded. "She'll find out tomorrow anyway. It's fine. Just — just tell her. I'm going to use the bathroom."

Mo got up and walked the short distance to the bathroom, closing the door behind her.

I got up from the bed and paced. "Sorry, I didn't mean to interfere or—"

"It's fine." Trace waved me off. "But you may need more wine." She grabbed my cup and filled it to the brim. "And I'd recommend sitting. I'm sorry. I really did think you knew."

"Knew what?" Okay, seriously. I was going to lose my mind and start shooting at things.

Trace took a large gulp and bit down on her lip, her eyes wide with… something. Was it fear?

"Mil… Tex is Vito Campisi's biological son."

The wine fell from my hand to the blood-red floor. It happened in slow motion, the wine hitting the ground, my shriek, and then I saw it again, the blood. Hell, there was so much blood.

"Mil!" Trace pushed me away from the wine as it splattered against my jeans. I stood motionless. Unable to really think clear enough to say anything or do anything — I stared.

"I'll get a towel." Trace cursed.

Time was still going by slow, so I wasn't sure if she was gone five seconds or five minutes, but soon, white towels covered the mess: the red of the wine seeping into the purity of the white color, soaking every last thread until the towel was just as hellish as the liquid that filled it.

I used to be that towel.

White.

"Maybe you should sit down." Trace pushed me onto the

bed just as Mo came out of the bathroom, her eyes puffy.

"Wow, you took that news well." Mo wiped her cheeks and smiled through fresh tears.

"His son?" I repeated. "But—"

"I'll give you the short version," Mo interrupted. "Tex was sent away when he was really little to stay with our family. A sort of mafia war or something broke out in parts of Sicily, and they thought the heir to the awesomeness that is the Campisi family would be safer in America with one of the most powerful families in the States."

Trace joined us on the bed, quiet as Mo continued the story.

"I don't know exactly what happened. I mean, we were all still in diapers, but the truce was broken by one of the families — either the Campisis or the Abandonatos. Nobody really knows, but in the end, um… in the end, Tex stayed until he was old enough to make a choice. See, he didn't really know his own family. Again, I don't know the whole story. Some say the Abandonatos stole the heir and caused an all-out war — another fun reason we don't ever deal directly with the Campisi family, but go through Luca, the minion, if you will."

I nodded, taking my time to process what she'd just said. "But what about five years ago? You said he's had five years to adjust."

"Right." Mo sniffled again. "Thanks to my jackass of a dad, nobody told Tex — or any of us — until five years ago. By then the choice was basically made for him. Turn his back on the family he's known his entire life, never to see them again, move to Sicily and take his place… or stay."

"And be cut off." Trace finished.

"Cut off?" I repeated. "What does that even mean?"

"He's not an Abandonato, and he's not technically a Campisi. — I mean, I guess he is. Blood and all that. He's just not recognized by them. Tex is a made man. His birthright is bluer than anyone in America, but to claim it means—"

"Losing everything," I finished. "So he stayed."

"And he gets paid handsomely," Mo said tightly. "But nothing like what he deserves."

After a few moments of silence, I giggled.

Trace's and Mo's eyes widened with horror, but I couldn't stop the fit of laughter erupting out of me.

Wow, I wasn't making any friends, but I couldn't help it. "After all that, you still want to eat everything in the mini-bar and charge it to his card?"

"Hey." Mo cracked a smile and then started laughing. "He could be a freaking saint, and I would still charge to his damn card. That guy is a pain in my ass!"

"But you still love him." Trace smiled, patting Mo's leg. "Admit it."

"I admit nothing." Mo closed her eyes and crossed her arms, then with a loud laugh said, "Except... I've been eyeing those stupid M&M's for the last ten minutes. I don't care who pays for them. I just need food. Too many tears were shed, and chocolate cures everything."

"And wine," I added. "Chocolate and wine."

"And hot men." Trace winked at me.

"Weird, because aren't the hot men what drive you toward the chocolate and wine? Yet after you're done with all that self-loathing, you crawl right back to the six-pack with a silly grin on your face and stars in your eyes."

"*Hmph*," we all said in unison. I took a swig of wine directly from the bottle.

"Speaking of six-packs." Trace cleared her throat. "How's Chase?"

The wine spewed out of my mouth, landing on the red floor. The dark carpet soaked up the red immediately leaving a large wet spot that looked more like water than anything.

"We're so going to have to pay damages." Mo shook her head. "And we've been here like fifteen minutes."

"Our damage is a wine stain in their red carpet. It's

Vegas. That's normal."

"Yeah," I agreed. "The boys' damage is gonna be blood."

We all looked at one another and then started laughing all over again. "Then again…" I stole an M&M from Mo. "It is Vegas."

"To Vegas!" Trace took the wine bottle from my hands and lifted it in the air.

"To six-packs!" Mo held up an M&M.

Both girls set their eyes on me, waiting. I laughed and lifted my one M&M into the air. "To the craziest honeymoon in history."

CHAPTER TWENTY-FIVE

Nixon

"That's enough, Chase." I jerked him away from the bloody mess and semi-mangled body. But Chase lunged again for William's face. "I said..." I gripped his shoulders and shoved him toward Tex. "...that's enough."

"Sorry." Chase stepped away from the rat bastard, a smirk of self-satisfaction plastered all over his face. "I didn't hear you."

"My ass," Tex said from the corner, grinning like an idiot as he took Chase's place and pulled out a switchblade. "Now, we can do this the easy way." He pointed to himself. "Or the hard way." He pointed to me and smirked. "And word to the wise? Always choose easy."

William spat in Tex's face.

With a laugh, Tex wiped his face, handed me the switchblade, then walked toward the bar and poured himself a drink. "He's all yours, man."

Smirking, I pulled the little freak to his feet and dragged him to the bathroom. "Don't feel like talking, hmm? Think you're tough? A mafia bad ass?"

I threw him against the wall, his head cracked against the tile. After a second push, blood ran from the back of his neck. I leaned in and growled, "You disgust me."

To his credit, the guy didn't even yell. Maybe he wanted to die, maybe he didn't care, but I couldn't take that chance. I needed to know for sure who he worked for because if it wasn't Campisi, someone else was tailing our every move.

I kicked his legs out from underneath him and pushed him into the shower, motioning for Chase to hold him against the floor. I grabbed a washcloth and put it over William Herald's face and then started the Jacuzzi tub. Chase's hands were on either side of William's body, holding him down as he choked and gasped for air.

"Enough," Tex said from behind me.

Obviously I'd done enough if Tex was the voice of reason. That happened once every ten years.

I turned off the water and pulled the washcloth from his face. "Ready to talk yet? A simple nod will do."

Hatred dripped from his eyes.

I tilted my head to the side. "Impressive."

With a grunt, I pushed him down again and motioned for Chase to hold his jaw open as I turned on the water, this time leaving it on twice as long. William's body started to shake.

Cursing, I turned off the water and pulled the cloth off for a second time. "Memory still fuzzy? Or you think we can have a nice little chat. Tell you what." I tapped his face with my hand. "I'll even pour you a drink, and when you're done spilling your guts, put you up in one of the nicest rooms in the hotel, William. How does that sound? I may even send you a nice call girl, someone real classy, maybe two. Hell, I'll send you three."

Snot mixed with spit trailed down William's chin and onto his chest. He gave a jerky nod. Chase got off of him and tugged him to his feet.

We walked in silence back to the main living room and each poured a drink. When I handed our guest his whiskey, he could barely hold it in his hand, let alone drink it without getting it all over his face. Maybe we'd beaten him too much. Or maybe he was just a really good actor.

"Spill," I pulled out my gun and aimed it at his face, "or this ends here and now."

"You'd kill me without knowing who sent me?" William threatened, his voice gravelly and hoarse.

"Absolutely." I laughed. "What's one less person in the world? Hell, what's one less hired man? You're replaceable, even to the people you're working for. You mean absolutely nothing. Damn shame, I doubt anyone would even mourn your passing. Ten bucks says when I bury your body out in the desert, people won't even file a missing person report for another two weeks."

His eyes flared to life, his lower lip trembling.

"Aw." I tilted my head. "Did I hurt your feelings? Strike a sore spot in that greedy little heart? Let me be very clear." I lowered my voice. "You don't matter. You never did, you never will. You're a joke. An idiot, actually. Tell me, how much did you get paid to spy on us? Were you even told what you were dealing with? As far as you're concerned, I'm the judge, jury, executioner, and the only prayer you have of walking out of this hotel alive. As it is, I'm debating whether or not I want to cut out your tongue first or start with your hands. It's an art form, you know... breaking the tiny bones in a person's fingers. You want to be sure to snap them at just the right angle to inflict enough pain and swelling to render a person utterly useless."

The man's leg shook as a stream of piss ran out of his pant leg and across his shoe into a puddle on the floor.

"I take that as a yes, then?" I grinned. "You feel like having a nice long chat now?"

"Y-yes," he stammered. "I didn't know."

"Know?"

"They didn't say who you were. I don't know who you are," he repeated. "I've been taking odd jobs for years from him. I got the tattoo after the first job. He said I was part of the family, that this was the last test."

Him. At first he said they, now he said him. Why? I stored that piece of information in my memory and asked, "How many years?"

"Six, maybe seven."

"You a local?" I bared my teeth and leaned in.

He nodded his mouth trembling again. "I never met with the main guy. My orders always came from someone else."

"Name?"

"I don't know."

I cocked the gun and pushed the point of it against his skull. "Name?"

"I don't know!" William whimpered, his teeth began to chatter uncontrollably.

Rolling my eyes, I rose from my seat and slowly approached him. With a grunt, I pulled William's arm out and twisted until I heard a pop. "Name?"

The man started screaming. I covered his mouth with my hand, muffling the sound.

"You can kill me." He dry heaved. "You can threaten me… all I know is he goes by Angel Santiago, but I think it's a made-up name."

"No shit." I dropped him to the floor and wiped my hands on my jeans.

"Hey." Tex pointed to the clock in our room. "Our meeting's in a few minutes. What's your call?"

I shrugged. "We take him with us. If he works for Campisi, we'll at least see some recognition on his face. If not, then we'll set him up in a room, put a few men outside, and let him eat his last meal."

William let out a low whimper from his spot on the floor.

Whoever he was, clearly he hadn't been broken before. The man was already dead and he didn't even know it.

"I'm not killing you." I rolled my eyes. "So stop being dramatic. Believe me, if I wanted you dead, your ass would be dead."

"Uplifting." Chase nodded in approval.

"Always." I popped my knuckles and stretched my arms high above my head. Tex yawned from the corner.

"Should I call the girls?"

A soft knock sounded at the door. I whipped my head around. "Shit." I held up my hand and motioned for the guys to be silent as I made my way toward the door and looked through the peep hole.

"Of course." I rolled my eyes and opened it wide as the girls all shuffled in. Trace's eyes bulged as she looked at William. I had to give it to her, she didn't even flinch. The guy was an absolute mess. Dislocated arm. Two swollen eyes, blood still spewing from parts of his body, and of course he still smelled like piss. Really he was a sight. Trace sighed, pressing her fingers to her temples briefly before flashing me a confident smile. God, I loved her. I loved her for dealing with this, for not running away screaming, for trusting me. Most of all? For seeing the ugly, and loving me anyway.

Mo was used to that type of scene. She was examining her nails while Mil stepped around her and stared in curiously.

William's face flinched just enough to give me pause, his eyes on Mil. "What? You recognize her?"

He shook his head violently.

Before anyone could say anything, I grabbed Mil by the elbow and thrust her into his face. "Think really hard."

"Nixon!" Chase yelled frantically. "Let her go."

"Think." I squeezed her arm, causing a little yelp of pain to escape her lips. In the corner of my vision I spotted Chase's lunge for me. As Tex tried to push him back, the man's eyes watered, and then he closed them as a tear slid down his cheek. Hell doesn't make him break, but an attractive girl makes him cry?

"I didn't recognize you," he muttered, almost like he was talking to himself.

Releasing Mil, I waited for the guy to talk more.

"She was so much younger in those days."

Mil looked at William in confusion. "I'm sorry. I don't know you."

"That is probably for the best," the man confessed. "Besides, we met in very... unusual circumstances."

"Two minutes." I nodded. "Give me the short version."

"Do you not know who she is?" the man sputtered, looking from me to Mil.

"Of course I know who she is." I felt a headache coming on. "But I want to know how you know."

"The Cave," he said simply. "Everyone knew of it."

"The C-cave." Mil's lower lip trembled. "Why does that—" Her face went completely pale, and I thought she was going to pass out. Instead she lunged away from me and punched him in the jaw, knocking him out cold.

"Hot," Tex muttered, pacing back and forth like a caged lion. Fights always left him on edge, like he'd just taken a shot of adrenaline and was ready for more.

"Mil..." Chase was at her side in an instant. "What was that about?"

Her lips were still trembling, but she forced a smile and shrugged. "Can't let you guys have all the fun. Don't we have a meeting?"

Her eyes met mine and held them. Fine. I'd get it out of her later.

"Don't want to be late!"

"Tex, grab the body," I ordered.

"Why do I have to carry the extra weight?" he whined.

"Um." Mo lifted her chin in his direction and flipped him

off. "Because you're an ass. Isn't that what they do? Kind of like a pack mule?"

Tex's face twisted in pain as he stood motionless in the middle of the floor as if waiting for Mo to take back the words. The room fell into an awkward, tense silence. It was as if she'd sucked all the life straight from his soul and left him defenseless. But that wasn't right. Hadn't he screwed her over? My head hurt just trying to figure it out.

"Just… do it." Chase hit Tex in the shoulder. "Alright?"

Tex popped his knuckles a few times then picked up the man.

"Question," Trace said once we were all in the hall. "How the hell are we going to carry around a body like this without getting caught?"

"Dude," Chase interrupted. "It's Vegas. This shit happens every day. Believe me, all we say is he got drunk and got in a bar fight. Case closed."

"Seriously?" Trace gripped my hand tighter. "That's it?"

We turned a corner and waited at the elevators. The meeting was going to take place in the other tower, which meant we had to walk a good five minutes into the rest of the hotel.

The elevators dinged open. A man with sunglasses eyed us and winced. "Rough night?"

I smiled. "You have no idea."

CHAPTER TWENTY-SIX

Mil

I clenched my hands behind my back to keep them from shaking. I didn't recognize the man. Then again, I wouldn't recognize any of the men. I'd purposefully pushed that memory so far into my subconscious that even a shrink couldn't pry it free.

The Cave.

My body shuddered — I felt cold and hot all at once. The walls of the elevator threatened to close in. Every breath I sucked in left me needing more, like I couldn't catch my breath if I tried. The tension was thick, making it worse. Chase's hands were on my waist and I couldn't deal. I was going to meet with Tanya, Chase was touching me, and The Cave. God, I'd forgotten about The Cave. I'd been dreaming about it but I hadn't known or wanted to believe it was… real. I'd pushed it away. Hoping that by denying the existence of the truth it would turn out to be a lie, or a horrible nightmare. I'd take either one. I needed to pull myself together. If I appeared weak, it wouldn't end well for anyone.

The doors opened to the twenty-second floor. We all quietly walked out. Luca and Frank were both leaning against the far wall. The rich smell of cigar smoke filled the air as they approached us.

"So..." Luca kept his eyes trained on me. "Shall we?"

I nodded.

"A friend of yours?" Frank motioned to the guy Tex was still carting around.

"Friend or enemy, not really sure yet." Chase spoke in low quiet tones. "Thought we'd take him in, just in case he's one of theirs."

Luca's eyes narrowed as he examined the man's face, his eye widened just a fraction before returning to their usual cool indifference.

I couldn't help it. I asked in a snotty voice, "Why? He a friend of yours, Luca?"

He gripped my wrist; pain sliced through my arm. I refused to make a sound as everyone walked ahead of us. "My dear, I'm merely surprised you didn't castrate him upon your meeting."

"Why would I do that?" The pain increased as his fingers pressed against the veins in my wrist, almost like he was separating them from one another.

Luca's face broke out into an evil grin. "No reason. My apologies."

I jerked my arm free and stormed past him. Chase turned around just as I reached his side. Flashing him a confident smile, I gripped his hand and tried to press my body as close to his as possible. Safe, he was safe.

Chase's arm wrapped around me protectively as we walked the rest of the way to the room. Nixon knocked twice.

"Want me to kill him for you?" Chase whispered across my ear, his face completely void of any emotion. It was as if he just asked me if I'd like to go to the movies or something.

"Not yet," I said in a shaky voice.

"Say the word." Chase's breath was hot against my neck. "And next time, Mil, when he touches you, use a knife."

"What?"

Luca's familiar cigar-infused scent permeated the air around us, meaning he'd finally caught up. I cleared my throat and looked at the door, willing it to open so I could get away from Luca and closer to my mom.

The door still didn't open.

With a curse, Luca pushed passed all of us to the front and banged on the door.

Nothing happened.

A maid and her cart came slowly down the hall. Without thinking, I walked toward her and tried to look as normal as possible. "Would it be possible for you to open the room for us?"

Her eyes darted from me to the group behind me, including the guy who'd just gotten the crap beat out of him by Nixon, Chase, and Tex. "Hotel policy says you have to go down to the lobby to get a new key."

"It's really important," I urged, sliding the knife from underneath my jacket, "that we get into that room."

"Miss, I don't think—"

The words died on her tongue as I held the knife to her neck. "The key card, now." I held out my hand.

Shaking, she pulled out a key card and handed it over.

"Thank you." I offered an apologetic smile. "And I'm sorry."

She nodded, her lips trembling.

When I turned, Chase was behind me. In an instant, he maneuvered around me and knocked the maid out with the back of his Glock. "No loose ends."

"Right," I huffed, feeling all sorts of horrible that she was going to wake up with a headache from hell.

"Besides," Chase took the card from my hands, "the less she knows the less danger she'll be in."

I gave a firm nod and followed him as he walked back to the door and slid the card into the slot. The green light blinked, the door swung open and in we all strolled, guns raised... waiting.

A black desk chair had been dragged to the center of the room. Sturdy yellow nylon zip ties wrapped around the arms and legs of a frantic-appearing woman, binding her hands and her feet to the chair. Her hair was matted to her face with blood. The bruises left on her chin made her appear deformed. Her head hung slightly to the side, and then her eyes flashed open. Dread turned my blood to ice. My mother stared directly at me. And I knew, it was over before it even began.

"Ma!" I tried to push through Nixon and Tex but was jerked back against Chase's chest. "Let me go!"

"No." He growled. "We don't know if it's a setup."

Tears streamed down her face as her head moved back and forth... in warning? What?

"Tanya Campisi?" Luca said in a low voice. "Did she do this to you?"

My mom shook her head no.

Luca swore and took a few steps closer to my mom's chair. She screamed like she was in pain, moving her head back and forth over and over again.

"Ma." I choked as Chase held me tighter against him. "Let me go!" I elbowed him in the stomach and tried kicking his shins, but he didn't release me.

"Mil." Nixon looked back at me. "You need to calm down. We're not untying her yet."

Ma's eyes looked wildly around the room, landing finally near the TV. She kept staring at that point. I followed the direction and gasped.

A homemade bomb was neatly tied next to the flat screen, right on the bar, as if someone had left it behind by accident. I swallowed the bile in my throat.

"What type of explosion?" Luca asked as Frank walked

over to the small device.

Frank leaned over and pulled out a pair of spectacles. "Let's just say it's a big enough boom to level half this floor."

"Trigger?"

"I don't see one. If it was the door or on some sort of timer, it would have gone off by now." Frank's mouth twisted into a firm line as he leaned in closer. "Believe me, whoever did this would not have wanted to wait for our murder. My guess is it's a pressure trigger. Not the floor, perhaps an object or—"

"Person," Luca finished, looking from my mom to me. "Well, it seems we're finished here."

"No!" I screamed. "We have to get her out."

"It's us or her," Nixon said quietly, as the room fell into a tense silence. My mom started sobbing all over again, this time nodding her head. So she knew. She knew it was us or her.

"Do you know who it was? Who did this to you?" I asked. My breathing was so uneven I was afraid I was going to pass out.

Ma shook her head sadly.

"Ma—"

She closed her eyes.

"Ma!" I yelled

Her eyes stayed closed.

"Mil," Chase said from behind me. "We have to go."

"Ma, open your eyes." My voice sounded so weak, so small. I felt like a little kid again, weak and confused. She opened them.

"I love you."

She nodded and then gasped as her eyes rolled back. Blood began pouring from her chest. She'd been shot. The glass from the window shattered on impact as my mom fell forward.

"Everyone out!" Nixon yelled pushing us toward the exit.

Chase yanked me against him and opened the door all

within a second. We started running down the hall toward the stairs. I counted to three, and then Chase covered me with his body as the hall exploded, sending us to the floor.

Alarms rang in the distance, but I couldn't tell if it was my ears ringing or actual fire alarms. Chase asked if I was okay, or at least it felt like that, but I couldn't hear him very well. Ringing pounded through my muffled ears. I nodded while he helped me to my feet and pushed me out the door to the stairwell. We didn't even wait to see if everyone was okay; we just ran down the stairs, down twenty-two flights of stairs. Legs like lead, I was so numb I didn't even feel the pain or the burn in my muscles. I had to keep going — I had to keep running. When we reached the bottom, Chase turned.

The rest of the group looked better off than I felt. Most of them were covered in dust with some scrapes and bruises.

"They'll evacuate the hotel," Luca said in a detached voice as people began flooding the stairwell, "I know a place. Grab your things."

"Where's the guy from before? William? And the maid?" I asked, even though I already knew the answer to the question.

Luca ignored me.

Which meant one thing. The maid had been caught in the explosion's line of fire, and they'd left the man they'd tortured earlier behind — to either get implicated or die.

Chase put his arm around my shoulders and squeezed. "Text directions to everyone, Luca. Make it fast. We need to split up. Now."

With a swift nod, he pushed past us and walked into the first floor lobby. Police were already everywhere. People were screaming. It was mass chaos, making it easy for us to slip by unnoticed. Chase gripped my hand and jerked me through the crowd. But it wasn't lost on me, as I looked at the terrified faces, it had been my fault. The death? On my head.
On my family's head.

CHAPTER TWENTY-SEVEN

Nixon

"Are you sure you're okay?" I asked for the millionth time while I drew the bath for Trace.

"Nixon." Her trembling hands reached out to grab mine. "I'll be fine. I just need to sit or do something so I don't completely lose my mind."

"Here." I helped her out of her ripped t-shirt and moved my hands to her jeans, pushing them to the floor so she could step out of them.

She was shivering. I pulled her into my arms, not saying anything, just willing the nightmare of our lives to go away. "Hey, it's going to be fine, Trace…"

"I know." Her body relaxed against mine. "I just wish this wasn't normal."

"It's not," I argued. "Nothing about strapping a bomb to a person and taking innocent lives is normal. Trace…" How did I explain that the mafia, while it got a bad rap for a lot of things, they weren't that stupid? Strapping bombs to people? Blowing up a Vegas hotel? Seriously? That was like waving a red flag in the middle of an FBI board meeting and then announcing to the world that you were a terrorist. "This isn't us," I argued. "The mafia? The Sicilians? This isn't how we handle things... Quiet, we like things quiet."

"Which means..." she whispered.

"Someone talked." I slammed the countertop with my hand, pain radiated from my thumb across my palm. "Either that, or whoever's responsible for what's going on is trying to silence every last person involved."

"Mil?" she asked.

"Shit." I groaned and kissed her head. "I don't know. I seriously have nothing to go off of. All I know is the minute we put her into power — things have gone to hell."

"She needs to talk." Trace pulled away from me. "You need to make her talk."

"Right." I snorted, stepping away from her long enough to turn the water off. "And say what exactly? Tell me all your repressed secrets or die?"

"That should work." Trace crossed her arms. "Or maybe something like, *I'll cut you if you don't start talking.*"

"I'll cut you?" I repeated, trying as hard as hell not to laugh out loud. "Who says that?"

Trace rolled her eyes. "You know, like in prison! They always say things like, *I'll cut you.*"

My eyebrows rose. "Oh? And how do you know that, little miss innocent? Been visiting some of the family in the state pen?"

She stuck out her tongue and smacked me in the chest. "What you say doesn't matter, Nixon. You just have to get *her* to say it."

"No, I don't."

"What do you mean?" She put her hair in a ponytail and watched me through the mirror.

"Chase." I cleared my throat and coughed. "He'll do it."

"Get her to talk?" Trace looked doubtful. "Good luck

with that. He's having issues kissing the girl, let alone using his seduction techniques to get her to talk. That would be like asking Nemo to fight Bruce. Chase officially lost all his bad-assness the minute he got married, leaving him the title of clown fish, and Mil—"

"Bruce?" I squinted at her. "Who the hell is Bruce?"

"The shark." Trace gave me a duh expression. "In Finding Nemo?"

"You're comparing their marriage to a Disney movie."

"Whatever." Trace waved me off and grabbed a towel. "The point is. Your chances of getting her to talk are completely diminished if you rely solely on Chase."

"Is that what you want?" I asked in a low voice. "For Chase to fail?"

Trace's hand paused on the fluffy towels. Without turning around, she answered, "I want him to succeed more than anyone, because I know how badly it sucks to lose the one you love, and I don't mean losing Chase. I mean thinking I'd lost you. Mil has lost everything. Chase deserves to be that constant person in her life. God knows he's done his time, don't you think?"

I'd stepped right into that one.

"Trace, I—"

"I'm gonna get in the bath."

"But—"

"Alone."

"Trace," I growled, angry that she was pushing me away. "Let me help you—"

"Out." She gave me a pitiful smile and ushered me toward the door. "And next time you open your mouth, try not to be such a jackass."

The door slammed in my face.

CHAPTER TWENTY-EIGHT

Chase

Nixon: *Get her to talk.*

The damn text pissed me off so much I wanted to shoot him in the leg for even thinking about that right now. Mil had just watched her mom die, basically in front of her face, and Nixon wanted me to get her to talk? What was his brilliant plan?

I groaned and threw my phone onto the bed.

Mil had been in the bathroom for the past half-hour. We were all supposed to meet at The Golden Nugget in two hours. Luca had said it was safer to stay in old Vegas anyway, at least safer for our kind. Right. Our kind, like we were some sort of fallen angels or messed-up vampires.

Some honeymoon.

"Mil?" I knocked on the door again.

No answer.

Worried out of my mind, I tried the door. It was unlocked. Steam billowed out as I pushed it open.

"Mil?"

"Here." Her voice was quiet, worried, so unlike her that my heart clenched in my chest. I pulled back the curtain to the shower. She was huddled in the corner, holding her knees to her chest, fully clothed.

"Mil." Her name erupted past my lips like an expletive. I was pissed, not at her but at myself. I'd failed to protect someone she loved. I'd failed again. "Come here." I stepped into the shower fully clothed and sat down next to her, extending my hand palm up.

She gripped it like a lifeline.

We stayed like that for a few minutes before she leaned her head against my shoulder. Hot water ran in streams down my face and arms, soothing my sore body. Even through my jeans and t-shirt, it still felt good.

"Chase…"

"Hmm?" I tapped my free hand against the tile to distract me from actually looking Mil in the face. She was too beautiful, too vulnerable, and I didn't want to be the jackass who ruined everything.

"What if I don't want it anymore? What if I want to run away? Run away from everything and abandon my family — does that make me a bad person?"

"No." I caressed her hand with my thumb. "It makes you human."

"A weak human." She laughed bitterly.

"Never weak." I let go of her hand and reached for her face, unable to keep myself from touching her, from looking into those damning eyes. The same eyes that made me want to say screw the world and just take her as my own. I tilted her chin in my hand as I lifted her face inches away from my mouth. "You are the bravest person I've ever met."

She closed her eyes.

I gripped her chin. "Open your damn eyes."

She tried to jerk back, so I squeezed harder.

"You're going to look at me when I talk to you."

Her lips trembled.

"You're incredible." I sighed, my thumb caressed her lower lip. "You're beautiful, strong, brave — and your mom? She has to be so damn proud of you to take over. Sweetheart, I know that the past isn't pretty for you. I know by being the leader you're fighting your own demons of what happened to you. I can only imagine—" I swore, softly as my forehead met hers. "Actually I can't, because your father was a damn monster. But, just know, that when I think of bravery, I think of you. When I think of a woman who should be president some day, your face comes to mind. When I think of someone I want on my team for capture the flag?" I released my grip and smirked. "You're it, baby."

"Chase." Mil leaned in so her lower lip grazed my chin.

"Hmm?" I told my body it wasn't time. My body refused to listen. Every nerve was on high alert as she moved to straddle me.

"Kiss me."

"Mil." I backpedaled, hoping that if I kept giving her excuses, I would be the good guy. She was weak, and she'd hate me later for taking advantage of her.

"I just saw my mom die," Mil said in a cold voice. "I'm literally on borrowed time myself. I'm straddling you. Wet. In. A. Shower. And I'm your wife. If you don't kiss me, I'll find some other guy man enough to make me forget—"

My mouth crushed against hers with so much force it hurt. But the pain was toxic, beautiful — addictive. She arched her body as my fingers gripped her t-shirt then snuck underneath and dug into the flesh on her back, pulling her toward me. Mil's hands pressed against the tile on either side of my head as her chest grazed mine. Wincing, I moved my hands to her hips, tugging her closer to my body.

"Mil—"

Her hands moved from the wall to the back of my head; her fingers dug into my hair as the friction of our bodies collided. I was fighting a losing battle, one I knew I wanted to be the loser of, because that meant I'd be happily naked with the most aggressive woman I'd ever met.

"What?" She reared back.

Wait, had I said something? What the hell? My brain was having a hard time catching up with the rest of my body. I shook my head and stared at her swollen mouth then her eyes. Big blue eyes framed with dark, thick lashes blinked back at me, as if asking for permission to go further. I swallowed, my body still humming from the buzz of her nails, her lips.

"Chase—"

I held my breath.

Mil carefully got to her feet and held out her hand. So apparently that was it. I waved goodbye to the moment of hyped emotions and sexual tension as it flew out the door and mentally kicked myself for thinking it had been anything more than that. She'd needed comfort.

And I'd given it to her.

I was *that* guy.

If you asked me — it was worse than the friend zone. I'd had the same exact issue with Trace.

I was *convenient*.

The guy you wanted on your team, just in case the star player didn't show up for practice or died during a game.

Second best.

Right-hand man.

The fixer.

So basically, I was nobody.

I could kiss her tears away. I could offer her my money, my body, all earthly possessions, and in the end, I would still be the one wanting more. Because I was already falling for pieces of her. Correction, I was becoming borderline obsessed with those jagged little pieces. Like a kid being told not to touch sharp glass lying shattered on the floor. But I was too damn curious not to touch, and the minute I did, I was addicted to the way the broken edges bit into the soft pads of my hands. Addicted to the difference between the cold smooth surface of the glass and my own reflection in it.

"Chase, I'm—" Mil put her hands on her hips and refused to look at me. "I'm sorry. That wasn't fair."

"Fair?" I choked.

Mil's eyes finally met mine. Sadness dripped from every single plane on her face. There was no crevice, no piece of her that looked whole. Broken. She was so broken that I hated myself for being selfish — for only thinking about my part of our partnership.

"To you," Mil continued. "When it happens—"

I shook my head interrupting her. "Mil, don't do this."

She kept talking, damn her. "When it happens, it should be because both of us are in the same mindset you know? It should—"

"Mil, really. I'm a big boy." I fake-laughed. "It's fine."

"Damn it!" Mil charged toward me and slammed my body against the tile wall. "Stop interrupting me, you jackass. I'm trying to share my emotions here, and you're bleeding like a damn martyr in the middle of a coliseum!"

Stunned, my mouth dropped open. My body hummed to life with pleasure at being scolded. Nobody scolded me. There was never a need to. I'd never had a girl actually yell at me before — I didn't count Trace because she was taken.

"You." Mil pointed her finger in my face. "Are. Mine."

I opened my mouth to speak.

And received a hard slap across my left cheek.

"I'm sorry!" Mil gasped, putting her hands over her mouth. "I just didn't want you interrupting me again!"

"So you slapped me?" I winced, rubbing my cheek. "Seriously?"

She glared. "I could have pulled a gun."

"Point taken." I cracked my jaw and crossed my arms. "So talk."

"Well, now you've got me all nervous, and I forgot my entire speech."

"So? You want me to piss you off again? Would that help?" I teased, slowly pushing away from the wall.

"You being an ass never helps, Chase. If you don't remember anything from this little conversation, remember that."

I smirked, unable to help my body's physical reaction to every damn thing that came from her hot-as-hell mouth. I took a few more steps, backing her into the corner where the shower was still running. I stopped when she was underneath the showerhead.

"Tilt back," I whispered.

"What?"

"Do it, Mil."

She rolled her eyes but complied. I lifted her t-shirt from her body, exposing a black silky bra, and fought the curse rising up in my throat as water dripped between her breasts. Next, I tugged her already wet jeans down to her ankles. Mil hesitated then stepped out.

Matching.

Black bra. Black lace panties? I had trouble focusing for a mere second before re-purposing myself to do my job — make her feel safe.

I washed her hair, letting the pieces of black silk slip through my fingers like it was the most precious thing I'd ever felt. When I was done, I kissed her on the cheek and removed my clothes. I grabbed a towel on the way out of the shower so she only saw my ass cheek at most.

"Chase!" My body responded to her yell like I'd just stepped on a live wire.

"Hmm?" I didn't turn around.

"Thank you."

"Anytime."

"I'm sorry I attacked you."

I turned slowly to face her as she peeked around the curtain. "You think that's why I'm upset?"

"Well, I, uh..." Her face started turning red as she closed her eyes and covered it with her hands. "I just I know that it's harder for guys, you know—"

"Mil?" Holy shit, I had to rein it in before I died laughing and embarrassed her more. "It's always harder for guys, kind of the point."

"Not that." She removed one hand and pointed at the towel wrapped around my waist. "I meant, it's harder to stop, and I know that... I could tell that you..."

She cursed and removed her hands from her eyes and glared. "I could tell that you—"

"Mil, stop before you give yourself an aneurism."

She glared, her cheeks so pink that it looked like she'd just gotten a sunburn from wandering the Vegas desert.

"Yes." I closed the distance between us. "I want you." I dropped my towel and purposefully looked down, waiting for her to follow suit. When her eyes dilated, I continued talking. "I think you know I want you. Did I want to throw you against the shower floor and have my way with you? Make you scream my name until you forget the horrors of what you just witnessed? Take you again and again and again until you no longer had any worries in the world? Hell yeah, I wanted that. I wanted that. But that isn't what you deserve. It isn't what I deserve. It's a moment, one moment, and then we're left with the rest of our lives. So yeah, you stopped the moment when I couldn't, and I'm glad you did. Granted, I could have done without the slap, but I'm into kinky, so it's fine."

At that she laughed, still not meeting my eyes.

"Mil, remember what I said about you looking at me."

"I can't."

"Why?"

"You're very, very naked." Her hand reached out to

touch my stomach, her knuckles grazing near my hip bone. Damn, but I wanted her fingers to slip so bad it hurt.

"You've seen other guys naked." How was it possible that her blush deepened? "Besides, I'm your husband."

"I'm sorry, Chase."

"For?"

"Ruining the moment."

"Don't be." I ran my fingers down the side of her jaw, memorizing the velvet feel of her skin. "Because I don't want a moment."

She gasped, her eyes instantly averted to the left.

"I want a lifetime."

Her head turned so fast I was afraid she was going to throw her neck out of place.

"Take a shower, Mil. I'll be waiting."

CHAPTER TWENTY-NINE

Nixon

I checked the time on my cell and leaned against the wall. The desert heat was not in any way helping my already tense mood and irritated disposition. A guy walked by, flicking his cigarette into the dirt. Note to self: you know you're edgy as hell when you're halfway tempted to grab said cigarette and suck the nicotine dry from the remains.

And I didn't even smoke.

Shhhit.

My head hurt, my muscles were sore, and Trace was pissed. I closed my eyes and leaned back against the building.

"Hey, there." A flirty voice interrupted my self-inflicted torture session. I opened one eye, then two. A blond-haired girl in six-inch heels and something I can only assume at one point had been a shirt, hanging over her shoulder, walked into my personal space. Her shirt-dress thing barely met her thighs.

"Yes?" I kept my sunglasses on. If I took them off and glared, she'd probably run screaming down the street, and I wasn't into scaring females... at least not in *that* way. I was downright pissed as hell and knew it showed.

"Just thought you looked lonely." She lifted her shoulder and offered a teasing smile. Did that really work on other guys?

"You thought wrong," I said simply. "I'm holding the wall up — like Samson."

"Samson?" She looked around as if waiting for another man to appear.

"From the Bible," I clarified.

"The what?"

"Gotta love Vegas," I muttered under my breath. "Look, I don't want any."

"Any what?" She ran a manicured nail down my chest, biting down on her lip at the same time. I could only imagine her point was to get me to stare at her lips, but all I felt was irritation. Damn Chase and Mil. I just wanted to go to bed. I inwardly winced at the bad phrasing. Damn it, where were they? I needed to talk to Chase before tomorrow.

"Sex," I clarified, my voice clipped. "I. Don't. Want. Any."

"But—" She twirled a piece of blond hair in her fingers.

"I'm gay."

She snorted. "Right."

"I'm into men."

"Oh really?" She closed the distance between us. Just as I was ready to seriously put my hands on her and push, I felt an arm wrap around my shoulder.

"Hey there, hot stuff." Tex said in a low voice as his hand grabbed my ass, cupping it with a little too much enthusiasm. "You ready?"

I ground my teeth together and forced a smile. "Yup."

"Oh…" The girl stepped back. "Um, sorry, you guys, uh, enjoy your night." She pushed past Tex so fast I was afraid she was going to teeter off her heels and get hit by a taxi.

"Tex…" I seethed.

"Hmm?" He took off his sunglasses and tilted his head as the girl hurried away.

"You can take your hand off my ass now."

He gripped it even harder, "Why? Afraid you like it too much?"

I pushed against him.

"Just embrace your feelings!" He shouted, earning the attention of a family walking by with their two little kids.

I grabbed him by the front of his shirt and threw him a few feet away from me, trying my damnedest not to smile.

"Admit it. You keep me around for comic relief." Tex nodded with a smirk.

"I admit nothing." I lost the war against smiling and barked out a strangled laugh. "But I do keep your ass away from Campisi, so remember that next time you start yelling about me being your lover."

"True." Tex grinned. "Oh, and P.S., don't knock it till you try it."

"P.S.," I repeated in the same voice. "Still pissed at you for screwing over my sister."

"Yeah well." Tex sobered. "It's for the best."

"Breaking her heart and bringing in whores is what's best for her?"

Tex lifted his hands into the air. "Look, I didn't say my methods were sound or that they were intelligent, just let us deal with it, okay? We're big kids."

"Kids." I gave a snort as the image of Tex as a menacing child filled my head. "That about sums it up."

A town car pulled up next to the curb. Chase got out and then held out his hand to Mil. My eyes narrowed; she looked... different. Happier.

Her mom had just died, and she'd survived a bombing.

And she was smiling like the Taliban had just declared world peace.

Chase gripped her so tight that I saw the white of his

knuckles.

I tilted my head, studying each of them when Tex said. "Dude, you get laid?"

"Tex," I snapped. "Go get something for their luggage."

"But—"

"Go."

Tex flipped me off, but ended up jogging over to the main entrance while I inspected both Mil and Chase. "I'm not saying this to be an ass—"

"Here we go." Mil crossed her arms a scowl formed across her swollen lips.

Chase waited.

I licked my lips and tried to appear indifferent. "But if you guys start screwing each other now, I may have to shoot one or both of you. It's not the time to play house, got it?"

"Play house," Chase repeated in a deadpan voice as he dipped his free hand into his back pocket, most likely clenching a pair of brass knuckles.

"I know it's your honeymoon," I continued. "But this little scenario you've got going on with the whole hot and cold is going to have to wait until everyone's safe. So Chase, keep it in your pants for once in your life, and Mil, stop trying to seduce the poor kid, alright? It's like dangling a damn fry in front of a seagull."

"Who's a fry?" Tex asked, pulling the luggage cart with him.

"Mil."

"Are we eating dinner or something? Because I have to admit—" Tex leaned against the cart. "—I'm freaking starving." He eyed Chase and Mil. "Then again, I'm sure you both are too. All those extracurriculars really take it out of ya."

Chase took off his sunglasses, his face twisting in irritation and annoyance, no smile. Nothing. He was pissed.

"Chase," I said slowly. "You know I'm right. You're the best I have. I need your focus to be on The Family. Your family. Then you can screw all you want, okay? Make a million babies, let her tie you up in scarves. Whatever shit you're into, fine. But not now."

Mil looked like she wanted to punch me in the face. Chase took a step forward, but she stopped him.

"Good talk." I exhaled. "Chase, I'll see you down in the bar in a half-hour, okay? We have business to discuss. Mil, you can go find the girls. They're having dinner out by the pool."

Nobody moved.

After a few seconds of tense silence where I was pretty sure Chase was trying to convince himself not to strangle me to death, Tex cleared his throat and pointed to the luggage. "You guys need help, then?"

"Yeah," Chase croaked. "Thanks."

We loaded them up and sent them on their way.

"Tell me," Tex asked once we were walking back toward the bar. "Is your only goal to see how far you can push Chase before he kills you in your sleep?"

I laughed, the tension escaping through every chuckle that ran through my body. "Hell no. But Mil's still the key in this entire scenario — we need her."

"Dude, let Chase do his job."

"Nah, I have a better plan."

"Anger? Castration? Drowning?"

I sat down at the bar and grinned. "How good is Chase in situations when he's told he can't do something or he can't have something?"

"Tortures himself until he—" Tex nodded. A slow smile suddenly appeared across his lips. I knew he'd eventually catch on to the brilliance of my plan. "You mean to dangle the carrot in front of the bunny until it dies from want."

"And when it gives in…"

Tex smirked. "Rotten bastard. When it gives in, the damn carrot and bunny are so inseparable it would take death for them to part."

"I'll drink to that."

CHAPTER THIRTY

Chase

Nixon was damn lucky I'd packed my gun in my suitcase at the last minute, meaning it wasn't easily accessible while he was harassing me in the street.

My fingers itched to punch something.

I hated that he was right.

Hated that the last thing I was focusing on was the fact that random people were after my wife, someone was stalking us, and Mil's mom had just been murdered.

But Mil was wearing a V-neck tank top.

I had the attention span of a pubescent sixth grader. Regardless of where my eyes were supposed to be trained, they'd eventually gone right back to her chest and stayed until she caught me. Then I'd jerked my head away — solidifying the whole sixth-grader theory, only to get caught staring again.

"You want me to flash you and get it over with?" Mil asked once we reached our room. Unfortunately, I'd just taken a sip of water. I choked it down and pounded my chest.

"Hey, caveman?" Mil snickered. "You gonna make it?"

"Yeah," I croaked. "Wrong lube."

"Lube?"

"Tube!" I shouted. "Shit."

Mil's entire face was frozen in a mocking grin, hands on hips, which, of course, drew my eyes to her chest. Again.

"I gotta go meet Nixon." I forced a smile and walked past her, grabbing the key card from the table on my way.

"Oh, and Chase," Mil called.

I turned.

She lifted her shirt, revealing a lacey pink bra that I could have sworn spoke to me. It said, *"Chase, stay. Chase, make love to me, Chase."*

"Chase," Mil interrupted. "Have fun at your meeting."

I must have looked like an idiot. My smile was so huge it actually hurt my face, but no matter what I did, I couldn't sober up. It was like I was drunk — only a hundred times better. "Thanks."

I half-walked half-staggered in a lust-filled dream all the way to the elevator.

The euphoric sensation lasted through the entire elevator ride.

And during my walk to the bar, flashes of pink invaded my senses making me drunk with lust.

And again as I took a seat, her face beckoned me, her body screamed. Damn it! I wanted to make her pay, hell I wanted to make us both suffer. The release alone would be my undoing.

"Chase..." Nixon cleared his throat. "You look happy. Hope that smile's for me and not because of your tardiness."

"Shit." Tex winked. "You cheating right in front of me, Nixon?"

"Huh?" That snapped me out of my stupor as I glanced between the two of them.

"Oh right, you weren't there. Let me catch you up..." Tex

leaned in and whispered in Nixon's ear. "Loverrr..."

"Stop purring in my ear, or I swear I'll cut your tongue out."

"Rawr."

"Tex," I interrupted. "If you ever — and I do mean ever — touch me the way you just touched Nixon, I will end your life and send your body parts back to Sicily in greeting card form. *Capiche?"*

Tex merely shrugged and ordered another beer.

"Luca and Frank still here?" I asked.

"Yeah." Nixon leaned back in his chair. The bar was located right next to the casino, meaning it was noisy as hell, but at least people weren't paying a lick of attention to us. "They're here for reinforcements, nothing more. Too many loose ends now."

I grunted. "Tell me about it."

We sat in silence.

"Chase." Nixon leaned forward clasping his hands together. "It's your call."

"What is?" Confused, I leaned forward, thinking I hadn't really heard him correctly.

"What you want to do." Nixon shrugged.

"I'm sorry. I still don't know what you mean."

"We could all go home," Nixon said in a low voice. "Live our lives, wait for them to come to us. Or we can draw them out."

My eyebrows pinched together. "How do you figure we draw them out?"

"The wife," Nixon said offering a casual shrug. "Tanya knows Mil. That was her connection." He popped his knuckles. "Obviously she knows how to contact her. Maybe the wife has information on what to do. It's possible we have more than one family after us. The dots need to be connected, and until we have any leads, we're sitting ducks. It's the only other way, beside going home and waiting to get shot at, which to be quite honest, might do Tex some good."

"Heard that," Tex grumbled.

"You were meant to," I fired back.

"So." I swallowed. "Get Mil to give me Tanya's information?"

"Simple, after all, the last thing the Campisi family wants on their hands is more blood, you know? I imagine they're hoping we'll just drop it." He took a long swig of beer. "Mil's mom has been estranged from the De Langes for such a long time. They're probably assuming she doesn't matter."

I groaned into my hands, hating every second that ticked by, because it meant I was that much closer to having to talk to Mil about her past — about her mom — things I knew she'd tucked away into her own personal Pandora's box. Her mom and dad had separated soon after Mil and I'd had our little Vegas romp.

Feeling a headache coming on, I drained the rest of my beer and stood. "I'll do what I can tonight and text you when I have answers — how long before everyone's flights leave?"

"Seven p.m. the day after tomorrow." Nixon rubbed the back of his head. Weariness wore at the edges of his mouth. "Good luck."

"Right. I think I need prayer more than luck."

"Well, I've got the Rosary memorized." He smirked as if hiding some private joke. "Couldn't hurt."

"Why'd you go and memorize that and make yourself a better Catholic?"

Nixon waved me off. "One of the Seven Deadly Sins got to me."

"Dude," Tex piped up laughing — he'd been silently listening the whole time. "One? How about all seven?"

"I'm too tired for this. See you guys later." I stood and gave half-hugs to both of them then made the trudge back to my room.

I had to keep myself from killing Nixon.

Keep my hands off my wife.
Keep it in my pants.
Discover all her secrets.
Get her to confide in me.
And do it all without looking at her breasts or thinking about sex.
Yeah, Rosary was right.

CHAPTER THIRTY-ONE

Nixon

I watched her.

Like a damn stalker from Criminal Minds.

She twirled her hair around her fingers and then threw her head back and laughed, exposing that long delicate neck — just one of the things I was obsessed with.

"Trace?" I licked my lips, suddenly nervous as hell to interrupt her girl time. "You ready for bed?"

"I think," she said, standing and wrapping her arms sloppily around my neck, "the correct answer is *are you ready for bed?*"

"Don't you mean question?"

"That's your answer!" She laughed and sagged against me.

"Shit. Who gave her wine?"

Mo and Mil both pointed at each other. I glared at my sister. She covered her mouth with her hand and hiccupped.

"Damn shame for a Sicilian to get drunk off two glasses of wine," I muttered.

"Sorry." Trace nuzzled her face in my neck. "I was just so stressed, and now I'm sleepy." There went all plans for seduction.

"It's okay, sweetheart." I kissed her forehead. "Why don't I carry you?"

"Nixon, it's fine. I'm—"

Ignoring her, I lifted her body into my arms and nodded to the girls. "See you tomorrow. Oh and Mil, Chase already went back to the room. He seemed... upset. You should go." Liar, liar, pants on fire. Holy shit, I was officially turning into Tex, all cheese and no seriousness. I needed some damn sleep.

"Oh." She stood so suddenly that I could tell she got dizzy. She grasped the chair and gave me a weak smile. "Uh, is it safe for me to—"

"No problem," I interrupted. "Vegas is basically the safest place for you to be. Cameras are everywhere, especially in this hotel. It's why Luca chose it."

"Thanks." Mil walked by me, leaving Mo all by herself.

"Should I send Tex?"

Trace was starting to get heavy, but clearly she didn't care. She was already sleeping against my chest.

"I'm a big girl." Mo took a drink of wine. "I'll go up when I'm ready."

"Text me if you need anything." I nodded and walked back into the hotel and down the hall to the Rush Tower.

"Nixon..." Trace moaned in my arms.

"What, sweetheart?" I hit the top floor button and slipped in my key card. The elevator jolted.

"Why won't you marry me like Chase?"

"Chase proposed?" I joked. Well, it was kind of a joke, as in, I would have laughed before I pulled the trigger.

"No, he's married." She pushed against my chest like she was irritated with me for not tracking. "I mean, why won't you and I marry?"

"Why won't we?"

"Mmm."

"Who says we won't?"

"Mo." Trace didn't open her eyes but they squinted as if she was trying to open them but lacked the energy. "She said your head's stuck in your ass."

At that I laughed. "Oh yeah? What else did my favorite twin say?"

"You're scared."

And there went all that beer I'd just drunk... threatening to come right back up. Because my brilliant twin sister had hit the nail right on the head. Damn her.

I was terrified.

Of losing Trace.

Of having her.

Of losing her again.

It always went in that order.

"You're drunk, Trace." The doors opened. I carried her to the penthouse and shifted my weight so I could slide the card into the slot without putting her down. Once we were inside and by the couch, I gently placed her on the cushions. A few sensor lights clicked on, causing a dim glow to invade the room.

Trace seemed totally alert. Her wide eyes examined me from head to toe before stopping at my mouth. "I love you."

"Trace." I growled, kneeling down so we were at eye level. "You know I love you. I'm obsessed with you. I can't live without you."

"Is that why you're scared?"

"Damn it." I let myself sink to the floor, leaning my back against the couch as her legs dangled by my shoulders. "I can't give you what you want, Trace."

"What do you think I want?"

"Out." I laughed without humor. "You want out. Out of this lifestyle, out of the family, out of the country, preferably anywhere but the US and Sicily."

"Oh?" It wasn't a good response; it reminded me of the way teachers answer you when you're in school. The *oh* sounded mocking, irritated, sarcastic, and hot as hell.

"I know you, Trace."

To be fair, I should have expected her to get upset; whenever she drank wine, she went from being bone weary to so aggressive I'd tied her up once.

Best night of my life.

Until she'd puked.

So it was a really good half hour.

"I hate you sometimes." Trace moved from the couch to my lap, smacking me lightly on the cheek. "I don't want out, you bastard."

What? "But, Trace, you asked on the plane—"

"I was being a woman." She all but shouted. "Yes, I wish circumstances were different, but leaving this life would be like leaving part of you behind, and I'm kind of a fan of every part."

I smirked. "Admit it, you have your favorites." I moved against her just to show her exactly what I was talking about then nipped her ear, slowly kissing down her neck and pulling back to gaze into her eyes.

"Ass." She punched my shoulder. "I swear, the more time you hang out with Chase and Tex, the more ridiculous you get."

"Part of my charm."

"You're not charming." She crossed her arms and looked away. "You're sexy but not charming."

"Charming and sexy," I corrected.

"Nixon..." Her hands cupped my face. "I just want you. Forever. That's what I want. I don't want to have to worry that you're going to run."

"So you do want to tie me up?"

Trace rolled her eyes. "Be serious."

"Fine." I kissed her mouth. "Tell you what. Anything —

and I do mean anything — you want is yours. So ask."

"I can't." Her face fell. "Because then it's not romantic."

"Romance isn't really a strong point for me. Sex? Absolutely, but romance?"

"Stop." She pushed against my chest. "You're better than you give yourself credit for. I just want to know that it's you and me for eternity, get it? I want proof of that."

"Proof." I repeated the word, letting it roll around on my tongue like slow, melting chocolate. And then, a light bulb went off. She was talking about marriage again. Romance? She wanted romance? In the middle of some unknown mafia war where we might all end up in caskets? Done. I could multitask. I was going to romance the hell out of her. "Done."

"What?" She reared back as if I'd just told her that her ass looked fat in her jeans.

"Done."

"But—"

"Now it's time for you to be patient. Can you do that?"

Her smile lit up the room, — scratch that, her smile lit up my freaking world.

"Yes."

I lost track of time as we sat on the floor talking, catching up, teasing each other... I was almost asleep when Trace asked, "Why are you being such an ass to Chase and Mil?"

With a sigh, I turned and pulled Trace into the curve of my body, resting my chin on her head. "You know Chase just as well as I do, sweetheart. You can't just order him to do things. It's hard for him. Hell, it's hard for me. They need each other. She needs to trust him, and he needs to allow himself to trust her to fall for her, if he can."

Trace let out a heavy sigh. My chest clenched at the thought that she wasn't okay with his relationship with Mil. I was damn possessive of her heart and hated that it was possible he still held a tiny sliver. I would start a war over that sliver. I would kill for it, steal for it, destroy for it.

"I'm glad."

"Hmm?" I pretended that my heart wasn't beating out of my chest, that my breathing hadn't hitched, that my damn mind wasn't ready to explode.

"That you're pushing them. It's what they need. It's why I love you."

"Because I push people?" I laughed nervously.

"Nah, because underneath that bad-ass mafia mojo, you really care, and you're willing to do anything, including killing your own damn happiness, to save the world."

I didn't think it was possible, but my heart beat faster.

"You're like my Superman."

"Whoa, let's not go putting me in tights or anything."

"It's the cape that does it for the girls, not the tights."

"Noted." I kissed her head. "Trace?"

"Hmm?"

"Do you still love him?"

No answer. I gripped her body harder, hoping and praying it was just my imagination, that I wasn't seriously thinking about marrying a girl I didn't completely have.

I was just about ready to pass out when she answered, "Yes."

My world exploded. If it were possible for a body to burst from the inside out to spontaneously combust on the impact of one simple word, mine would have.

"But not how you think," she clasped her hands together pausing too long for my comfort. "Chase was my best friend — you were my soul mate. There's a difference. It's like asking me if I love Tex or Mo. I love them, I even love Mil. Chase will always shave a special place in my heart, but he doesn't own it — you do."

Amazing how the human body can go from overdrive to complete serenity in six seconds. Even more amazing? That my physical reaction was caused by something completely emotional. On the outside I probably looked fine, but on the inside I was completely destroyed, just like Phoenix had been by his father and the ridiculous life he'd put him through.

I had no idea why Trace's confession was making me think of Phoenix, but there it was. Maybe because in that moment, when I was hanging on Trace's every word, I could almost glimpse into how he must have felt when his dad had told him…

"It's complicated." Phoenix broke the beer bottle against the rocks and stuffed his hands into his pockets. His sister had just gotten shipped off to boarding school. He said he wanted to talk — said he was having a rough time with it, which was just weird, considering they weren't even that close.

"So try to explain it." I took a seat on the rock and watched as the waters of Lake Michigan lapped around the rocky terrain.

"My father, he's been into some messed up stuff and finally — he finally got desperate, like real desperate."

"How desperate?"

"Let's just leave it at that." Phoenix sniffed and rubbed a gloved hand under his nose. "I think he was going to use Mil."

"Use?"

"In his prostitution ring. One of the men asked if she was available, like it wasn't a big deal. Like she was some whore." He cursed and picked up a rock, throwing it into the ocean. "When I asked him about it later, he laughed it off. Said to mind my own shit."

"Did you tell Mil?"

Phoenix winced. "Didn't have to. Somehow, her ma caught wind of it. When I asked my step-mom if I could help, she said no, that she already had a plan."

"A plan? Which means that clearly your father was—"

"I know," Phoenix interrupted. "Can we not talk about him, though? It's Mil I'm worried about… after Vegas, after Chase, she's just… not the same. It's like something happened to her, like Chase did something."

"He didn't," I snapped. "He wouldn't."

"Look." Phoenix's eyes looked crazed. "When she got back from Vegas she had cuts up and down her arms and a scar on her wrist, an ugly-as-hell scar that looked like someone had burned a cigar into her skin. I'm not saying Chase did it. I'm just not saying he didn't, either."

"That why you're being such an ass?"

"Well that." Phoenix smirked. "And he did sleep with my sister." His face sobered. "It's a strange feeling."

"What is?"

"Wanting to kill someone yet be their friend at the same time. Sometimes I'm scared of my own brain, my own emotions. I swear everything keeps building inside me, Nixon and I don't know how long I can keep it all in."

I slapped him on the back. "Don't be dramatic. You'll be fine."

But after that conversation he'd changed. Everything had changed. He wasn't the same Phoenix. And he died before I could find out the truth of what had changed him. The only clue was Mil.

Something had happened to her. Something Phoenix was protecting her from. I jerked away from Trace and grabbed my cell. No calls from Chase.

"What's wrong?" Trace mumbled sleepily.

"Nothing." I sent Chase a quick text. "Go to sleep."

Me: *Get her to trust you then ask her what caused the scars — mention Phoenix, but be ready.*

CHAPTER THIRTY-TWO

Mil

By the time I got back to the room, Chase was in the bathroom. The shower was running, and I could have sworn I heard him singing some sort of Frank Sinatra song, but it's entirely possible I made it up. Trace hadn't been the only one drinking wine.

With a flourish I fell across the bed and let out a huge sigh — the type of sigh a girl lets out when she's trying to let the person next to her know that something's not right.

Lucky me. All I had was a wall.

Right, so I was sighing at a damn wall.

I sighed again.

Well, no time like the present. I wasn't sure which side of Chase I was going to get tonight. The hot-as-hell arrogant asshole, who made me want to slap him almost as much as I wanted to kiss him? Or the funny, easy-going, hormonal teenager, who had left earlier this evening after staring at my boobs like he was twelve?

I smirked at the thought. Me and my sigh would take

either one. The water turned off in the bathroom. The door swung open. I glanced and almost fell off the bed.

Chase naked.

Chase. Was. Naked.

Clearly he wasn't aware that I was in the room. He didn't turn, just ran the fluffy white towel around his dripping body. Licking my lips, I felt my pulse jump as he wiped a few droplets that streamed down his face. Damn, I wanted to run my tongue along the trails the water created. My breathing picked up — and I swore under my breath as that same towel ran down his ridiculously tight abs. I was completely wrecked, my body strung so tight I was afraid to keep breathing — afraid that it was too loud — and I didn't want the show to end.

"How were the girls?" Chase asked without turning around.

Aw, crap. Embarrassed, I cleared my throat and scolded my eyes for continuing to remain on his muscled body. Just one more look, I promised myself, and then I'd be fine.

"Good." I continued my bold stare. His ass was fine. Seriously. Fine.

"You get some wine and food?" he asked, wrapping the towel around his waist. Bummer.

"Yup," I squeaked, my voice sounding all kinds of immature.

"So," he padded over to the bed and sat, "dinner and a show, huh?"

"I, uh—" Laughing, I scooted away from him toward the pillows. "I was going to say something, but—"

"Cut the shit, Mil." Chase smirked. "You were ogling."

"Girls don't ogle."

"Oh?" That gorgeously perfect idiotic face mocked me with every ounce of hotness. Damn Chase Winter. Damn beautiful man. God should have at least taken pity on the female race and made him short or fat or anything but what I was staring at. A muscled god with dark skin, bright green eyes, and a smile that made a girl immediately want to do anything she could to trap him into marriage.

"What'cha thinking about?" He smirked again.

"Stop smirking!" I yelled then covered my face with my hands. Stupid wine making me loose-lipped and ready to attack my husband with every ounce of strength my five-foot-ten body possessed.

His smile fell.

And immediately I wished I could take it back.

Chase smirking was one thing. Chase devouring me with his eyes? Yeah, totally not something I was sure my body could handle. He hadn't even touched me, and I was buzzing with pleasure. My skin felt so sensitive I could have sworn someone had put something in my drink, and I was just now feeling the effects of it. Warmth spread all the way to my toes, melting every defense I'd carefully erected when it came to Chase.

A moment. He'd said he didn't want a moment. He wanted forever. But how do you do forever with someone who doesn't even know the real you? I could offer him a moment, and he'd take it thinking it was more than that. And I'd feel like crap knowing that I was keeping everything from him. I self-consciously rubbed the scar on my wrist. Like a reminder, of what I had done in the first place when I'd asked Chase to marry me. Protection. Safety. If he only knew how he'd really saved me when I was fourteen. How he'd saved my life.

"Mil?" Chase closed the distance between us. Desperate, I threw a pillow down between our bodies, like a freaking teenager.

Chase snorted. "You think a pillow's gonna stop me?"

"No." I gulped.

Crap! I pulled into myself, wrapping my arms around my knees as if to protect my body from his close examination. My self-control was always at a zero when it came to Chase, and right now, all I wanted was for him to tell me everything was going to be okay. I wanted a repeat of our first time together — only I wanted it to mean something more. Did I even deserve to have that with him?

Liar, my brain shouted at me. *You're a liar.*

Chase tossed the pillow to the floor and walked to the edge of the bed tugged my feet so hard my legs straightened, then he and his towel decided to straddle me. My body shook as he pulled the towel from his waist — it happily joined the pillow on the floor. Stupid towel. I was jealous of a towel because it had touched Chase. It had wrapped itself around him. And given the chance, I'd do the same thing — well given the chance, I'd probably do exactly what I was doing.

Panic.

"Mil..." Was the man a damn exhibitionist? I kept my eyes trained on his, burning with embarrassment as his body pressed against mine. A small moan escaped my lips before I could stop it.

Chase grinned, that same smug grin that made me want to scratch his eyes out while mauling him with my mouth.

"Take off your shirt," he ordered, still straddling me.

I didn't move.

Chase, however, did. It was as if he knew exactly what I needed and wanted, but recognized the sheer terror behind his question and took matters into his own hands.

Cold air bit at my sensitive skin as he tugged my tank top off and threw it onto the floor. That damn towel was getting quite a show.

"Jeans." Chase's hands moved to the button of my jeans. I swear the sound of my jeans being unzipped by someone other than me was the most terrifying thing I'd ever heard.

With a grunt, he moved off of me and walked to the end of the bed where he tugged the hems of my jeans until my legs were completely bare. Chilled air from the air conditioning vent blew across my heated skin. Holding my gaze, he tossed the jeans into the laundry heap he'd created.

I was lying on the bed, shaking, in nothing but my pink bra and underwear, and hoping to God that I didn't look as scared as I felt. Sure, I was excited, but with excitement came the idea that the power of our relationship would shift if we slept together. I'd be done. I'd be owned, branded, wrecked, and then he'd want to know everything that woke me up at night — the scars that still haunted me.

He'd know my shame.

I closed my eyes.

"Look at me," Chase ordered.

I opened one eye, then two as Chase's smile went from smug to warm, trusting, loving, perfect.

"You're freaking beautiful, Mil." He slowly crawled back onto the bed. His mouth touched my leg, and I jerked with pleasure. His tongue made an appearance, swirling its way up my thigh. I whimpered. My body trembled as his hands moved to my hips. It was as if my body fit perfectly in his hands — in his care.

"Let it go." Chase laid his head on my hip. His hot breath ran across my belly button making me shiver. "Whatever it is, Mil. Just let it go. You can trust me — I'll protect you until I die. If you remember one thing from these lips, it's this. I'll die before letting you go."

Tension soared out of my body at his words.

He kissed my stomach and worked his way up to the crevice between my breasts. And then he laughed.

"What?" Was he seriously making fun of my body?

"Wait." Chase kept laughing, his face at eye-level with my chest. "It's not you."

Oh great the *it's not you, it's me* speech.

"Do you even realize how uncomfortable it was for me to ride down the elevator and meet with Nixon while flashes of this," he asked as he fingered the lacy strap of my bra, "kept slamming into my head?" His hands grazed the top of my breasts as he sighed and kissed where his fingers had just been, "I swear I almost turned around to come back a dozen times. Pink bra... hmm, may have special powers." He grinned. "I was so turned on I had to drink. You turned me to alcohol with just a glance. One look and I was drowning my sorrows in beer. You're lucky I didn't pass out and suffocate."

A laugh escaped my lips. "Sorry."

"Don't lie," Chase scolded, biting down on the flesh on my collarbone then licking where his teeth had just been. "You couldn't care less about putting me through hell."

"True." I breathed.

"And I deserved it."

"You did," I agreed.

"Because I was ogling."

"To be fair," I moaned, arching against his hand as he cupped my neck, "I did flash you."

"Which isn't really playing fair, now is it, Mil?" He chuckled against my ear and then swiped his tongue around the upper shell like he was licking an ice cream cone.

"No?" My voice shook as chills wracked my body. How was he able to have a conversation right now?

"Mil..." Chase shifted his focus and his mouth brushed mine lightly, the scrape of his five o'clock shadow had me trembling with desire.

I wanted more. I wanted to grab him by his ridiculously handsome face and never let go.

"I'll stop, if you want, but know that if I do, I may have to spend the night in the bathroom. Door locked. With visions of a naked Tex running through my head so I don't come in here and take advantage of you."

"What happened to the moment?"

"This is it." Chase's mouth met mine again. "The first moment in a lifetime of moments. I'm going to collect them."

"You can do that?" I teased, feeling more comfortable

with his naked body pressed against mine. "Collect moments?"

"I'm doing it now." His green eyes flashed. "Bee-stung lips, high cheekbones, perfect skin that feels like velvet, scents of vanilla here," he tapped my ear, "and here." His hand ran down the middle of my chest. "Legs that go on forever." He grinned. "A smile that could both start a war and end it. And the most beautiful eyes, I've ever seen." He pressed a kiss at the corner of my mouth. "God, I love your eyes."

"I love yours," I echoed in a small voice.

Those same green eyes widened as a smile broke out across his face; it hurt to look at him. Just being with Chase was overwhelming.

"Say something now, Mil." His finger traced from my mouth to my jaw line. "Because I can only keep myself from you for so long."

"Now." I shrugged, a teasing smile dancing on my lips.

"Now?" He repeated and then like a light bulb or, in Chase's case, a bull taking over his brain, he tugged at my bra and then my underwear. It was just us. Hot as fire, skin against skin.

Safe.

Home.

Protected.

And that part of my heart he'd held for so long finally found its home — in his arms.

CHAPTER THIRTY-THREE

Chase

I'd lost complete control of myself when I'd caught Mil watching me, and then teasing her had done nothing except the inevitable. It had led me to this moment, where I was at a crossroads. I wanted her so bad — my body did. But my heart? I wasn't sure where it stood.

All I knew is for the first time in a really long time, I saw Mil's face, her face, not Trace's. When I felt Mil's body with my hands, she consumed my everything, and I wanted to wreck her for anyone else.

I wanted to brand her with my touch.

I wanted to sear her with my kiss, sealing her mouth with such strong memories of what my lips felt like against hers that she'd never forget as long as she lived.

Holding her in my arms, feeling her heartbeat against my hand as I removed the last shred of her lingerie.

It was the best feeling in the world. I wasn't worrying about Nixon or Trace or some damn love triangle — it was just me and Mil. Just me and my wife, and I wanted — no I needed to love her like she deserved.

I closed my eyes… finally releasing the last part of me that was clinging to Trace. And when I opened my eyes? I felt like I could soar, as Mil looked up through thick black lashes, asking me the question every girl does when she's in a vulnerable position. Will you love me? Will you leave me? Or will you give your body while you take all of mine?

I flipped over onto my back, pulling Mil on top of me. I figured she'd need to feel in control; she wasn't one to give up herself willingly. But the minute she was on top of me, it was as if she was confused about what to do. Damn, my body was having no issues remembering what to do. I almost wished it would have, because then it wouldn't be the fastest sexual experience of my life.

"Mil." I cupped her face, dragging my mouth slowly across hers, memorizing her taste, then dipping my tongue into her mouth. She kissed me back, hard. Her hands tangled in my hair as her body moved slowly against mine.

I groaned — trying to rein it in. She was driving me crazy. Her nails dug into my shoulders as she moved her mouth to my neck. Holy shit. She bit me. Damn, that pain felt good. She bit again and again then sucked.

I just died.

They were going to find my body in this exact position come tomorrow morning, and my soul would be giving me a high five from heaven.

The friction between our bodies was driving me absolutely insane. I flipped her over onto her back, but she fought me. Wrestling match, party of two. I laughed when she slapped my ass, and almost bowed down to worship her when she winked and crushed my mouth with hers again.

"Mil, I can take about five more seconds of kissing you before I spontaneously combust," I admitted honestly, my voice low and strained.

The little minx grinned like I'd just given her the keys to

heaven, and maybe I had, because she reached for me and guided me to exactly where I wanted to be.

With a groan, I tried to go slow.

Then realized... I had to.

Confusion smacked me in the face like a two-by-four.

"Um, Mil..." My eyes searched hers.

Her face turned red, and then with a smirk, she jerked me against her, making my world explode in a thousand different rays of light.

I didn't want to hurt her, but having her body surround me? Yeah, it was the best damn feeling I'd ever had, and with my self-control being that of negative ten... I moved against her, faster and faster until — she screamed.

I hoped to God it was a good scream. I hoped to God I hadn't done some sort of irreversible damage and—

Tension built from my center, rendering me incapable of hoping anything else. Pure primal need took over. My blood heated, exploded to every inch of my body, through my veins. It pounded in my ears, roared. On the edge of my consciousness, I heard her whimper as she clutched my shoulders, her nails digging into my skin. All sense of rationality completely deserted me as we took each other over the edge.

With a shudder, I slumped against her, trying to keep my body weight off of her. "Tell me," I croaked when I stopped gasping for breath.

"No, I need to—"

I held her firm. Her body shivered.

"How many guys, Mil?"

Her eyes closed as a single tear ran down her cheek. "You... only you."

"Damn."

"Are you mad?" she whispered.

I burst out laughing. "Yes, I'm pissed I'm the only guy who's ever touched you here." I placed my hands against her breasts. "The only man who's kissed you here?" I trailed my fingertips down her stomach, in between our bodies. "Made love to you here."

She shuddered, closing her eyes. I brushed a soft kiss against her lips. "Are you insane?" I kissed her again, this time harder, with possession. "I don't think I could be happier. It's possible I was already looking into any of your last boyfriends, you know, to find social security numbers and whatnot just in case—"

"You were going to order hits on my ex-boyfriends?"

"To keep you safe." I nodded. "And to keep me sane, yes."

"I think I may actually like you, Chase Winter."

"Murder? That's all it took to get you hot? Killing your ex-boyfriends?"

"No." Her smile widened.

I nipped her lower lip. "Because I'm really good at sex?"

"No, and I wouldn't know anyway."

"Then why?"

"Because you gave me one moment — but you promised more. And..." she licked her lips. "...I believe you."

My heart rammed against my chest as if it was trying to break free. I smiled, tucking pieces of her hair behind her ear, and kissed her neck. What was I supposed to say to that? Words lodged in my throat. I ran my hands down her arm and paused on her wrist, hovering over her scar.

"Are you ready to tell me?"

Mil tensed beneath me. I held up my hand. "Wait, before you say anything, I've got an idea." Still fully naked, I got off the bed and grabbed the phone to call room service.

"Yeah, can I get a bottle of champagne and an assortment of—" I paused and smirked at Mil. "Chocolate. Lots of chocolate. Whatever you have."

Mil's eyes watered. I wasn't sure if it was because of sexual excitement or just being excited about chocolate-covered strawberries.

"You. Stay." I pointed at the bed.

"Oh?" Her eyebrows shot up.

Right. It was Mil. Telling her to stay was basically like throwing down the gauntlet, challenging her to do the complete opposite. "Please?"

Her eyes narrowed.

"Let me take care of you."

Her entire body relaxed, as if I'd just told her I was going to save the world, and all she had to do was sleep through the battle until it was won.

"Five minutes." I held up my hand and walked into the bathroom and started the bath water in the Jacuzzi tub. After a few minutes, it was full enough for Mil to sit in. Without saying anything, I walked back into the bedroom, scooped her up into my arms, even when she beat against my chest playfully, and placed her in the soothing water.

The knock on the door was soft, discreet.

"Stay." I kissed her forehead and grabbed a bathrobe, tightening it around my waist as I opened the door. Without letting the guy in, I handed him a twenty-dollar bill and pulled the cart the rest of the way, locking the door behind me.

When I walked into the bathroom, champagne and food in hand, Mil was humming to herself.

"You hum?" I asked stupidly.

"Huh?"

"Hum?"

"What?"

I rolled my eyes. "You were humming."

"Is that against Chase Winter's rules? Humming in the tub? What would you rather I do?"

My body roared to life. "Well…"

"Stop." Mil held up her hand. "Forget I asked."

"Aw, baby, that's like turning the key to an engine and then deciding not to drive… it's just… cruel to the car."

"Are you calling me a tease or a racecar driver? I'm confused."

Sending her a smug smile, I set the full champagne glasses onto the counter and dropped my bathrobe. "Still confused?"

"Little chilly, Chase?" Mil reached for the champagne. I smacked her hand lightly.

"Little eager, Mil?"

"Ass."

"Tease."

She sighed, but I could tell it was a happy sigh. Mil was trying to act tough, like always, but I was beginning to see that second layer to her. All women, in my experience, were complicated. Each had her secrets and every single one had a way of hiding them. Mil's fierceness was her armor — and it killed me to think that I could have possibly been responsible for making her gun shy when it came to men.

"I'm getting in the tub."

"Does that mean you're kicking me out?"

"No." I stepped in behind her and slowly slid down the porcelain. "It just means things are going to be snug."

"I'm not so sure I can handle snug."

I let out a hiss when the hot water surrounded me and a soft groan escaped from deep in my throat as I pulled her roughly against me. "If I can handle snug, you sure as hell can handle snug."

Her soft sigh fanned across my chest, raising goose bumps that had nothing to do with being cold and everything to do with wanting a repeat performance of the last hour we'd spent together. She leaned her head over my heart. I reached out and tucked her hair behind her ear and kissed her temple.

"I want to know, Mil."

My fingers lightly grazed that same scar again, this time pushing against it, as if by adding pressure, the words would come out of her mouth, the fear would dissipate, and she'd trust me.

"What if I tell you and you hate me?"

My heart clenched. "Mil, I could never hate you."

"You could," she said in a small voice. "You might."

"Trust me."

A few seconds of silence passed, and then Mil said, so quietly I almost didn't hear her, "I was fourteen…"

CHAPTER THIRTY-FOUR

Mil

I couldn't believe that I was actually telling him. Never in a million years had I planned on cutting open past wounds and letting myself bleed out onto the ground.

But for some reason, Chase made me want to share. He made me believe that if I told him about my demons, he wouldn't run away screaming; instead he'd help me conquer them.

"Fourteen?" Chase repeated. "Before or after you and I—" His voice died off.

I could feel the tension in his body as silence filled the bathroom.

"Before," I whispered. The memories surfaced slowly, and then it was impossible to stop the pain as it pinched my chest. That's how demons destroyed a person. The minute you opened the door to one, the rest of them followed suit, leaving you defenseless and desperate to do anything to get the door to close again.

"Mil." Chase rubbed my arms. "It's okay, I'm here."

I was shaking, and although the bath water was still searing hot, I had goose bumps all over. Chase continued rubbing my arms as I talked.

"My dad... he wasn't right in the head."

"Understatement of the century," he grumbled.

"Not like that." My body felt heavy. "I'm sure Phoenix told you about the prostitution ring. Not only was he into selling young girls, but he liked to break them in himself."

Chase's fingers dug into my arms. My world stopped. Would he be disgusted? Maybe I *was* all of those things my dad had said to me.

"Mil?" Chase kissed my temple, his lips hovering over my skin as he whispered, "It's okay, keep going."

"One day, one of his men came and said my dad needed me for something. He was at The Cave and had forgotten his cell phone on the counter. So, being the dutiful daughter that I was, I went with the man to drop off the cell phone and ask my dad what he needed."

Terror filled every square inch of my body. "I remember that it was really dark. They didn't call it The Cave for fun. It was an abandoned warehouse that had lights which flickered on and off. My dad was in the middle of some circle, surrounded by a few men in suits. He asked me to come forward, so I did."

Chase was quiet, so I kept talking. "I'm still not sure if it was his plan all along, but one of the men asked how much I was. And then another offered money for me. Someone else shouted in a gravelly voice that he'd pay over two million." I shook my head. "It was such an astronomical amount that I thought they had to be joking. But they weren't. My dad didn't even hesitate. He turned to the man with the raspy voice and asked him what the catch was. The man was standing in the shadows, but I remember that he was really big, as in, for a second I thought he was a giant, but his voice... it never changed. It was gravelly, almost as if he'd somehow lost the ability to speak."

Chase released his grip a bit on me and kissed my head again. "Did he touch you?"

"No." I shook my head. "My dad told me to go home, but he stayed out all night. When he got home, it was the first time in years that he actually smiled at me. The next week was the best week I'd ever experienced with him. He took me shopping, kissed my mom in front of all of us, and was honestly acting like the dad I'd always wanted. Even Phoenix had been impressed. We left for Vegas later that week and that was when my mom told me."

"She said my dad was going to sell my virginity to a horrible man. She said if I didn't do something about it, I would die."

"Wow," Chase interrupted. "Dramatic much? Couldn't she have at least lessened the blow?"

"Would that have made what I had to do any better, Chase? Yes, she freaked me out, but it also lit a fire under my ass. Later that night we all met for dinner."

Chase sighed. "You were wearing the prettiest blue dress I'd ever seen." He laughed. "I remember, I assumed you were Phoenix's cousin. No way could a girl that pretty be related to him. It didn't seem logical. I mean, he was just so Phoenix and you were so…" He paused. "So damn beautiful it hurt to stare at you."

I smiled at his memory.

Chase's mouth found my ear. "I'm pretty sure I propositioned you that night, and you tried to slap me."

Laughing, I pulled away and shifted in the water so I could see part of his face. Looking at Chase would probably go down as one of my favorite things to do in the world. His beautiful smile made my stomach drop.

He lifted his hand to my cheek. "What made you choose me?"

I looked down, feeling the shame of that moment tenfold.

"I didn't."

Chase pulled his hand back.

"My mom did."

"Your mom picked me out? The same one who just—"

"Died." I choked on the word. "Yeah, she pulled me aside and told me not to screw things up. She said you were safe, said you'd protect me. And then she left. Luckily, you took that opportunity to seduce me."

"I'm an ass."

"No." I gave Chase a weak smile. "You did what I needed you to do—"

"Mil, I used you as a Vegas one-night stand."

"Right." I shrugged. "But I needed you."

"I left you."

"I know." I couldn't look at him in the face.

"Mil." Chase tilted my chin toward him. "If it was all a ploy, why were you so upset with me when I didn't want to take the relationship further?"

Because you made me fall for you. Because you protected me when nobody else did. Because the minute you took my heart, I didn't ever want it back. Because the minute you touched me, my life was never the same.

"I was fourteen." I shrugged. "And I am a girl. We tend to get emotional when sex is involved."

His eyes narrowed. I cleared my throat and looked away. "At any rate, Phoenix told my dad he found us in bed together, and that's where the story ends."

"And the scar?" He grabbed my wrist.

I tried to pull away.

"Mil—" Chase's teeth ground together. "Tell me all of it. Now."

"He was upset." My body convulsed at the memory. "Please don't make me say it—"

"Damn it, Mil, did he touch you? Did he do this to you?" He grabbed my wrist hard in his hand, his eyes wild with fury.

I nodded. "He beat me and then he used a knife to cut this scar into my wrist, he finished it off with a branding on top of the scar, burning it against my skin, covering what he did. He said I was a marked woman, that anyone who saw this scar would know who I should have belonged to. He said it was only a matter of time—"

I choked on my words. "Only a matter of time before I was killed. He said I ruined everything. He called me a damn Helen of Troy and laughed." Hot tears ran down my cheeks. "He laughed the entire time he cut the scar on my wrist, no matter how many times I screamed or yelled. Nobody came. Nobody saved me. I was fourteen, Chase. I thought that's how life worked, just like the movies... someone hurt me, but the person I cared about the most would rescue me. I kept thinking of your face, but the door never opened. The next day he sent me to an all girls academy."

At Chase's sharp intake of breath I knew it was time to get out of the tub. The story was finished. He either accepted the truth as it was — or dug further. I preferred for him to let it go.

I tried to stand.

Chase gripped my wrist and held me firmly against his body. "You're not going anywhere."

"Chase—"

His mouth silenced any sort of complaint I would have had. When he pulled back, his eyes darkened. He cursed and let me go. "We need to contact Tanya."

"I know," I said in a small voice. "She was my mom's only friend after the separation. She never forgave Phoenix's dad for sending me away. And I never forgave him for making it so the first and last time I talked to my mom in years. And now she's dead."

Chase cleared his throat. "The sooner we get to the bottom of this the better everything will be, okay?"

I nodded, not feeling very confident. Where did it end? With Tanya? With Campisi? Did he even have the power to make everything go away?

"Text her." Chase kissed my temple. "Tell her you want to meet. Tell her something bad happened and you need her help."

"Okay."

Wordlessly, Chase rose from the bathtub and wrapped me in a towel, drying me off as if I was nothing but a small child. I'd never been taken care of so tenderly before. Nobody had ever cared. Nobody had ever even touched me as much as Chase did. I'd always thought I was one of those people who didn't need physical touch. You know, almost like there was something wrong with my body, because every time a guy hit on me, all I wanted to do was slit his throat. But when it came to Chase, it wasn't ever enough. It was terrifying how much I craved him, how much my body had come to depend on him, and how much my heart needed his consistent encouragement to keep beating strongly.

Once I was dry, I threw on a bathrobe and walked out into the main living area. My sleek iPhone mocked me as it stayed charged on the nightstand. Before I could punk out, I grabbed it and sent a quick text to Tanya.

Me: *Something went horribly wrong. Can we meet tomorrow morning?*

I waited, anxious for her response. Sweat pooled at my temples as the phone burned against my hand. Finally the text alert went off, her text flashed in front of me.

Tanya: *Not a good idea.*

Me: *I don't care if it's not a good idea! My mom's dead!*

Two minutes later my cell phone lit up again.

Tanya: *You're right. My apologies for being so insensitive. Where would you like to meet?*

I chewed my lower lip. Public places were always best.

Me: *The Golden Nugget Night Club. 1 hour.*

Tanya: *Done.*

Shaking, I put the phone back on the desk and massaged my temples. One hour before I was meeting the wife of Campisi. And there was a fifty-fifty chance she was responsible for everything that had gone to hell in the past twelve hours.

No other explanation would come.

We were stuck.

Going home meant waiting it out until someone planted a car bomb or tried to shoot me in the head. I'd always been the type of girl to face danger head-on. I didn't like hiding, and I wasn't about to now.

A text alert went off. I picked up my phone, but it wasn't mine that had gone off. Not thinking, I walked over to the opposite nightstand where Chase's phone was. I clicked on it and was given the privilege of seeing the last three text messages.

All from Nixon.

Each one making me sicker than the last as I read.

"Ask her about her scars?" I repeated out loud. *"Get her to trust you?"* Shaking, I read the last one. *"Chase, do whatever it takes, and I do mean whatever it takes."*

I dropped the phone onto the bed and barely made it to the trashcan before I threw up the strawberries Chase had just hand-fed me. It was as if they'd gone sour in my stomach. I tried to keep the hot tears from pouring down my cheeks. But they came anyway, mixing with my spit and falling into the trashcan, mocking me with every salty drop that fell from my face.

"Bastard!" I clenched my fists, unable to keep my body from trembling as I knelt onto the floor, feeling absolutely broken and betrayed.

The man that promised to save me.

Had done the exact opposite.

He'd used me.

And broken me in the process.

CHAPTER THIRTY-FIVE

Chase

I was whistling.

Like a damn fool.

If Nixon could see me now, he'd think I'd completely lost it. My grin got wider at the thought. Damn, if I didn't watch it, I was going to break something in my face.

The hot water poured over my achy body. Being with Mil had been... amazing, effortless, obsessive. Already, I was eager for another round. My body flared to life at just the thought of touching her again, of kissing her, squeezing her flesh between my hands as I ran my tongue down her—

"You piece of shit!" Mil screamed. I stepped out of the shower only to find her standing in front of me, a gun aimed directly at my chest. "I trusted you!"

"Mil, put the gun down." I lifted my hands into the air like a guilty ass and looked frantically around the bathroom for the reason behind her anger.

"If I didn't need you so damn bad, I'd shoot you in the head." She choked, tears running down her cheeks.

"Baby, what happened?" I took a cautious step toward her.

She shook the gun harder, this time pressing it against my wet chest.

"Mil?"

"No." Her lips trembled.

"What the hell happened?" I whispered. "Are you hurt? Did someone hurt you?"

She nodded, dropping the gun onto the floor. It clattered against the tile making such a loud noise that I winced.

"Baby—"

"Don't call me that." Her voice was low, emotionless. "We have to meet Tanya in less than an hour. Grab your shit and put some clothes on."

"Mil—"

"Here's your phone." She forced a smile that looked more like she was baring her teeth. "Hope you got all the information you needed." She pushed the phone against my chest and stalked out of the bathroom. I grabbed it before it also crashed to the floor and looked at the screen.

"Shit." I wiped my face with my free hand as I scrolled through the messages. Damn Nixon. Did he have to ruin everything? Seriously? Running after Mil would do nothing. She'd just think I was lying to her like everyone else in her life. So instead, I listened to her orders. I followed her out of the bathroom, put my jeans, grabbed my gun and wallet — or *my shit* as she lovingly called it — and stuffed my phone back into my pocket.

"Aren't you gonna text Nixon and let him know what's going on?" Mil asked, without looking at me directly in the eyes.

"Nah." I felt like an ass, even though I'd done nothing wrong. "Some things should be kept just between us. Tanya isn't much of a threat, you know? We're just going to do a meeting in a public place. It's not like she's going to try to shoot us. Then again..." I sighed, things hadn't gone how I thought they would, "It may be wise to have backup."

"Fine, do whatever you need to do." Mil's voice caught in her throat.

"It will be," I whispered, reaching for her hand.

She jerked back and shook her head.

"I didn't betray you. I know you don't believe me, but if you remember correctly, I was a little distracted these past twelve hours. When would I have had time to even look at my phone? And you know how iPhones work. If the message is checked, it doesn't show up on the home screen anymore."

Mil stared at the carpet, her fingers twitching at her side.

"I just wanted to say my peace so you'd know."

Her head jerked up. "Know?"

"Yeah, Mil." I stalked toward her and pushed her against the wall, nearly knocking off the artsy picture by the door. "I want you to know. I want you to freaking feel. I want you to believe me when I say I want you. I like you. I trust you. I live to protect you. And I only do what I want to do. My cousin can go to hell for all I care. I chose to be with you... I wasn't forced, nor will I ever be forced. And if I am, I'll take the punishment with open arms. So pick up the broken pieces to your tragically shattered heart. Let me glue them back together again so you can get that damn look off your face and let me kiss you."

"Is that how this works?" she said, her voice thick with tears. "You kiss me then tattle to Nixon."

I pinned her arms behind her back, exposing her neck and mouth to mine as I slowly leaned forward, my forehead touching hers. "I have given you absolutely no reason not to trust me, Mil. When this is all over with and I walk away, just know it won't be because I want to, but because I could only handle so much rejection and distrust before you forced me to give up and I'm not a man that gives up. I'm it. I'm all you have. So stop being so damn insecure."

She closed her eyes.

"Look at me."

Mil's lower lip trembled.

I kissed her mouth and whispered across her lips, "Trust me. I need you to trust in me."

"Okay." She opened her eyes. "But no secrets."

"Mil." I released her hands and gave her a sad look, tilting her chin so I could feel the smoothness of her skin. "I think we both know who's harboring secrets between the two of us, and it sure as hell isn't me." With a sigh, I released her chin.

I pulled on a white T-shirt and my black suit jacket that could easily conceal a gun without looking too weird. Then I turned back to Mil.

"Where to?"

"The Golden Nugget Nightclub."

My eyebrows arched in amusement. "Mixing business with pleasure, huh?"

Rolling her eyes, Mil snatched a knife from the table. She stomped over to her suitcase, and paused long enough to pull out a short black cocktail dress. With slow movements that I'm sure she did on purpose in order to teach me a lesson and get me so hot for her I was ready to forget about meeting Tanya anywhere, she let the robe drop from her body and shimmied into the tight dress. It was like a freaking second skin as it snaked around her body. It shimmered in the light with each movement; I seriously wanted nothing more than to remove the dress.

I licked my lips in anticipation. Damn, she was beautiful.

Mil walked over to me and turned. Shaking, I fingered the zipper and slowly zipped her dress up, fighting the desire to unzip the entire time.

"Ready." She threw on a pair of red heels and then wrapped a holster around her thigh, strapping her knife in just in case.

"I'd say you were." I whistled.

Her eyes narrowed. "I'm still pissed."

"Good." I focused in on her eyes. "Use it."

I could tell she was nervous. She kept pressing her palms against the front of the dress, smoothing it down.

With a curse I walked over to her and grabbed her hands. "It's going to be fine, I promise."

"And if it's not?" Her voice wavered.

"Then at least we had tonight."

She pushed against my chest, a smile playing at the corner of her lips. "Do you always have to be such an ass?"

"Yes. Especially when you look like you're about to shit a brick. It's going to be fine. I've got your back, and we'll have Luca, Frank, Nixon, and Tex watching from the shadows. Or in Tex's case, distracting the would-be assassins by dropping it like it's hot on the dance floor."

"Right." Mil snorted. "Like that won't get us killed."

"It may get him shot." I shrugged. "But it will be a good distraction."

Mil checked her phone. "We have a half hour to notify everyone and get down to the club."

"Alright." I opened my own phone and began typing a group text. "I'm going to fill everyone in on the details via text. Something about us all meeting at a public place kind of rubs me the wrong way."

"I thought it didn't matter which way you were rubbed?" Her eyes teased.

"Aw, there she is. I knew you'd make a comeback." I winked. "Like I said, use the fear. Think of it this way. The only reason Tex acts like a complete jackass most the time is because he's scared shitless. He has more to lose than anyone."

"Yeah." Mil nodded, her eyebrows drawing together in concern. "Trace kind of told me."

"Let's hope this is about you more than it is about him," I said sourly. "Because if Tanya Campisi recognizes the prodigal son, we may have a full-out war on our hands."

"How do you figure?" Mil asked, wrapping her hair around her head into a tight bun.

Damn, I liked it loose and wavy, but loose and wavy meant some freak assassin could pull her hair and drag her away. Bun it was. Bun was safe.

I tried to look nonchalant, even though something in me twitched with fear. "Tanya never forgave the Abandonatos for taking away her sweet boy. She felt that we brainwashed him with our American ways."

"Hmm." Mil smeared or rubbed or whatever the hell girls called it — lipstick across her luscious lips and pouted in the mirror. Was her entire plan to get me so aroused before we went to the club that I was rendered useless?

"'Kay, now I'm ready."

"Me too," I grumbled.

"Later." She gave me a shy smile, pink gracing her high cheekbones.

"Promise?"

"Swear."

"Pinky it." I held out my pinky.

She stared at my pinky and let out a sigh. I tilted my head, waiting. With an exaggerated eye-roll she latched onto my finger with her own pinky. "I swear, sometimes it's like I'm married to an adolescent."

"Amazing how you can make a man lose his arousal with one sly comment. Thanks though. I needed that, like a bucket of cold water thrown on my body." I chuckled and opened the door, looking down the hallway for anything suspicious. After I ensured the coast was clear, I let Mil walk in front. "After you."

CHAPTER THIRTY-SIX

Nixon

"I don't like it," I mumbled to Trace for probably the tenth time as I toyed with my drink at the bar. The dance club was too loud, too dark, too everything. I still couldn't see Tex, even though he'd promised he wouldn't dance too far away from the crowd. Frank and Luca were sitting over in the corner looking more uncomfortable by the minute.

"There he is." Trace nodded in the direction of the door as Chase and Mil made their way through the crowds to the opposite end of the bar.

Damn, Chase was earning points for looking so hopelessly in love. He trailed after Mil with wide eyes and a smile that said he'd just gotten lucky. Then he touched her ass, and she grinned and grabbed the hand and lifted it off of her with a smile and shake of her head.

"They look relaxed," Trace said loudly in my ear.

"Yeah well, sex has a way of doing that to a person." I couldn't decide if I was frustrated that he'd let his guard down or proud that he'd done what it had taken to get answers out of her. It still felt wrong. Every damn thing felt wrong about the club, from the way my clothes were pressed against my body to the music they were playing.

Chase held up his hand and motioned for the bartender and laughed with Mil, every once in a while touching her knee with his hand.

His smile faded when a figure walked up to them. I didn't recognize him; he was tall, clean-shaven, and had dark hair. His suit was expensive, from what I could tell, and he seemed distant but friendly.

Chase eyed me across the bar, lifted his drink one last time, and grabbed Mil's hand as they were led to a back door.

"Shit." I pushed away from the bar then, remembering Trace, doubled back and pointed at her face. "You. Stay."

"Staying." She raised an eyebrow.

I glanced up, made eye contact with Frank, and then motioned for Luca to follow me.

Trace froze and I turned back to her. Recognition flared in her wide eyes, but she was looking over my right shoulder. Something hard pressed into the small of my back, and the cold steel of a gun filtered through my shirt. Well shit, didn't see that coming.

"Let's go." the voice said, the gun pushing harder into my back.

Grimly, I nodded and reached for Trace. She held my hand as we all walked out of the club. Nobody noticed — or if they did, nobody cared that there was a gun pointed at me. Just as it seemed nobody noticed my smile was tense or that Trace looked like she'd just swallowed a bug.

I caught Luca and Frank in the corner of my eye and stretched my neck to the left, which was the usual sign for them to follow. They slowly walked toward us but feigned disinterest. I couldn't look directly at them so I wasn't sure if they recognized who was escorting us out, or if they were getting ready to put a few bullets in our captor's chest. Out of the corner of my eye, though, they seemed not to be interested.

Once we were out in the street, I was pushed into Trace's arms and heard the click of a gun. Shit.

Turning, I guarded her with my body and looked into the eyes of our captor.

"You should have stayed in Chicago," Sergio said, his voice sad. "Why, Nixon, is it that you can't just leave things alone?"

"But you're a ghost…" Trace's voice wavered. "You help us!"

Not to mention the fact that he was blood. Did he have a death wish?

"What the hell do you think you're doing?" I spat.

Sergio laughed and scratched his head with the tip of his gun. "You mean other than saving your pathetic life?"

"What?"

"Ten," Sergio said in a cold voice. "Ten men. All with guns trained on you and your little mafia princess." He licked his lips and closed his eyes, cursing into the night sky. "It's bad, Nixon."

"Bad?" Trace repeated.

"How bad?" came another male voice I recognized as Frank's. Luca stood next to him, his expression grim.

"Bad enough," Luca muttered, "that one of our ghosts had to come out and play, I imagine."

"The footage. From the night Chase and Mil were attacked at the hotel." Sergio shook his head. "There were marks on the insides of those men's wrists."

My head snapped up as every nerve twitched with awareness. "What kind of marks?" I glared at his hand. "And put your damn gun away."

"Oh, sorry." Sergio put the gun back into his jacket. "I needed to make it look like I was capturing you guys before you got your heads blown into what I can only assume is the worst techno music to ever be produced."

"Thanks," I said through clenched teeth. "The marks?"

Sergio clicked through his cell phone pictures and finally settled on one of the bodies; he expanded it until the fuzzy mark came into focus. It looked familiar, like a face I couldn't quite place it.

"Think hard," Sergio said. "I'm sure it will come to you."

"Let me see." Luca snatched the phone and then did something I'd never seen him do in my entire life. He showed fear. He handed the phone back to Sergio and looked at me straight in the eyes. "We're all going to die."

CHAPTER THIRTY-SEVEN

Chase

"Hey," I joked. "These clothes are new. Be careful." I tried to appear like I didn't have a clue in hell why we were getting escorted out of the club at gunpoint and into a waiting black Escalade.

"Get in," the man said gruffly, shoving me against the car before opening the door and pushing both me and Mil inside. I stumbled over her and let out a loud laugh. I figured the more I played the stupid role the easier it would be for me to snap his neck and get Mil the hell away.

"You've grown," came a gravelly feminine voice.

"Tanya?" Mil said surprised. "Was this necessary?"

"Keeping you alive?" Her laugh was evil. It sounded like something out of a horror story, as if someone had crushed her voice box and then played Frankenstein with it, putting it back together but completely tattered. "I believe so."

I swallowed. Her face was covered in moonlight. She shifted in her seat, and I got a brief glimpse of cold grey eyes and salt-and-pepper hair. The car didn't move. So clearly we were doing this little meeting on the street as if that was safe.

"This must be Chase?"

"It is." My teeth ground together.

"Handsome."

"I'd like to think so." I smiled tensely.

"And he has a sense of humor."

I almost lunged for her right then and there.

"My mom's dead," Mil said in a cold voice. "So unless you have some helpful information, we're done."

Tanya sighed. "It was you who contacted me. Not the other way around. I can only answer what you ask." She hesitated. "You've changed." Tanya's voice dripped with sadness. *What? The bitch suddenly developed a heart?* "I'd always wondered what happened to you after—"

"After?" I asked quickly.

"After she was beaten by her father."

"You knew?"

Mil lunged across the seat, but I grabbed her, pulling her back into my arms.

"In those days? We all knew the workings of your father, Emiliana. We simply turned the other way when things became too ugly. Not all of us, mind you, but most of us."

"And my mother?" Mil asked quietly.

"Wrong place, wrong time," Tanya said sadly. "I was supposed to be in that hotel room as well. Your mother and I were meeting an hour before to order room service and catch up. I walked as far as the elevator and happened to break part of my heel. I bent down to grab the damn thing, looked up, and came face-to-face with three men in suits, nice shoes — Italian, of course — all getting on the same elevator."

"Why didn't you call her? Why didn't you warn her?"

"Because I'm selfish," Tanya said quickly. "Because one phone call meant both our deaths." She sniffled. "I walked away. Within fifty minutes, I heard the explosion and knew... I knew he'd gotten to her."

"He?"

"Aw..." Tanya reached into her purse and pulled out a cigarette. "You mean to tell me you still don't know?"

"Know what?" Mil shouted.

I gripped her hand. Hard.

"I wonder..." Tanya took a long drag, "...if repressed memories can cause a person to go insane. Chase?" She eyed me coolly. "What do you think? Should I tell her?"

I assessed her from head to toe. "If you don't, I'll cut out your tongue and feed it to your favorite bodyguard, so sure, I'd start talking."

"I like him." She turned away from me and tilted her head, as if she had nothing but pity for Mil. "My dear, your father marked you."

"I know." Mil rubbed her scar and leaned further into me.

"You've been on borrowed time since you were fourteen, and he's finally called up his marker. After all, he paid two million dollars for you, and we all know what happens when a debt hasn't been paid."

Mil squirmed in her seat. "But why now?"

"Because now you have what he wants."

"A husband?"

Tanya's eyes turned into tiny slits. "No. You have leadership of the De Langes. You're the boss of the family he's been wanting to keep quiet for over twenty years. After all, they know all his secrets, and it's only a matter of time before you do too." She shrugged. "Besides, you also have three mafia bosses at your fingertips. Tell me, will they come for you? Will little Chase fight your battles? Will Nixon fall all over himself to protect his own family?"

"No." Mil shook her head. "They couldn't care less about me. It's a business arrangement, that's all."

"Really?"

Mil nodded.

Tanya lunged for her, but I was quicker. I kneed Tanya in the chest, caught her in the mouth with my elbow, pulled out my gun, and held it to her head.

Blood spewed from her mouth. "Go ahead. He's just going to kill me anyway."

I slammed her head back against the seat. Her hand came up and gripped my wrist, and that's when I saw it.

The exact same mark that was on Mil's wrist.

"So," Tanya sputtered, blood caking her teeth from my hit. "Now you know."

"Chase?" Mil asked.

"We need to go now." I jerked away from Tanya and grabbed Mil's hand, pulling her out of the car before we could do anything. I was taking her away. I was running. Because no place in the freaking United States would be safe for her. Not now, not for any of us.

The dry desert air hit me in the face as I jerked Mil toward my body with one arm and shot the bodyguard in the chest. No loose ends.

Mil gasped, probably horrified that I could be so cold, but it didn't matter. I didn't even hesitate, because it wasn't my life hanging in the balance. It was hers, and suddenly, every single puzzle piece finally fused together. My time with Mil, our past, our history, our marriage — it had all led to this. Even things with Trace. Had I met Mil all over again and hadn't had my heart stomped on, I wouldn't have treasured her as much as I did now.

That's what she was to me. She was a treasure. One I wanted to keep for myself, one I would die saving. If it was the last thing I did.

"Come on." I tucked the gun back into my jeans and gripped her hand and squeezed.

Luckily, the street was more of an alleyway so it wasn't exactly flooded with people, and Vegas was full of crazies. We got as far as Freemont when I got a text from Nixon. They

were waiting for us back at the hotel.
At least they hadn't been captured. Not yet.

CHAPTER THIRTY-EIGHT

Nixon

The restaurant back at The Golden Nugget wasn't crowded in the least. We took a booth in the very back and sat. Nobody spoke for a while. I'd never seen Luca so quiet in my entire life. I mean, this was Luca we were talking about. He fed on small children and laughed when people bled out. I wasn't looking at the same man. I was looking at a man afraid — and to see a man as terrifying as Luca afraid? It didn't sit well with me. It made me think that maybe this was bigger than I'd originally thought.

I slid a small Glock .9 toward Trace; her eyes flickered shut before she gave a quick nod and put it in her purse. She knew what I was asking her — what I was communicating to her. I needed her to protect herself at all costs.

We'd gone over her escape plan more times than I'd like to count. She had seven passports that would gain her access into the countries I'd previously chosen. Countries where I knew she'd be given asylum. I'd also assigned two men who would leave with her and protect her until the day I could either find her again or until the day we were reunited, that is, if God even let people like me into Heaven. If not, at least Trace would be there. I could live with that. A private account had been set up so that she would never want for anything. She'd hated me for it. But it was necessary. If she wasn't safe... Hell, I couldn't even think about it. My mind couldn't wrap around the idea of a world where she was no longer breathing, a world where her heartbeat wasn't slow and steady next to mine.

"I think we need to talk." Frank ordered a bottle of wine and placed his weathered hands on the table.

Luca shook his head. "Talking like a bunch of women will accomplish nothing."

"Try," I urged through clenched teeth.

Tex plopped down on the other side of Trace and crooked his finger at Mo. Wordless, she took a seat and waited in silence like the rest of us.

"We wait." Luca nodded. "For Mil and Chase." He nodded again as if he was convincing himself that it was the best plan imaginable. Then he pulled out a cigar and began puffing on it like it was his only lifeline.

"Here they are," Trace whispered.

I turned around. Mil's face was white as a sheet, and Chase looked like he needed something a hell of a lot stronger than wine. His gaze flickered to mine and then back to Mil as he put his arm around her and pulled out a chair.

Now that was interesting. Usually he looked at me, then at Trace, and then back to me again. What had changed?

"Loose ends?" Luca said without looking up.

"None." Chase swallowed. "One dead."

"Anyone important?" Sergio spoke up for the first time. We were huddled in a dark booth where we were all facing out so that we could see anyone or anything that dared approach us. They'd be dead before they could open their mouth in greeting.

"No." Mil's voice shook. "Just Tanya's bodyguard."

"And Mrs. Campisi? How does she fair?" Luca blotted out his cigar and poured himself a healthy glass of wine.

"We left her." Chase cleared his throat and popped his knuckles. "She's dead anyway." His knuckles were caked with blood, but other than that he seemed clean, so he must have been telling the truth. Then again, Chase's style of killing was cleaner than mine. While I'd rather beat the shit out of someone and torture them until either my name or God's was the last on their lips, Chase used guns.

He liked guns.

Guns liked him.

They had a good relationship. Chase hated loose ends, and he hated getting his hands dirty when the gun could do the job for him. To each his own, I guess.

Trace placed her hand on my thigh. I reached down and gripped it, each of us waiting for someone to say something that would be helpful.

After taking another sip of wine, Luca spoke. "You were young when you were both chosen. Rare for a boss to fall into power at eighteen, Nixon, even rarer to earn the respect of your elders at fourteen when your own father nearly killed you." Luca shook his head. "You and your friends were all sons of bosses, important men, too important for us not to initiate you into the family once we deemed you old enough to know what was going on. I thought of it as a brainwashing. What fourteen-year-old doesn't want to bring pride to his family? Luca swallowed. "And you, Nixon? You did not scream."

"What?" Trace whispered.

"He didn't scream." Luca gave a sad smile. "When his father crushed his skull. Not one single tear either." He bit down on his bottom lip. "My own men were terrified. They asked, 'Who is this boy? Where does he find his strength?' I envied you."

I winced. "I set off airport security with my metal plate, not much to envy."

Frank pinched the bridge of his nose as if the violent talk about the Abandonato family was too much for him to take.

"We initiated the four of you that next week." Luca nodded. "Phoenix followed, as well as Chase and Tex."

I remembered it all too clearly. The dark room, the metallic smell of blood, and the knives. Never in the family's history had they initiated mere teenagers. We'd been forced to grow up before our time. Forced to become men, when we should have been playing baseball and going to the movies…

A knife sat to my right, a gun to my left.

"Prick your trigger finger with the knife," Luca instructed. His voice sounded confident and smooth to my fourteen-year-old ears.

I did as he said, hands shaking the entire time. When the blood pooled around my fingertip, he squeezed until a drop of it fell onto a card he held in his hand. He repeated the process for each of my friends.

"You are now family," he said in a low voice. "By this blood you are united, by this blood you will die. You live by this very knife." Luca picked up the knife. "You die by this knife. Do you accept?"

"Yes," we said in unison, our voices cracking because they'd barely begun to change. I knew the seriousness of what was happening. My father watched from the corner of the room, his smile predatory. It took everything in me not to grab the knife and throw it at his head. I was going to be boss someday, and when I was, the first thing I was going to do was kill the very man who claimed to be my father. I would end his life, and I would smile when his warm blood ran cold through my fingers.

Luca handed me the card with my patron saint, Blessed Saint Antonio Lucci. I held it in my hand, my blood dripped on the card.

Luca lit a candle and then held it out to me. "Repeat after me." He held the flame beneath the card and spoke in a low voice. "As burns this saint, so burns my soul. I enter alive, and I will have to get out dead."

I repeated the words, knowing that getting out meant my death. But getting in? That meant my survival. It meant my revenge...

"Sorry." Tex shook his head. "Not that I mind going down memory lane, but what the hell does this have to do with the fact that Luca looks ready to run for the hills?"

Tex had reasons for hating that memory. When he should have been initiated as a Campisi, he'd been initiated as a made man, initiated into a family who, even though we'd said was his blood, was nothing like it.

Luca looked at the wine in his glass. He swirled it around and sighed. Some liquid dripped off the edge of the glass; it reminded me of blood, of the blood that would continue to spill if we didn't fix what was happening.

"Each man takes this very oath. Each man is given a saint during the initiation ceremony. Some men may tattoo the symbol somewhere private, or they may build a type of shrine in their home, lighting candles next to the picture of their saint, in thanks for making it through another day without being killed, or worse, becoming marked.

"One man, in particular, made his very own symbol of the saint. He used it as a way to mark people. As a way to remind that person and anyone else who comes into contact with them that they are a marked man, meant for dead, cursed."

"What does the mark look like?" Mil asked in a small voice.

Luca reached across the table and grabbed her wrist then flipped it over. "This. It looks like this."

Mil tried to jerk her arm away, but Luca held it captive as his trigger finger traced the outline of the scar. It almost looked like pentagram minus the circle; instead there was a small triangle toward the top and really long sides.

"The Albatross," Frank whispered, gripping the same hand and flipping it to the side. The scar made an A-shape with an N where the triangle had been. "He's branded you."

"My father," Mil whispered, her lips trembling. "He said I was meant for *him*."

"You remember nothing of The Cave, Mil?" Luca asked, a touch of tenderness inflected, as if he actually did give a rat's ass what she did or didn't remember.

"It was dark." Mil shifted in her seat and jerked her arm back. "And there were lots of men."

"But only one that mattered." Luca swore. "Did you ever see him?"

"Who is *him*?" Chase asked slowly.

"The Capo," Luca said slowly. "Vito Campisi. He is the only one who makes the mark of the Albatross. If you were meant for him, it means only one thing."

Mil began rocking back and forth in her seat.

"What the hell?" Chase pulled her to his chest as Mil started whimpering nonsense about it being cold.

"What are you doing to her?" Chase swore again and pulled out his gun, aiming it at Luca's head.

"Chase," I growled. "Put the gun away. I'll shoot Luca myself if he doesn't start talking."

"Her virginity." Luca laughed humorously. "That bastard must have bid on her."

"Bid?" I swallowed the bile in my throat.

"The prostitution ring was very illegal, even by our standards." Luca nodded. "I visited twice. Both times I was witness to things I can only assume are reserved for the darkest deepest circles of hell."

"You were there?" I whispered.

Mil nodded. "Once that I remember. My dad, he forgot his phone and—"

"I was there that day." Luca sighed, interrupting her. "The minute your father auctioned you off, I walked out the door, not caring that I could be shot where I stood. I was banished to Sicily anyway, thanks to the Abandonatos and

Alferos thinking my family had overstayed their welcome." He shot a glare to Frank. "At any rate, it was too dark to see faces. The De Langes were good about keeping identities a secret. One could be in The Cave with the President of the United States and still not know who was standing next to him."

"Because of the lighting?" I asked.

"No," Luca said slowly, his eyes flickering from mine to Mil's. "Because of the masks."

"No!" Mil screamed.

Chase stood, knocking over some of his water, and reached for his gun. I grabbed his hand, to keep him from doing something stupid, and swore.

"Luca — this isn't helping."

"She needs to remember."

"And if she dies in the process? Loses her freaking mind because she wasn't ever supposed to remember in the first place?" I shouted.

"Nixon." Trace shook her head slowly. "I think it will help."

"Mo?" I was grasping at straws, waiting for one of the girls to say something, waiting for one of them to say it would be too hard for a girl to talk about things that were better left buried in the ground.

"His voice sounded like gravel," Mil whispered against Chase's chest. "He was really big. And his mask..." She shuddered. "I saw his eyes."

"What color?" Frank asked.

"Blue. Like ice."

Sergio swore.

"Dead." Luca lifted his glass into the air as if cheering our demise.

"Why does that make us dead?"

"Because it seems our Capo has decided that he doesn't want the sins of his past to come out. Seems he's hell-bent on destroying anyone close to the girl, including us. And believe me, he's good at what he does."

"He's been in retirement," Frank offered.

Luca snorted. "We retire when we're dead and buried."

"Something's not adding up," I said. "Why not kill her? Why keep her alive all this time?"

"Oh, Nixon." Luca swore. "Sometimes I wonder about you, kid."

"I'm not a kid."

"You are a child." He spat. "And the Capo knows you'd do anything to protect your love, as well as your family, including Chase and his new bride. By default, that means I must protect my family, which now includes all of you as well as Frank, the bastard, and Tex." He swore again. "Perhaps he'll bury us together."

"That won't happen," Tex said in a quiet voice. "I won't let him."

"You won't let him?" Mo all but shouted. "What are you going to do, Tex? Waltz into the airport, fly your way over to Sicily, and kill him?"

"I won't have to." Tex licked his lips. "My bet's on him being here."

"So you plan on doing what? Putting his number in your phone and tracking him with GPS?" Mo was all up in his face, her lips trembling as she waited for his response.

"I won't have to."

Luca raised his hands to his temples and massaged. "He has yet to find us. But he will. The best we can do is be ready."

"Ready?" Trace repeated.

"For war." Luca nodded. "Many lives will be lost. If we survive, and that's a giant *if*, I plan on leaving you crazy Americans and going back to Sicily. I've had enough inter-family drama to last me a lifetime."

I listened as everyone began talking at once. And then an idea hit me.

"How much money do we have altogether?"

Frank laughed. "You must be joking? We could buy the US outright, pay off the debts, and still be sitting nicely."

Luca rolled his eyes. "While I wouldn't go that far, we are quite nicely settled, why?"

"We order a hit."

Luca began choking on his wine while Frank patted his back. "You've lost your damn mind!"

"No." I grinned. "We offer twenty million."

"Twenty million?" Trace sputtered. "Dollars?"

"No. Goats," Tex interjected. "What else would we give them?"

I sucked on my lip ring and laughed. "Tell me his own right-hand man won't be jumping at the chance to shoot that bastard in the face. Tell me his wife won't try to kill him before the week's up. Tell me we won't have half the mafia after him." I leaned in. "Hell. Tell me the half of Sicily won't fly into New York by Friday and take care of it for us."

"To order a hit of that magnitude is a death wish." Luca swore.

"As you said." I shrugged. "We're already dead."

"I can do it," A small voice said. I looked over at Mil, just because I wasn't sure it was her talking or if my imagination was running wild.

"Do what?" Chase pulled her away from his chest and tilted her chin toward him.

"I'll spread the news."

"And you think you can do a better job than us on ordering a hit?"

Mil grinned, probably for the first time in hours. "Oh, I know I can."

"How's that?"

She shrugged. "I am the De Lange boss."

"And an hour ago we thought they wanted you dead. Your cousins had his branding."

"They were probably given no choice. Either kill or be killed. The only reason he would brand them would be to mark them," Mil said slowly. "My family is your only hope to get out of this alive. He won't expect it to come from me."

"The element of surprise," I muttered with approval.

"That…" Her mouth tilted into a smile. "…and my family's been dealing drugs to the Mexico cartel for the past ten years. This shit's going to go worldwide. The connections go into the Irish and Russian mob — weapons dealers." Mil swallowed. "I'm not telling you all of this so you hate my family even more, but to show you they're desperate. I mean, last I heard they were going to sell all you guys out to the feds. What if I give them a truce?"

Luca's eyes narrowed. "What kind of truce?"

"The other four families stop going after the De Langes, and the De Langes promise not to go to the feds. In the meantime, I order the first real respectable hit of my career — and I go balls to the wall." Mil's face hardened. "Cementing the De Langes as a power force once more."

Luca's eyes lit up. Frank started clapping his hands. And I couldn't have been more proud had the woman just declared world peace. I imagined it would only take five seconds for Chase to throw his wife against the wall and maul her… his gratitude and all that. By the looks of it, he was ready to do it now.

"Well…" I sighed. "I think we have a plan. Mil—" I tapped my fingers against the countertop and nodded. "Make the call."

Luca stood. "No sleep tonight, ladies and gentleman. One person awake at all times. Keep your phones close."

"So what happens next?" Trace asked. "She makes the call and then what?"

Frank winked. "We wait."

CHAPTER THIRTY-NINE

Mil

"You don't have to do this," Chase whispered for the third time once we got back to our room.

I had my cell phone out and the number dialed. All I needed to do was press send. But my damn hands kept shaking.

"We'll find another way."

"There is no other way." My body wouldn't stop trembling. "This fixes everything, don't you get it?" I stared at my phone. "The De Langes will trust me. Your family won't take the blame. In the end it works."

"Listen." Chase grabbed the phone and threw it onto the bed, his hands cupping my face. "I. Can't. Lose. You."

"Chase." My voice cracked. "I'm not going anywhere."

His green eyes pooled with tears. He looked fierce, like he was ready to go into battle, sword raised. "Promise me something."

"What?"

His mouth covered mine for a brief hot kiss.

"Promise me that when I tell you to get down, when I tell you to get out of the way, when I yell at you to move so I can take a bullet for you, promise me you'll move."

"Chase," I forced a smile, "you're not going to have to take a bullet for me."

"Please," he whispered, his lips touching mine again. "Please don't choose that moment to be brave or stubborn. Please let me protect what's mine. I didn't protect you all those years ago when your dad beat you. I wasn't there. I never got the chance to play the white knight."

"So that's what this is about? You want to be the white knight?"

Chase shook his head and swore. "Screw the white knight." He gripped my chin in his hand. "I want to be your savior."

"Oh." I inhaled, choking on the air as his mouth collided with mine again. His tongue tasted like wine. It was a taste I was starting to crave. Everything about Chase's kisses were possessive, warm, obsessive. My body crumbled beneath his touch. What had I done before Chase? I couldn't remember, didn't want to.

"Make the call, Mil." Chase handed me the phone. "And when you're done, I'm going to give you a new brand."

"A new brand?" I asked, confused.

He touched the ridges of my scar. "I'm going to destroy that bastard, but before I destroy him, I'm going to love you."

I didn't trust myself to speak, so I nodded my head instead. Chase walked over to the bathroom, turned, and winked. "Good luck. I'll just be taking another long shower while you have that conversation. I know you can do it, but you need to do it without me looking over your shoulder."

"Okay."

"Mil?"

My head snapped up. "Yes?"

"You're a bad ass, just remember that. You're a De Lange.

You eat nails for breakfast, right?"

"Right."

"Go get 'em, tiger."

He shut the door behind him, leaving me blanketed in silence. I looked at the green dial button and pressed it.

It was answered on the second ring.

"So, the boss finally calls? You going to tell us to stop dealing with the feds? Or were you going to offer up yourself and your new little family as a sacrifice?"

My uncle had always been a jackass, but at least he didn't beat his children. I knew he was bitter because the De Langes, for the most part, had agreed to let me be the boss, though half of them hadn't even been present for the meeting Luca had strung together. Most of them had been paid off because, yes, they were just that desperate for money.

"Joe," I said dryly. "Always such a pleasure."

He snorted. "Make it quick. I'm busy."

I swallowed and looked at the bathroom door then closed my eyes. "I have a job for you."

The phone went silent.

"Joe?"

He cleared his throat. "I'm listening."

"I need someone taken care of."

"Name."

"Vito Campisi."

"I'm sorry, could you repeat the name? It sounded a hell of a lot like you just asked me to kill the closest thing to a godfather the five families have seen in a hundred years."

"I did," I said firmly. "Twenty million for his body. I want him injured, but alive. He should be in Vegas. Oh, and Joe?"

"Twenty mil?" His ability to use the F-word in so many ways was quite impressive. "What's the catch?"

"No catch." I cleared my throat. "I need it to be clean. No tracing it back to us."

"Where you getting the money?"

"Since when have you cared?"

"Since the feds have been breathing down our necks after Lonnie promised information on the rest of the families."

"That's just the thing, Joe. This is being funded by the Alferos."

More cursing.

"The Nicolosis."

He was going to go to hell for all that cursing.

"And the Abandonatos."

"So let me get this straight." His voice strained. "You mean to bring the head down on the five arms... to what gain?"

"To end what my father started," I said in a low voice. "Campisi was the one, Joe."

"The one?"

"He was the one who bid on me. He bid two million dollars for my virginity and for our family's blood. My father was going to sell our family out to him. He's been pulling the strings from the beginning, and I mean to end it right here, right now."

"We'll either die trying, or it will go down as the greatest kill in our family's history," Joe said, his voice softening.

"There are other assassins I can—"

"I'll put out the contract." He cleared his throat. "Does it need to be us or can it be—"

"Get the Russians. Get the Irish. Get the damn Mexican drug cartel. I want them all. Do you hear me, Joe? I want the man to be so damn terrified of his own shadow that he ends his own life. I want him to be so petrified of taking a piss in the dark that he carries his gun to the damn toilet. Are you understanding what I'm saying?"

"Yes," Joe clipped. "Yes, boss. I do."

"Get it done."

"Consider it finished."

The phone line went dead. I was grinning like an idiot because the pieces were finally falling into place, and it was my family helping me put them back together. If my brother were still alive, I think he'd be proud of me. I think he'd tell me I was insane, and he'd probably be doing a lot of yelling like Chase had. But he would have hugged me afterward and told me I was a bad ass, just like Chase had.

Phoenix's memory would live on because I was going to finish what he'd started. I was going to redeem our family if it was the last thing I did, and I wasn't going to be afraid anymore.

I rubbed my scar. The man didn't own me. He may have branded me, but hell was coming for him in a blazing chariot of fire — and I was the effing driver.

CHAPTER FORTY

Chase

The water dripped down my body, but I hardly felt it. In that moment, I wished for spider senses or super-hearing so I could see how Mil did. It wasn't that I doubted her; I just knew that this was some scary shit. I also knew that if I had to do what she was about to, I'd have to take a couple of shots of whiskey and wave my gun around like I was some bad ass before I ordered a hit on one of the toughest sons-of-bitches I'd ever heard about.

In my mind, ordering a hit on the Capo was like ordering a hit on the devil; somehow, he'd just find a way to drag you back to hell with him.

I leaned against the shower and waited five, maybe ten minutes. I should probably get out soon, but I wanted to give her enough privacy to do what she had to do. As much as I wanted to be her strength I knew I couldn't. This was something she had to do on her own. It was her first act as boss.

I ran my hands over my face and nearly fell on my ass

when I felt breasts press against my back.

Holy shit. Either I'd died and gone to heaven, or my wife was a goddess sent by the angels. I turned, slowly.

She just stood there, a look of pure joy radiated from her face as water cascaded down the valley of her breasts across her flat stomach and down her long lean legs. My lungs burned. I realized too late that I'd forgotten to inhale. My focus had been so intent on the perfection in front of me that I'd literally stopped breathing. I pulled in a shaky breath and with my eyes followed the trail of her long wet dark hair as it fell across that perfect skin. I watched in eagerness as water dripped from that same hair and slowly slid down to her navel. My knees almost buckled when I followed the water trails all the way down to exactly where I wanted to be.

My body tightened.

Mine. That was mine. She'd been mine since I was fourteen. She'd been mine since the first time I kissed her. I was the first to explore those breasts, to kiss that neck, and I'd be damned if anyone else would ever get the opportunity to touch what was mine again. *Mine. Mine. Mine.* My body hummed with the primal urge to claim her.

I licked my lips in anticipation as my body burned in ways I'd never experienced before. First hot and then cold as if it couldn't decide what it was but knew only one solution — Mil. Her gaze hungrily swept over my nakedness, pausing at my chest and quickly moving on, finally settling on me and all my glory. With a twist of her lips and lift of her eyebrow she tilted her head and whispered huskily, "You gonna use that thing?"

Yeah, like that wasn't just like playing with a loaded gun.

I didn't even realize I was moving until my lips crushed hers in a frenzy to taste, to explore, to claim over and over again until she begged for rest. I pressed her against the tiled wall. She sucked in a sharp breath as our legs tangled together. My tongue stroked her neck then nibbled, but it wasn't enough. Would it ever be enough? With a feral growl I shifted her weight and it was all I needed. I lifted her higher, angling myself perfectly and thrust into her hard and fast, not thinking about anything but marking her as mine, being hers and nobody else's.

Each give. Mine.

Each take. Mine.

Each scream. Mine.

This was it for me, everything I'd always needed and wanted, found in the one girl I never realized I was missing. In that moment, pieces of the puzzle that was Chase Winter, shattered to the ground. The past? Didn't matter. But right now? Feeling her warmth, tasting her desire? It was everything. I pushed harder, faster, she met me with each thrust, grabbing my body tighter against hers.

She screamed my name as we both found our release, a freaking explosion that robbed me of my vision, balance, and sense of time. I'd have held her just like that. Forever. I wanted to freaking set up camp in that shower and never leave. But she slumped against me, boneless, most likely exhausted. She slid slowly down my body, a sexy smile dancing across her lips. "Well, that was nice."

"Nice?" I repeated.

She nodded and shimmied by me, collecting what was left of the soap I was using and started lathering it across her body. Hot damn. The tease moved the soap down her hips, around her ass, my eyes trained on that soap like it held the secrets to the world. Her hands moved to her breasts and I swear I almost blacked out as the soap lathered around one of my most favorite parts of her body, playing hide and seek.

Dear God, I was going to pass out on the spot. Already my body was responding to her again — how was that even possible? She handed me the soap and turned around. Growling in frustration, I told myself to calm down and helped wash her back, when really all I wanted to do was grab that mop of black hair and give a little tug while pleasuring her again.

I finished with her back then moved the soap down one of her perfectly formed legs. I went up and down in rhythmic motion then stopped when I reached the inside of her thigh. I let the water cascade down her then moved my mouth to where the soap had been. With a gasp her head fell back as she grabbed my hair and pulled, pushing me harder against her core. Groaning, I don't know how the hell it happened but I was ready for her. Again. Immediately. Damn, it really wouldn't ever be enough, would it? I stood and gripped her hips.

"Wrap your legs around me," I demanded.

"So we can hug?" she asked innocently.

"Right. I'm going to hug you so damn hard you get pregnant."

"Chase!" She smacked me in the arm.

I was serious as hell. I turned off the shower and wrapped her in a towel, quickly drying the both of us off, and then lifted her onto the counter, again not taking any time to do it right. I nudged her legs aside and pushed into her. I really wasn't in the mood for romance and flowers. This was need. Primal need. I was in the mood to make her forget everything about what she'd just done — about what we'd both be facing within the next twenty-four hours.

If I died, I wanted the last name on my lips to be hers.

If I got shot, the last image I wanted flickering through my head would be of her naked body, of her smile, of her luscious lips, and of those damn blue eyes.

"Chase..." Mil moaned as my lips slid down her neck, sucking the water droplets with my mouth and teasing her with my tongue. Her head fell back against the mirror.

"I have something to tell you." I moved inside her, slowly, and then faster.

"Can you make it fast?"

"Can you not distract me?" I groaned.

"S-sorry." Her body tightened around mine and she shook. Then she sighed and leaned against my chest as my body climaxed and then shuddered against hers.

"I love you." I'd said it twice in my life. Once to Trace and now to my wife.

"Come again?"

I smirked. "You think I can't?"

She smacked me in the shoulder.

"What?" I said innocently.

"You're such an ass sometimes."

"I think that's why you love me back?" I whispered in a hopeful voice.

Mil's eyes were clear as day, so blue and striking that I sucked in a breath to make sure I really hadn't died. "I've loved you since I was fourteen."

"Really?" I lifted her off the counter so she could stand in front of me and so I could hold her in my arms. "You aren't saying that to stroke my ego?"

"The last thing you need is more stroking." Her eyebrows arched in amusement. "And I mean it. When my dad hit me. It was your face I saw. When he..." She choked. "When he branded me, when you didn't come for me, I pretended that you did." A fat round tear slid down her cheek. "I closed my eyes and pretended that it was just a nightmare, an alternate reality. I dreamed I was still in your arms. You kissed me and told me it was going to be okay. Earlier you said you didn't want to be a white knight. It's funny, because in my book, you really have always been my savior. You've been my everything. I was just too angry to admit it."

"And now?" I whispered, my voice hoarse.

"Now I can't help it." Her hands caressed my face, rubbing over the stubble that had started making its presence known since I hadn't shaved that day. "I can't help but want you. I can't help but need you. I can't help but depend on you.

It wasn't my own stubborn will that kept me alive all these years, Chase. It was you. It's only ever been. You."

My heart about burst.

And I finally knew the difference. Before, I'd thought I'd been in love. It had hurt like hell, but that love? The love I felt for Trace? I realize now it was mostly lust and a deep unrelenting friendship, nothing more. I'd loved her with my whole heart. I still did, but not the way I loved Mil.

I was obsessed with Mil.

I wanted to freaking collect her eyelashes and stare at them like a lunatic — they were that long and beautiful.

Every time she breathed, I was jealous of the air because it was touching parts of her that I hadn't had a chance to explore.

She was my beginning — my end. The woman I wanted by my side until we were two cranky old people who still carried weapons and shot at squirrels when they ran in front of us.

I wanted a future with her.

I wanted a present with her.

I just wanted her.

"You seem to be thinking really hard." she whispered.

"How do people survive this?" I asked in a low voice. "How do they survive when someone they love dies? How do they go on when the other half of their soul is missing?"

"A lot don't," Mil said in a sad voice. "But us? We'd be fine. You know why?"

"Why?" This I had to hear.

"You're too much of an ass to go and die on me, and I'm too stubborn to sit around and watch while death defeats you."

"Oh, good." I nodded. "So we have a plan then?"

"A plan?"

"Right." I pulled her hands from my face and clenched them in mine. "We don't let each other die until it's time, and when it's time we die together, notebook-style."

"Since when do guys watch The Notebook?"

"Since I was given Trace duty for three months, and she slowly tortured me with chick flicks."

"You cry?"

"Hell no!" I blustered.

"Liar."

"There were a few tears," I said gruffly. "But it was more an allergy to the popcorn and... salt."

"Salt?"

"Leave it, Mil."

She lifted her hands in innocence.

"We should get dressed, just in case we're needed. They probably don't want us running around the hotel naked."

"Bummer." Mil dropped her towel.

"Damn it, woman!" I turned around. "Stop trying to give me an early death. I can't take your nakedness. It makes me horny as hell, and I'm supposed to be holding a gun."

"Which gun?" she whispered as her hands wrapped around my waist and headed south.

I barely escaped, then I turned and gave her a pointed look. "Clothes. Now."

"Since when are you the voice of reason, Chase Winter?"

"Since I want my wife to live," I said seriously. "And since I've just had sex with you twice in the past three hours, and I'm pretty sure men's parts fall off if they use them too much in a ninety-minute period."

"Misinformation."

"I'm attached to my parts."

"Me too."

"So we're agreed." I crossed my arms. "Clothes, then I may let you cuddle, but I get dibs on being the big spoon."

She seemed to think about it a minute then held out her hand. "Shake on it?"

"Sure!" I said stupidly, reaching for her hand. But it was

too late. Before I knew it, my body was again responding to her nakedness, and I felt cold air as my towel dropped. "Oh the hell with it."

CHAPTER FORTY-ONE

Nixon

"This is so not romancing," Trace said once we'd reached our room.

I'd promised to romance her, and now we were waiting to see if the hit had been carried out or if Vito was going to pop out of hiding long enough for someone to aim for his head.

"Yeah it is." I pulled Trace into my arms. "Think of it this way, we get all this time to ourselves."

"Nixon." Trace's irritation was evident in the way her voice lowered. "We're waiting for death."

"Only sort of," I argued. "Come on, admit it, it's kind of hot."

"In what way?" she said, exasperated.

"Oh, you know, this could be our last night together." I grinned smugly. "What would you do if this was your last night with me?"

"It's still too soon, Nixon," Trace whispered.

Aw hell, I was trying to lighten the mood, not make her

go crazy with worry. I'd done that enough after faking my own murder.

I cleared my throat. "Come here."

We sat on the bed together. I wrapped my arms around her as she leaned back against me.

"You already know what I did," I said in a low voice. "I wanted to spend my last moments with you. In your arms, loving you, cherishing you, possessing you. I kept thinking that if it ended badly, if I really did end up dead, the last memory I wanted was of you."

Trace sighed. "I'd want the same thing. Though I'd probably want it differently."

"Differently?"

"It's unfair to give your body and soul to one person, while asking for everything that person has to offer in return, knowing that you may not be able to follow through with the promise you're making."

"But I did—"

"You could have died," she said slowly. "And you were willing to take every part of me with you to that grave. I wouldn't have moved on. I couldn't have. While I love Chase, it was never the love I had for you Nixon. So although I don't blame you, a part of me still hates you for gambling not just your life, but mine too."

Humbled. All I could do was sit there. Sit and feel like a total and complete ass for doing that to her. "I hadn't thought of that."

"You're a guy." She toyed with my hands, twisting my ring around my finger. "You wanted to make me yours, and you did. But you weren't there to see me after—"

"I saw you in his arms."

"You pushed me into his arms." She sighed. "You didn't see me toy with the gun in my room for the two hours Chase was gone." My arms stiffened around her. "You didn't see me point it at myself and then freak out that I was even contemplating something like that. You see, I've never been one of those girls, the type that get all dramatic and freaks out. You know me, Nixon. I just... I couldn't imagine living in a world where you and I weren't together. The love that I have for you isn't something that's going to go away. It's real. I was lucky enough to have it once — and knew I'd only be getting a sliver of it if I grasped at what Chase was offering. But I was desperate for that completion, because when you left me, you left me broken and he was offering to fix me."

"The bastard would have ruined you."

Trace chuckled. "Stop being jealous of something that doesn't even matter."

"You're right."

"I am?"

I closed my eyes against vision of Trace holding a gun, contemplating suicide, all because I'd been careless with her heart, and careless with her love and trust. I loved that woman. I would die for her. I breathed for her, lived every day to make sure she was happy and safe.

"Trace?"

"Hmm?"

"I'm sorry."

"Nixon, it's—"

"I swear, if you say it's okay, I'm going to lose my shit," I spat.

"Whoa there." She snuggled closer to me. "I was going to say it's fine."

"It will be," I vowed.

"What?"

"Marry me."

I'd never truly understood the expression of air being *thick with tension.* I mean, I'd been in some pretty freaking tense situations but nothing, nothing compared to the way my heart was ramming against my chest when Trace didn't respond right away. Did I just propose? Was she really not answering? My hands began to sweat as I waited for the woman to say something, damn it, anything!

Finally… just as my heart was getting ready to give out, I felt her shudder against me. Holy shit, was she crying? Was the idea of marrying me making her that upset?

And then her arms flew around my neck as she twisted her body in my lap and began sobbing against my chest. "I love you s-so much! Of course I'll marry you!"

I exhaled and dropped a few expletives before I was able to form a sentence. "I swear you just took fifteen years off my life."

"I think you deserved a long pause."

"That was an eternal pause, as in, I think time actually stood still."

"Good." She sobbed some more. "Now you know a sliver of what I felt when you were dead."

"Point taken, damn it, but for future reference can we just nip all long pauses right here and now? I'll freaking put it in a contract and sign it in blood, just no more pauses. From here on out, you need to say yes sir, immediately."

"I never call you sir," Trace teased.

"Lies," I murmured against her hair. "You called me sir last night."

"Entirely different circumstances."

"Really? You mean when we were—"

She covered my mouth with her hand. I bit it.

Her eyes flared to life as they trained on my lips.

I licked her palm.

She flicked my lip ring.

I sucked on her fingertips and then winked. Trace raised her hand to smack my chest, but I grabbed her wrist and twisted her onto her back, hovering over her. "I think it's time to celebrate."

"What did you have in mind?" She wiggled beneath me.

With a groan, I crushed my mouth against hers. "Oh you

know…" I started lifting her shirt when I heard a knock on the door.

"Probably room service," Trace whispered against my mouth. "Make them go away."

I nodded and jumped off of her. "Don't move."

"Not moving." She lifted her hands in the air.

"We didn't order any damn room serv—" I opened the door to Mo collapsing into my arms.

"He's gone!"

I gripped her shoulders. "Who's gone? What happened?"

"Tex!" She wailed. "He just… he got a text, said he'd only be a minute, and then I saw him get basically ambushed by four really big guys. I mean they were huge and the—"

"License plate number?" I snatched my phone while Mo rattled it off. She was always good with numbers. "Got it."

I dialed Sergio first to track the car and then sent out a group text to everyone else. It seemed retribution was going to come a hell of a lot sooner than we'd thought.

I was going to end Campisi's life if he touched a hair on Tex's stupid-assed head. I was going to end his line. I would cleanse every last family member, if that's what it took to get his attention, and I would do it cheerfully.

Chase texted me back right away.

Chase: *How's Mo?*

Me: *She needs us.*

Chase: *Lobby.*

"Trace, stay here and—"

"Hell no."

Trace had pulled the gun out of her purse and made sure it was loaded. What the hell kind of monster had I created?

"We end this together. You guys can do whatever the hell you want. Go storm the castle, but us girls? We're going to be in another car, waiting to call in the cavalry if need be. We aren't abandoning you."

"Fine," I said through clenched teeth. "But if you step

foot into whatever shit-hole that man's hiding in. I'll shoot you to keep you from putting yourself in more danger."

"Ah, the romance." She fanned herself with her gun.

Mo wiped at her cheeks while she checked her own gun and then pulled out a few knives I knew she liked to throw at people when she was pissed. It was why Tex had a scar on his thigh. She had killer-aim now, though.

She fanned them out and then stuffed one in each boot and up her sleeves, finally stashing the last one in her purse. "Let's go."

CHAPTER FORTY-TWO

Tex

I knew they would come for me. I wasn't an idiot. I mean, I played nonchalant better than Henry Cavill played Superman. Look too smart? People start to talk. Look too dumb and people won't use you. So I liked to stay right in the middle.

The middle was safe.

The middle kept my adopted family safe.

But the minute my real father's name had been dropped, I knew there wouldn't be a safe place for any of them. Not until he was dead. So it didn't shock me when the car pulled up. That was why I didn't run. Why run from your destiny? It was a cowardly thing to do, and I wasn't a coward — no, that would be my father. After all, he was going to use me as bait. I mean, how stupid could he be?

I'd flipped on my GPS the minute I got back to my hotel room. I'd assumed they'd just shoot me to make it so I couldn't run. Instead, the men who'd grabbed me had been polite, a bit gruff, but they hadn't slapped me around. Not that

I would have cared.

What did I really have to live for?

The woman I loved hated me, and my own family had abandoned me when I was a child.

Right. So my life? Not worth a hell of a lot.

"So…" I toyed with the nylon cable ties they'd used on my wrists. Idiots. How'd they know I didn't have a knife stashed in my sleeve? I rolled my eyes. "We going to the Strip? Or did you guys wanna do some shots first?"

The guy to my left chuckled while the one to my right punched me in the jaw. Ah, there it was. I was beginning to think the Campisi family had gone all soft.

"Fine." I sighed. "We'll go to the gay bar, but only because you punched me. Geez, why didn't you just say you had a preference?"

That earned me two more punches, one to the gut and one to the face.

Blood spewed from my mouth; I laughed and spat it at the guy to my left who was using me as his personal punching bag. Tattoo on his neck, metal stud in his left ear, a scar down the right side of his cheek attached to a nose that looked like it had been broken at least three times. His teeth ground together, and from the stench of his breath, he hadn't brushed in a few days. I sloppily fell against him, breathing in the scent of his clothes. He pushed me off of him, but not before I got a whiff of something musty. They'd been either underground or in an abandoned building. Then again, Vegas had a dry climate. I squinted at the man again; a few beads of sweat trickled down his temple. My bet was that he was petrified of me.

"You know who I am?" I said in a cold voice.

"Everyone knows who you are," the man said in a thickly accented voice. Hmm, Sicilian who still sounded like one. This should be interesting.

"Say my name."

"I'm not saying your name." The guy swore under his breath.

The thing about my name? Nobody uttered it. I was living in my own version of Harry Potter. The one who shall not be named was my actual title to most people in the Campisi family. For some reason, it had been spread that I'd been sent away to live in the states because I was cursed. So they thought of me as a bad omen. I was the Campisi family's version of seeing a black cat on Halloween.

And saying my name was basically like uttering Bloody Mary three times in your bathroom mirror.

It actually cheered me up to think of the guy shitting his pants if I started arching my back and foaming at the mouth.

"Well." I sighed. "This is a lively group."

The two men in the front seat exchanged a glance.

"Tex," I continued. "They call me Tex for short. But my real name? It was passed down from my father." I allowed for a long pause. "Vito Nicio Campisi, Junior."

"Shut up!" the man next to me yelled.

"It's a mouthful," I added, spreading my legs wide enough to push both bastards further against the doors of the car. "And the minute I got to the States, I became obsessed with everything Texas had to offer, big cows, big hats, big hair, big—" I earned another punch to the stomach. It hurt like hell but I kept talking once I could catch my breath. "So you can imagine that the minute I hit puberty and noticed how big I was — and how much I had to offer the big bad world, I asked to be called Tex. Though to be fair, in the bedroom the ladies just call me Big."

"Does this kid ever stop talking?" The guy to the right muttered.

"Would you rather I shit my pants and rock back and forth?" I spat in a low tone. "I'm the son to one of the most powerful men in your sad, pathetic, little world. He owns you, therefore, I own you. I'm a trained assassin." I purposefully narrowed my gaze as if I was looking down on all of them and thought them beneath me, which technically they were. "By your silence I can assume you were told I was a half-assed village idiot who smiled more than he talked and screwed women for fun." I rolled my eyes. "I could kill all of you like this." I snapped. "I wouldn't even blink and neither would my father. The only reason you guys are still alive is because the longer my father takes with me, the longer that fun little contracted hit hangs over his head. Hell, he may be dead by the time we get to the location."

The guy to my right held a gun to my head. "Still confident you could kill us? Shit, you talk a lot."

I smirked. "You irritate me." I turned to the guy on my left. "And you smell like you ate shit for breakfast, and I don't mean that as an exaggeration. You actually smell like you woke up at six a.m., took a crap in the toilet, dipped your grubby little hands into your own bowl and fished out a prize."

"That's it!" The guy to my left lunged for me, which really was unfortunate for him, considering I'd already managed to saw the zip ties off my hands.

I used the same knife to slice his throat. His eyes went wide and he gurgled something as a crimson waterfall gushed from his neck. Pity. It was hell getting stains out of white. Then I wrestled his gun out of his clenched fist and fired it right-handed at the guy next to me. Poor bastard slumped in his seat, a look of pure horror crossed his face before his body stilled.

Two seconds.

That's how long it took me.

The one choked his last breath while the other slumped against the window. The driver slammed on the brakes, while the guy in the passenger seat turned around and aimed a gun for my head.

I was too busy wiping my hands on the guy next to me to

care. Once they were semi-clean, I looked up and shrugged. "Please, don't stop on my account. Like I said, the one kept punching me and the other smelled. Tell me you didn't smell him. I did you a favor. Is it my imagination, or are the made men these days lacking in the hygiene department?"

The guy in the front seat took his gun off of me. "He was right about you."

"Who?" I asked innocently as the car started going again.

"Your father."

"Oh, and what did Papa have to say about his abandoned son?"

The guy smirked in the rearview mirror. "He said he should have killed you when you were an infant."

I smirked right back. "For once, he's right."

CHAPTER FORTY-THREE

Chase

"He kept his GPS on." I muttered tapping my phone as it found Tex's location. He was at Lake Mead. Though his signal was fading. Either they were tossing him into the water or he was going underground. "Are there any tunnels? Old abandoned buildings?" I asked Sergio.

He clicked the keyboard into his iPad and began going to town. "I'm not seeing anything glaring other than a few old houses, some old caves."

"Wait." Frank held up his hand. "He's superstitious."

"What?"

"Albatross," Luca said for him. "And houses on the lake are another superstition. The man has a thing about bad omens and curses. My bet is he went underground or into an abandoned cave."

"Searching." Sergio's hands flew across the keyboard. "Okay, so the only thing I'm finding is an old abandoned boathouse. Everything else is either a nice house, hotel, or restaurant. None of those places are even close to the location he disappeared at."

"Old boathouse it is."

Sergio smirked.

"What?" I asked.

He looked up from his computer. "The old boathouse. It's called The Albatross."

"Good work." Nixon exhaled. "Girls, you're going to drive separate with Frank. You're safer with us than hiding out at the hotel. They could be drawing us out to kill us or drawing us out to get to you. I'm not taking any chances." He turned to Frank. "Follow, but not too close. If you don't hear from us within a few hours, call this number."

"What is it?" Frank asked.

Nixon's eyes fell. "The airline. If you don't hear from us, you go off-grid, you go to the first location stated in Trace's plan. She has the information you guys would need to go into hiding. If we make it out, we'll meet you there. If we don't..." His voice died off.

"You've thought of everything," Mo said, her voice sounding hollow.

Nixon pulled her into his arms. "We're blood. We protect blood."

When he released her, I stepped up to him and held out my hand. "Blood in. Blood out."

Luca and Frank shook our hands, repeating the sentiment as each of us kissed one another's cheeks.

I'd never been one to think about the whole patron saint thing, but in that moment, I pulled out the cross that I'd made when I was fifteen. It had Saint Paul scribbled across it.

"May God protect us," Nixon mumbled, making a cross motion with his fingers in front of him.

Frank nodded. "He protects the just."

Mil leaned against me. "And those who rape little girls, sell their virginity, or worse yet, purchase it for their own gain? What does he do to them?"

I squeezed her. "He gives them their just reward."

Luca nodded. "An eternity in hell."

"Ready?" I whispered in her ear.

"Yeah."

"I love you."

She nodded and then wrapped her arms around me. "I love you too."

Stepping away from her, knowing it was entirely possible it would be the last time I'd be in her arms, was one of the hardest things I'd ever done. It was necessary. I was going to war — for her. And even if I died, I'd die with peace, knowing my last action had been saving her from monsters and demons. My last battle cry... would be her name on my lips.

CHAPTER FORTY-FOUR

Mil

Frank pulled the black Escalade up to the curb and waited as all of us girls piled in. We were safe with him. He wasn't just Trace's grandpa; he was the boss of the Alfero family. He was also old enough to let the younger generation run in, guns blazing, but not too old to not be able to protect us. He was in his seventies but looked more like his fifties.

"You girls will listen to me," he said, his voice slightly accented. "You will not run into the building when you hear gunshots. You will not cry when you see blood. If need be, you will kill. You will kill swiftly. You will kill smoothly. Do you understand?"

"Yes," we mumbled in unison.

"Do you all have ammo?"

"Yeah," I said.

Trace and Mo repeated the same thing.

"And knives?"

Mo grinned. "My specialty."

"Fantastic."

Weird. It was like he was proud that we were heavily armed and ready to kill on a dime. What a life.

I sent a quick text to Joe, telling him what was going on. Not to put us in more jeopardy, but because I figured that the guys would need all the help they could get.

Me: *If you don't hear from me in 40 minutes. Come to this address, guns blazing.*

Joe: *How many men do you need?*

Me: *Every last one you have.*

Joe: *Should I be concerned?*

Me: *We found Campisi. I wouldn't be against you bringing hell to his doorstep.*

Joe: *And to think I wanted to kill you a few days ago.*

Me: *Um, thank you?*

Joe: *It was a compliment. Keep in touch, boss.*

"Do you trust them?" Trace whispered next to me.

I nodded. "Right now? We have no choice but to trust them. And if they turned on us, they'd bring four of the most powerful families down onto their heads. They have more to gain by joining us than going against us."

Trace squeezed my hand. "Good thinking."

Mo leaned forward so that she was touching both of our shoulders. "Girls, I love you both but I think I'm going to be sick."

"Nerves?"

Mo shook her head. "He could be dead."

"He's not dead," Trace reassured her instantly. "You know Tex. He's smart. He's very, very capable."

"That's just the problem," Mo grumbled. "He talks way too much."

"But he's good, right?" I asked lamely. "I mean, he can hold his own?"

The girls both burst out laughing.

"What am I missing?"

"Don't get me wrong," Mo said. "It's scary as hell that

they have him. My heart hasn't stopped racing since I saw the exchange, but Tex kills people. It's what he does."

"Don't they all kill people?" I asked confused.

"They do." Mo nodded. "But to Nixon and Chase, it's a necessity. Nixon likes hitting things, Chase likes shooting things, and Tex? He's like an artist. It's not a profession to him. It's a lifestyle, something to perfect. He would do well as a gun-for-hire because nobody could trace him." Mo laughed. "I remember the first time I watched the stupid Jason Bourne movies I asked Tex if he was taking special serum."

We all giggled.

"Is he?" I asked.

"Negative." Mo shook her head. "Though he did say they should make a serum out of his genes."

"Of course."

"Almost there, ladies." Frank said from the front seat. "Be sure to keep alert, and remember, shoot first, ask questions later."

"You're a great grandpa." Trace patted his shoulder.

"Trying to soften me up before battle?"

"Never." Trace swore. "Just glad you're finally okay with me shooting things."

"Well, let's hope those lessons with Nixon paid off. A shotgun is a hell of a lot different than a pistol."

"Me and Annie will be just fine." She patted her own gun and smirked.

"You named your gun?" I asked.

She nodded. "Makes it seem less violent."

"Women," Frank muttered under his breath.

CHAPTER FORTY-FIVE

Tex

We arrived at our destination. A nice little warehouse that had a possessed-looking bird on the side of it. The paint was chipping and, as I'd predicted, the location was next to water. Great. Were they going to drown me or just shoot me? I wonder if I'll be given a preference? Probably not.

"Out." The man opened the door, pointing the gun at my face. I lifted up my hands and blew him a kiss.

I strutted in the middle of the two remaining men. They knocked three times on the door. It flew open and I was pulled inside. A bag was put over my head — it smelled like the man I'd just killed and had to sit next to for a few minutes. Lucky me. Even in his death, his stench was haunting me.

"So," a gravelly voice said. "This is—"

"The man who shall not be named." I tried to sound bored. "But everyone just calls me Tex. I wonder if they're afraid of the curse."

"The curse?"

"Yeah, the one that says that whatever family who is

responsible for my death has blood that can't be cleansed from their hands — their souls will rot in hell for eternity. Their children, their families — completely killed off."

"Lies," the voice spat. "We made that up for our pride."

"Oh, so now he admits it." I shook my head. "Really, Pops, you think you could come up with a better story? I mean, I'm a freaking legend because of that curse. Why couldn't you have given me magic powers or something?"

"You do talk a lot."

"One of my many flaws, other than being sired by the Capo himself."

Air whooshed by my ears, and then the bag was pulled from my head. I could actually — for the first time in my entire existence — get a look at the bastard who'd abandoned me; I could look directly into his cold icy eyes.

He glared.

I glared right back and then forced a smile. "My apologies. Did you want me to cry?"

"No."

"I might be able to conjure up a tear if one of your guards gets a feather and starts tickling me, but I think that would be frowned upon."

"Your mouth will be the death of you."

"Funny, that's exactly what that guy's mom said when I screwed her last night, though I think it was the other way around. Something like my mouth will be the death of her."

The guard I'd pointed at just glared then rolled his eyes. "Thinks he's funny."

"I know I'm funny." I winked. "Thinking has nothing to do with it. I'm freaking hilarious, and the longer you listen to me talk, the shorter the time is before you die."

"Me?" My father laughed. "Who's going to kill me? You? Your little friends?"

"My little friends. It almost sounds like a play date, only with guns, and knives, and well... Chase does have this weird bomb fantasy, but whatever."

"They will come for you," my dad said coldly. "And I will end what I should have ended years go."

"Just out of curiosity…" I leaned forward. "What would that be?"

"The list is quite long." He scratched his face and took a step forward into the light.

He was a large man, and by large, I meant large. Over three-hundred pounds and at least six-and-a-half-feet tall. His dark hair was thinning around the crown of his head, and I could tell he hadn't shaved for a few days.

"Been running, Pops? Or have you just let yourself go now that Mom's finally left you."

"Your mother is dead." He said it so matter-of-fact that my first reaction was to laugh, and then I wanted to cry because I'd never met her, and I'd been so freaking close that it destroyed me to know I would never see her smile.

"So?" I shrugged, lying my ass off. "I didn't know her."

"You look like her."

"She must have been very attractive."

"She was a conniving bitch."

"Ah well, I'm more of a conniving ass, so I guess I must have inherited that from your side. Can't have it all, looks and smarts. How would that be fair?"

"Sir?" One of the guards rushed to my father's side. "A car pulled up to the restaurant a few minutes ago. We think it's them."

"O-oh, them," I mocked. "Tell me Nicolasi doesn't make you want to shit your pants right here, right now, and I'll let you shoot me."

"Nicolasi?" My father's eyes narrowed. "With an Alfero? And an Abandonato?" He chuckled. "The world is not big enough for those three to be in the same place at the same time, my son."

"I have no father," I said quietly. "And you have no son."

"We'll see."

My response was to smile and pretend like what I'd said wasn't something I'd recited over and over in my head since I'd been old enough to form an actual thought...

I said it in the mirror when I was four. Nixon overheard me and asked why I was so upset. I told him it was stupid that he and Chase looked so much like everyone else, while I had stormy blue eyes and weird-colored hair.

He said it was the Spanish in my Italian heritage.

I cried.

And told him I didn't know what Spanish was, but was Spanish mean too? Did he not want me either?

Nixon hugged me like a brother.

Chase came in and did the same thing. We played Legos for a few hours afterward, and they promised that even though I didn't look like them, I'd always be family...

So my real father?

He could rot for all I cared.

"Check it out, Marco." Father nodded toward the door. "And keep eyes on the perimeter."

"How many men?" I asked casually.

"Pardon?"

"How many men do you have here, protecting you? You're a cocky son-of-a-bitch. I assume you can't imagine a world where some of the families you helped build would turn on you."

"It would never happen." My father set his gun out on the metal table and took off his rings. "I am the Capo. To kill me would be like killing God."

"Holy shit, I'm surprised you haven't been struck by lightning yet, you blasphemous idiot."

"He put me in this position." My father closed his eyes and lifted his hands into the air. "He put me on this earth to create order, to make money, to make a better life for my family."

"Question." I winced. "Did His plan also include you buying a fourteen-year-old's virginity so you could gain control over her family as well as buy silence for involving yourself in what's been known as the sickest prostitution ring known to the underground?"

He slapped me so hard across the face that I fell to the ground. Blood dripped from my face onto the dirt floor causing a cementing mixture to attach to my face. I spat onto the ground and laughed. So violent, I wonder if he even realized how long I could withstand torture? He punched like a bitch and I craved to tell him that. I touched my lower lip. Great. Now I'd never be able to get a lip ring like Nixon. I'd look like a fool. Damn pipe dreams.

"Who told you that?"

"The girl you tried to kill." I got up to my knees and made it to my metal chair. "The one you sent the De Langes to kill."

"I helped the De Langes." He popped his knuckles. "After all, they came to me, bitching and complaining that a mere woman had been named boss. The few that agreed to it were too terrified of Nicolasi to say no and too greedy about the money he used to buy them off. A few of the members approached one of my associates and asked if I could help." He grinned. "After all, I am a very helpful man."

"Oh I can see that." I saluted him.

"I gave them the location of the girl. It was a win-win. She dies, they die, no loose ends."

"Misjudged Chase a bit, you think?" I laughed. And got slapped. Again. Damn it.

But this time I got back into my chair I was more irritated than in pain over my throbbing cheek.

"I wasn't informed of his skill set."

I raised my hand. "It's the same as mine. We kill people. We assassinate. What else is there to know?"

"So do the De Langes." He cursed. "Clearly this Chase

was better."

"And the branding? I mean, was that totally necessary?"

"Easy." He chuckled. "I brand any associate who works with me or for me. That way, if they ever piss me off, I put a hit on their head. The contracted men know who to kill because of that mark. As I said, I'm a fair man. It wouldn't be right to kill those who don't deserve it."

"Wow, you really should be sainted."

"The church said no."

"Shocking." I put my hand over my heart. "So what's this about? You want to shut everyone up? Me included? Because it's not going to happen. It's—"

He gripped me by the throat and lifted me off the chair. Holy green giant.

"The American mafia is a joke!" He spat. "A pimple on the land of Sicily! I will put a stop to your fighting, your childish bickering, inability to stay out of prison, hard-headed ways for good!" His eyes flashed with something. At first I thought it was anger, then I looked again.

"You're terrified," I croaked. "You're scared shitless of what the De Langes have on you."

He dropped me to the ground and kicked me.

"The only way out is blood," I muttered. "And it's going to be yours."

CHAPTER FORTY-SIX

Nixon

It looked empty. But I knew better. It was probably crawling with associates just waiting to get another kill in so they could be made men. I rolled my eyes and strapped another magazine to the holster around my chest.

"It's a good night to die." Chase looked up at the sky and made a cross into the air with his finger.

I handed him a magazine. "It's also a good night to live."

"Well said," Luca commented, coming up from behind us. "Though, I'd rather we stop having to kill mafia bosses. It's really tarnishing my reputation."

"As a hard ass?" I offered.

"Your reputation is that you're blacker than sin and each time you get shot, your own soul is refused entrance into the afterlife." Chase rolled his eyes.

"I've only been shot three times. All times flesh wounds. Truly, people exaggerate." He waved us off and stomped out his cigar. The last thing we needed was a flicker of light to give us away.

"It was a good idea to park the car next door. They'll investigate, leaving only a few guards near the entrance." I pulled out my binoculars. "And there they go."

Three men strutted outside and slowly walked toward the abandoned car.

I waited until they were close enough and hit the button.

The car exploded, throwing all three men at least thirty feet.

"Gotta love explosives," Luca muttered under his breath. "Though by the looks of it, we're only going to have thirty minutes to get in and out before the feds come."

"Well, let's hope they respond to our little invitation." I smiled and aimed my gun at the door.

Sure enough, five more men ran out of the building.

"Shit, it's almost too easy." Chase picked off the first three.

"Like playing video games with guns and real people." I hit the last two men and waited. The door opened again, and this time it was Tex's head that poked out, followed by Campisi. He looked in our direction and gave us the bird.

"Geez, he could have at least offered us dinner or something," Chase joked. I smirked and hit him on the back.

"That's our cue." I winked at Luca. "Go back to the car. Make sure the girls are safe."

"On it. And have fun, boys. Do save a few for me."

"Always," I promised.

Chase and I slowly approached the building from our viewpoint on the lake. Our hands were both up, guns out of our hands. We were going in without guns blazing, and I hoped to God it would be enough to throw Vito off.

"Ah, so the cavalry has arrived," Tex said, his lip swollen and both eyes bloody, but otherwise looking like his assy self.

"Honey, we're home." I blew him a kiss.

He caught it mid-air.

"Bunch of idiots!" Vito spat, throwing Tex back into a

metal chair and aiming his gun in the direction of me and Chase. "This is not how business is done! We do not joke around. We do not make light of these situations. Do you not realize I will kill you? I will bring hell down to earth to destroy you."

I nodded. "Just a ray of sunshine, aren't you, Capo?"

"At least you respect your elders."

"Oh, sorry." I winced. "I wasn't saying it as a term of respect. I meant to say *Crappo*."

"Shit for brains," Vito mumbled. "And now you will die."

"Okay." I nodded. "You okay with that, Chase?"

"I'm good." He stood his ground. "Should I close my eyes or something?"

"Eyes open," Tex said from the chair. "It always goes better that way."

"Idiots!" Vito yelled.

"Where are all your men?" I asked in a calm voice. "A Capo? In the States? And you have what? Fifteen men?" I looked around the room. "Maybe less, since we just killed seven in under two minutes."

The men that were still standing behind Vito started looking around the room nervously.

"And by the looks of them, they're B-team at best. Not made men. Just associates. A made man wouldn't run out of a warehouse waving his gun all over the place. A made man wouldn't get close enough to a car to even be touched by a bomb."

Vito's eyes narrowed in hatred. "A twenty-million-dollar bounty causes some to question their loyalty. And apparently good news — or news about money — travels fast. I imagine my phone was ringing before you even hit end on the call. So I chose to go into hiding until I killed you. Seemed a more intelligent choice."

"Oh sorry." I lifted up my hands in surrender. "I wasn't

aware of your plan, but now that I am, I have to admit to something."

"What?" He waved his gun at me again.

I hadn't counted on him being terrified. Then again, he was old. He was on his way out. Twenty million did that to people. And the fact that the De Langes, the very family that he'd tried to control all those years ago, had ordered the hit? That meant the De Langes, the bottom of the totem pole, had risen to the top, which basically just made our families look like the toughest shit ever to hit Chicago.

And it made Vito defenseless.

All within twenty-four hours. We had successfully brought down an empire that should have never been erected in the first place. No man should have so much power; no man should think of himself as more than that — a mere man. A mortal, given the chance to share the same air that God used to breathe when he walked the earth.

Shouts filtered from the outside.

And then the doors opened.

Mo, Mil, Frank, Luca, and Trace — damn it. Trace. They were all being escorted very nicely into the warehouse, at gunpoint.

"Shit," I heard Chase mumble.

"A bit of a miscount?" Vito laughed.

We were outnumbered, not by a lot, but enough to sway the odds. If it turned into a gun fight, lives would be lost.

"Forty," I offered. "I'll give forty million dollars to the first person to hit the bull's-eye."

"He's bluffing!" Vito shouted! A vein pulsated across his forehead. "He's a lying prick! The Abandonatos stole my son!" He began pacing. "I just want him back! All I want is my son back, and I'll leave. I'll leave! No more killing. My old heart, it just can't—"

"Lies," Tex spat, pushing away from the chair and approaching his father. "Say my name."

"No."

"Afraid of a little curse?"

"For the last time, it is not real!"

"Vito Nicio Campisi, Junior," a female voice said from behind me. It was too late before I realized it was Mil. I yelled as Vito raised his gun, directing it at her head. She stood firm.

The warehouse doors burst open again, and what can only be described as a miracle took place, as men I'd never seen before in my life poured in. Most of them looked like they'd seen better days. But there were sixty of them. And they were heavily armed.

"Hey, Joe." Mil shrugged. "What took you so long?"

"Oh, you know." He cocked his gun. "Vegas traffic."

"No!" Vito fired.

Chase yelled and ran in Mil's direction then fell to the ground in a heap. More gunshots rang out. I ran toward Trace, but paused when she pulled out her own gun and started firing at Vito's men.

I hated how turned on I was at the sight.

Within seconds, it was all over with. No lives lost on our side — at least… not yet.

CHAPTER FORTY-SEVEN

Chase

I'd always wondered what it would be like — to sacrifice yourself so another person could live. It wasn't like I was morbid or anything, but in my line of work it was just a daily reality. You don't work for the mafia and not think about it. Death was at your door constantly. Shit, it practically camped there.

I just thought it would come knocking a little bit later in life, you know? Every muscle in my body tensed as the second gunshot rang out.

Funny, how at the end of your life, you think about the beginning. Even crazier? It was her smile that had first attracted me to her. The way her entire face lit up, the way her eyes said she'd eat me alive if I didn't watch it. Damn, but so many things had changed over the course of a few weeks.

I don't even know how it happened, how she'd maneuvered her way into my soul, how she'd made it so that I was overcome with madness for her — a type of obsession that I never wanted to be done with. She had destroyed me, and in my destruction, I'd found my salvation.

I touched my chest and examined my fingers. My blood was wet and sticky. Slowly, I fell to my knees. I heard shouting around me but it seemed to come from far away. A foreign grunt came from my lips as my body slumped against the ground. Nixon came running, then Trace, and finally *her*, my tough as shit, Mil.

My wife.

And now... a widow.

"I'm s-sorry." My breaths were coming in sharp, as if there was too much pressure on my lungs to breathe. Every gasp hurt like the fires of hell. I was getting choked by the pressure in my chest, pushing and tearing, just waiting to pull me into the fiery pit.

"Don't talk. You're going to be fine, Chase, you have to be fine!" Mil pressed her hand hard over mine. Tears splashed onto my chest — her tears. "Damn it, Chase! Fight!'

"It's not cold..." I sighed happily as the pain started to dissipate leaving me in a state of shock. "It's so warm." And it was. Death was warm, not cold as I'd always thought.

Mil slapped me hard across the cheek. "And it's gonna get hotter than hell if you don't listen to me. You have to fight, Chase Winter. I refuse to live without you."

"Okay." I smiled. I would have probably rolled my eyes too but moving anything more seemed too much of an effort. She would be fine. She was a fighter, after all. "Love you..." And then I succumbed to the blackness of my warm death. At least I knew, in those last few seconds, that for once in my life, I would have done nothing different.

Because every damn road had led me to *her*.

"Chase!" Something pounded on my chest. Shit, that hurt. I blinked a few times, thinking I'd really lost my mind when my wife stood over me without a shirt on, clad only in her bra and jeans, holding something to my side. Damn, my side hurt — and my chest. It felt like someone was sitting on it.

"Move," another voice said.

"But he'll bleed out!" Nixon snapped.

Damn right! I wanted to shout. *Listen to Nixon! It's not a flesh wound!* I felt my body weakening from blood loss.

"I'm a doctor," Joe snapped.

I would have laughed had I had the energy.

The room fell silent, or at least it felt like it.

Joe, or whoever he was, grabbed something and wrapped it around my leg; it was so tight I winced, or I think I winced. And then he started talking in Sicilian about alcohol and something else about lifting my body and not letting me stand because then I would bleed out. Wow, thanks genius, I appreciated that.

"Shit!" I wailed.

Oh, wow! So I wasn't dead. I was able to yell. "Shit. Shit. Shit. Shit." Let's not over-do it. "Damn it!" My body hurt like hell. I'd been shot before, but never like this. What the hell type of poison did that man dip his bullets into? It felt like my body was getting ripped apart.

"We can't take him to a hospital." Nixon looked freaked.

Should I be freaked too?

I blinked a few times and mouthed, *"It's okay."* Or at least I think I did.

Joe snorted. "Some of us don't live and breathe the mafia and have to make a living somehow, you asses."

I wanted to give him a high five but figured it would probably be the death of me — literally.

Somehow, I was floating in the air. Oh shit, just don't go into the light. I almost puked as I was carried into a car. I nearly shit my pants when the lights turned on because I thought I was getting called home. It didn't help that the heater was blasting so it felt like the fires of hell were licking my heels, just waiting for me with bated breath.

"Hold on," Mil whispered near my ear. "Please, Chase, please God, just hold on, can you do that?"

"Yes," I whispered hoarsely. "Love you, Mil."

"Love you too." And then she leaned down and whispered in my ear. "My savior."

CHAPTER FORTY-EIGHT

Tex

He was dead.

My father was dead.

And my best friend was getting a hands-on demonstration of why the game of Operation was scary as hell.

"How are you holding up?" Nixon asked, handing me a cup of coffee. Chase had been in surgery for four hours already. Somehow my bastard of a father had missed his first shot at Mil, but had succeeded in hitting Chase three times. Once in the lower back, dangerously close to his kidneys, one through the side, and another through the left shoulder. Had it been any closer to his heart, and he would have died instantly.

"I'm fantastic." I took the coffee. "Just another day in paradise."

"Please don't start singing." He sat down next to me. "I'd probably end up punching you in the face."

"Sorry…" I muttered. "…lover."

"Do you ever quit?"

"No." I sighed. "I'm cursed for a reason."

"You aren't cursed." Nixon swore. "You just talk so much I want to put duct tape over your mouth."

"Sure came in handy during my captivity."

"Did you... um..." Nixon lowered his voice as Mil looked over at us with tear-stained eyes. "...find out any more information?"

"Not from Vito." I couldn't call him father now. Not even in my head. He'd almost killed my best friend. Besides, it was unfair to give him the respect of that name when his own son was the person who had pulled the trigger.

I'd knocked him over and turned his own gun on him. He'd damned me to hell, and I'd told him he'd be there in a few seconds. I pulled the trigger twice.

I wanted to empty the gun into the bastard, but I'd heard Mil's scream and I'd known they needed me. The life had left my father, and I'd like to imagine that the world — our world — had finally gotten to him. He'd finally cracked and lost control; he'd started becoming careless and had thought himself a deity, when in all reality, maybe he'd just wanted to get caught, maybe he'd wanted someone to end his miserable existence. After all, you can only live and kill for so long, until you want to be in the cold wet ground.

"Joe was some help." I sniffed. After Joe had explained to the doctors about our *hunting accident,* he'd sat in the corner and spilled his guts.

They had been desperate. The feds were sniffing around, offering them deals if they'd give information on the other families.

And then the feds had discovered the prostitution ring.

"It was bad." I sighed. "Most girls who went through The Cave didn't make it out alive. The ones who did were sold to the highest bidder and usually dead within the first year. They were all underage — it was why they earned so much money. Underage girls earned more than older women."

"Sick bastards," Nixon muttered under his breath.

"It gets worse." I flinched and explained. "My father helped them get the girls. He wasn't just finding them off the streets. He was taking them from some of the more prominent families in Italy and then offering them for ransom. If the family could afford the payoff, the girl would be raped and returned. If not, then the girl was sold. The De Langes used it as a way to earn back the money they'd lost."

"Why would Vito help?"

"He took the girls from families who refused to pay for the protection of the Campisi family. It was to teach them a lesson. Then he'd look like the hero when he returned the girl. Then he'd ask them to keep making their payments. *After all,* he'd say, *it's a dangerous world.*"

"Did Joe try to get out?"

I looked around the corner at Joe, who was sitting next to Mil. "He says the minute Mil's father told him everything he threatened to come to one of the families."

"And?"

"His wife was found dead the next day. Suicide."

Nixon swore. "When will it end?"

I shook my head. "Who knows? But at least the monster is gone. Cut off the head…"

"Let's hope he was the head." Nixon nodded. "Otherwise, I imagine more nights like this. We need a vacation."

At that I laughed. "Since when was the last time you took a vacation? Try never. Do you even know what that means? And you can't bring your gun."

"I know." His eyes were trained on Trace. I wanted to look away, but I couldn't. Jealously flared to life. Not because of Trace, but because of Mo. I could never have her, and she could never know the real reason. I truly believed myself to be cursed. After all, my father's blood ran through my veins. That alone made me scum to her. And she deserved more than that;

any future children deserved more than that. I was killing the bad seed. Cutting off my own head. I wasn't going to get married. I refused to have children. It wasn't happening. It just... it wasn't.

"I think I may try it."

"Try what?" I asked, lost in my own thoughts of Mo and how sexy she'd look in a wedding dress.

"A vacation."

I rolled my eyes.

Nixon smacked me in the arm. "I'm serious. But I think it will be more of a honeymoon."

"Huh?"

"We are in Vegas," he muttered then got up and walked over to Trace.

Hmm.

CHAPTER FORTY-NINE

Mil

I wanted to smack Chase on the head then kiss him senseless. I was trying to figure out which one to do first when his eyes flickered open.

"Hey," he said in a hoarse voice. "Stop eye-screwing me. I'm in a hospital bed and defenseless. Show a little decorum." His smile was loving as he reached out his hand.

I took it in mine. And burst into tears.

"Aw, baby." He pulled me close. "Come here."

"You almost died!"

"I told you I would take a bullet for you."

"Not funny. You took three!" I sniffled. "You hear that, Chase?" I smacked his arm. "Not funny, damn it!"

"Ouch!" He rubbed his arm. "I did almost die!"

I started sobbing all over again.

"Too soon?" He winced.

"You think?" I wiped my tears and tried to lie down next to him without pulling out his IV. Those things always freaked me out. Blood freaked me out, but only my own.

"What can I do to make it better?" He kissed my hair. "I could sing you a song, but I have a crap voice."

"Are you on a morphine drip?" I asked.

"Don't be sad, don't you cry..." Chase started singing. "Wait, I forgot the words."

"Because it's not a real song, and you're high."

"I feel no pain!" He pumped his fist in the air. "Well, that's not true. Physically I feel no pain, and yes, for some stupid reason I want to sing to you. What can I say? It sounds like a good idea. But my heart..." He sighed. "Damn, it hurts."

"Should I call the doctor?" I started to get up, but he pulled me gently back into the curve of his warm body.

"No, I think I know the cure."

"What?" I whispered.

"You." His eyes fluttered closed. "I never want to be without you again, okay? And I swear, I'm getting you a damn bulletproof vest after today."

"That would look too obvious."

"I'll freaking wrap you in bubble tape with a bulletproof vest. I don't care if you look like a circus freak." Chase snorted. "I can't lose you."

"You were the one who almost left me..." I cupped his face. "I'm just glad you're okay."

"Fine." He yawned, his eyes still closed. I traced his strong jaw then dipped my hands into his dark shaggy hair. Even on a hospital bed, he looked like a freaking underwear model with tattoos. "I saw your face."

"What?"

"I didn't want to go toward the light." His brow furrowed. "But I kept seeing your face, and I told myself I would die trying to reach it."

A few tears streamed down my face before I could wipe them away. "I'm glad you succeeded."

"Me too."

We lay in silence until his breathing deepened. I knew he

needed his sleep. He'd only gotten out of surgery a few hours before, but I hadn't been able to wait to see him. He was my life — the other part of my soul. I never imagined love would feel like this — it was wrecking me. Making me feel like I wasn't the same person I'd been a few weeks ago.

I kissed his forehead and laughed. "Some honeymoon."

"Viva Las Vegas," he whispered hoarsely, lifting his fist into the air. I rolled my eyes and bumped it.

"Sleep."

"Will you be here when I wake up?"

"Always." I swore. "I will always be there when you open your eyes."

"Good." He smiled, eyes still closed, and drifted off to sleep again.

"How is he?" a male voice said behind me.

I knew it was Nixon, just from the way the air stirred around me; he had a way of causing tension to build in a room until you wanted to slam your head against the wall.

"Tired." I cleared my throat.

"Can we talk?"

"Depends." I turned around and stuffed my hands in my jeans pockets. "Are you planning on threatening me or shooting me again?"

Nixon's face broke out into a gorgeous smile, his white teeth sparkling against his dark skin and lip ring. I almost took a step back. I'd only ever seen him save his smiles for Trace, and now that I'd received one, I kind of wanted to keep it forever. It changed his entire demeanor.

"Come here," he whispered.

Slowly I walked over to the door.

In an instant I was in his arms. He was hugging me tight. After the shock wore off, I was able to relax in his bulky frame. He towered over me. I laid my head against his chest and sighed, feeling the need to cry a bit.

"I'm sorry, Mil." he said gruffly. "I know my methods

may seem a bit insane and harsh, but I needed you to step up, and you did it beautifully. Can you forgive me?"

"Y-yes," I stuttered, holding back the tears.

"Mil..." Nixon pulled away from me and started shifting on his feet, his eyes flickering to the floor while he sucked nervously on his lip ring. "There's something I need to give you."

"What?"

"I don't know how..." Nixon smiled sadly. "Maybe I don't want to know. But Phoenix, he, um, he left some things for you. I didn't know he was the type to keep a journal, but in it, he wrote an entry almost like a letter to you. I ripped it out so you could have it. I thought... I thought maybe it would give you closure."

He pulled out a piece of paper and handed it to me. "You need to know one thing, Mil."

I took the paper and clenched it in my hands.

"He would have been so damn proud of you." Nixon shook his head, his eyes pooling with tears. "He wasn't right in the end. Not in the end. But he wanted so badly to make things better. He wanted a life for you, wanted to protect you. The things he saw... He couldn't block them out, Mil. I truly believe God granted him peace for the first time in twenty-one years when he finally took him home. I believe men like Phoenix, ones who do bad things then ask for forgiveness, I believe they're granted it. We all make mistakes. We all have ugly within us. We're all capable of acting out in the darkness. What sets people like Phoenix apart is, the moment it truly matters, they finally choose light, and in that moment, their souls are redeemed."

Tears blurred my vision.

Nixon pulled me toward him again, kissing my forehead. "Don't doubt that he's resting in peace — I know for a fact he is. Heaven isn't reserved for people like Vito, ones who think themselves a god. It's reserved for the broken, the humbled, the ugly, the unlovely, who finally see in themselves what God had made them capable of when he created them — greatness."

I nodded. Words weren't really coming, and I was shocked that Nixon knew me that well — knew that my mind was still conjuring up images of Phoenix living in that type of atmosphere, day in and day out, with no escape in sight. And then to discover that his little sister, step or not, was going to be sold to someone? All in the name of what? Money? Greed?

Nixon nodded and walked out of the room, leaving me alone with a sleeping Chase and a note that was burning a hole through my hand.

I closed the door to the room and walked over to the chair. With shaking hands, I opened the journal entry.

> *I can't protect her anymore. I want to. But I can't. I don't know what the hell to do. Mil, if you're reading this, you're either a sneaky bitch, or I'm dead. What other reason would you have to go through my stuff? You'd want clues. You'd want to know about our family's history even though I've sent you as much information as I can without getting totally blacklisted.*
>
> *It sucks.*
>
> *Life sucks.*
>
> *I'd die happy if I knew you were happy. Funny, I'd always thought of myself as being a purely selfish individual, until my father married your mother. Then this fierceness took over, this desire to shield you from the ugly of the world. Your fifth birthday you wanted a pony and got yelled at for being such a child. Remember? Later that day, I asked Nixon if Mo had any old pony toys. She did, of course, because the girl was obsessed with horses, just like you. I wrapped up two ponies and put them under your pillow.*
>
> *For five years I did that.*
>
> *Five years you had ponies under your pillow. You*

were devastated when you turned ten and found out that there was no such thing as a pony fairy.

I wanted to keep you innocent like that.

I wanted you to always believe in the pony fairy. Funny, because when you discovered it was me — your eyes were as big as saucers, almost like I was your hero, when I knew I would end up being the exact opposite. Things with Dad were getting progressively worse, the nightmares, The Cave. All of it. It made me sick.

And then a girl was brought into the cave who looked just like you.

I lost my shit.

I beat Father within an inch of his life.

That's when I knew I would have to kill him. I went to Tony Abandonato for help. You know what he did? He sold me out.

I would never be free.

But I knew one day you would. I know I'm getting off track here, but I guess... wow, if I could say a few last words. What would I want to say? Most people don't get to plan their own funeral, and I know this is depressing as hell. But my wish? My desire? Is that you find a man crazy enough to put ponies under your pillow. A guy that loves you just as you are, a guy that makes you laugh with your whole body. Someone who would sing you a song, just because he thought it would bring a smile to your face. A man that would take a bullet for you.

I saved the white horse for last.

It's somewhere in my room. Who knows if it's even there anymore? I could be eighty, and you could be reading this now. At any rate. I figured the white horse would be last. For when you got married. I'd give it to the lucky bastard as a joke then punch him in the face for sleeping with my sister.

I hope you found him, sis. I hope you found someone

who would make you happy. And I hope you find peace. Spending your life trying to find light within the darkness isn't in vain — it's why we have hope. When you've lost hope, you have nothing. I lost mine awhile ago. I hope to God you still have yours—

Phoenix.

The sobs started heaving so hard that I couldn't control the whimpers coming from my throat. I hugged my knees to my chest and rocked back and forth. He'd died too young. He'd made so many mistakes. But he'd wanted — he'd wanted so much for me.

"Mil?" Chase whispered. "Are you okay? Sweetheart? Are you crying?"

He flinched as he pushed himself up onto his elbows and then reached out a hand.

I didn't need to be asked twice. I launched myself into his arms and sobbed against his chest. I told him about the letter.

And Chase, my Chase, after a few minutes of silence said, "I'm going to find that damn white horse if it's the last thing I do."

I laughed. So did he. And it felt good to laugh. It felt good to be free. I said a prayer for Phoenix. A prayer of thanks — a prayer of love.

CHAPTER FIFTY

Nixon

I fidgeted with my tie and slapped Tex's hands away as I fixed my hair. I looked like a total idiot. A black suit? What the hell had I been thinking?

"You look hot." Tex nodded. "She'll totally marry you in this."

"You're not helping."

Tex grinned.

"Ready?" Mo clapped, looking right through Tex to me.

"Yes. I think." I started pacing. "What if she thinks it's a terrible idea?"

"She won't," Mo said while Tex said, "She may."

"Nixon?" Mil walked into the waiting room. "I think everything's ready to go."

"Thanks, Mil." I was relieved the tension was gone between us. Well, as gone as tension can be when you've shot at the person your best friend married. Whoops. "Is Chase ready?"

Mil saluted. "Clothed in his best-man clothes and

grinning like a fool."

"Damn morphine."

"He uh…" Mil's eyes bore into mine. "He forwent his pain meds this last hour. He wanted to remember everything."

"I bet he did." I laughed. "Okay, let's do this."

I went into the small hospital chapel, followed by Mil and Tex. Mo was on Trace-duty. She'd lied to Trace and told her we were going out to a really nice dinner. She'd even taken her to a stylist so she could pick out a kick-ass dress. My way of apologizing, again, for a vacation that had ended up in bloodshed.

"Why are we here again?" Trace's voice echoed down the hall.

"Oh, I thought we should say goodbye to everyone. They decided to hang out with Chase since he's so bored."

"Chase gets bored all the time. What else is new? And did they move his room?"

Chase chuckled from the front pew.

"Here they are!" The doors to the chapel burst open.

Mo may have overdone it with the surprise in her voice, but it was all worth it to see Trace's face. Her eyes narrowed in on the flowers filling the room, and then she looked at Mil, dressed in a pink flowing dress, Chase dressed in a tux, Tex in a tux, and then me.

"What's going on? Are we all going to dinner or something? And why are we in a church? Oh my gosh." Her face paled, "Chase, you're okay, right?"

"Ready?" Luca cleared his throat ignoring Trace. He walked to the front and held out a Bible.

Really, it was shocking that he was allowed to even hold a Bible, let alone conduct a ceremony. Then again, my whole life I'd played by the rules. I'd bled for them. I'd fought for them. For once, I wanted to break them. I was going to break Catholic tradition. I was going to break the whole long engagement tradition, and I was going to marry my lover, my best friend, in a hospital, with one of the scariest men I'd ever known conducting the ceremony.

"Do you have the rings?" he asked.

"Rings?" Trace whispered, her lower lip trembling.

"You did say yes." I stalked toward her. "Didn't you?"

She nodded her head, a solitary tear streaming down her right cheek. I caught it. I would catch every tear. Every piece of sadness. I'd catch — and never release.

"I want to marry you," I whispered. "Here. Right now."

"But that's so romantic!"

Chase burst out laughing. I turned around and glared. He held up his hands in surrender. Damn it, where was my gun?

"I found a little romance." I winked.

Trace took my outstretched arm and walked with me, but I held up my finger. "Frank?"

"Here." He stepped into the chapel. "Sorry I was late." He had tears brimming at the corners of his eyes as he held out his hands to Trace. "Now, I believe it's time to escort my favorite granddaughter down the aisle."

Trace ran into his arms and hugged him. He kissed her cheek and embraced her. "Your grandmother would be so proud."

"She'd be proud of both of us." Trace stepped back and looped her arm in his. "Now we're ready."

Luca grinned. "Who has the rings?"

"I do." Chase's voice was loud — clear — strong. He stood from the pew and slowly walked over to Trace's side. He still wasn't a hundred percent, but he swore he could make it a few feet without breaking any stitches. He wanted to do this. He was part of her life too. And I would never deny him that, no matter how many times his love for her had almost destroyed me.

"Trace." Chase reached for her hands. "I wanted to give you away." He looked behind her to Frank and sighed. "But it seems I was beat." He grinned. "I wanted to give you away because I love you. You helped me realize what love was. Being your best friend, being with you — it prepared me for Mil. For my wife. I love you with my whole heart. I love Nixon too. Never in a million years would I have guessed that this is how our story would end. But it's better than I could have ever imagined. I'm so damn proud of the woman you've become, the man you make Nixon be. So I bless you, on your wedding day." He kissed her right cheek, then her left. "May you have many more years filled with love, happiness, laughter…" He laughed. "…and wine. Lots of wine."

"Here, here." Mo cheered.

Trace hugged Chase tight and kissed him back on the cheek. He walked back over to Mil and kissed her full on the mouth.

Our story was evidence that sometimes when you try to write it yourself, you get stuck. You can't see every possible outcome. Maybe that's why it's better to let life happen — because sometimes it surprises you.

"Do you, Trace Alfero, take Nixon Abandonato to be your loving husband from this day forward, in sickness and health, through gunfire and hell—"

I shot a glare to an amused Luca.

"—for as long as you both shall live?"

"Yes," Trace whispered. "Even through gunfire."

Her wink about had me mauling her.

"And Nixon." Luca cleared his throat. "Do you take this woman, from this day forward, in sickness and health, through gunfire, hell, your terrible moods, inability to calm your temper and—"

I put up my hand; he winked.

"—for as long as you both shall live?"

"Forever. I take her for as many lifetimes as she'll give me."

"Then, by the power vested in me by the Internet and the lovely state of Nevada, I now pronounce you man and wife.

You may kiss your—"

I drowned him out.

Her. I just wanted to kiss her. Love her. Be hers.

Trace wrapped her arms around my neck and sighed.

"So, Mrs. Abandonato." I licked my lips. "How's that for romance?"

"You're getting better." She teased. "What's next?"

"Dinner." I shot her a smug smile. "And then who knows? Maybe a nice long vacation."

"Amen," Luca muttered under his breath.

CHAPTER FIFTY-ONE

Tex

"What crawled up your ass and died?" Chase threw a tennis ball at my face and winked.

"I'm here providing entertainment to your poor broken body, and you're making fun of me?" I taunted, throwing the ball harder, not to hurt him. No, I just wanted to warn him not to mess with me.

"Whoa there." Chase chuckled. "Low blood sugar? Grouchy because you need food? The girls will be here soon. Do you need like a cracker or something?"

"Stop talking."

"Wow, you know something's wrong when the kettle's pissed about its own color."

"Dude—"

"And a dude comment?" Chase's eyebrows rose as he threw the ball back at me.

I was seriously going to abandon my Good Samaritan nature and actually lose my shit for the first time in years if he didn't stop poking me.

"I'm just tired." I'd been tired for months. Ever since Mo had broken my heart by actually walking away when I told her it was what was best. I'd figured she'd fight for me. I'd figured she'd at least yell and throw a fit and tell me that she wasn't going anywhere.

But she'd walked away.

She'd actually listened to me. She'd done the smart thing for once in her life. The one time I'd wanted someone — no, needed someone — to shut the hell up. And she'd easily left.

When I heard her crying in her room, I'd wanted to make it better.

So I'd brought over girl after girl in hopes that instead of being sad — she'd hate me. I wanted her hate. Craved it like a man starving in the desert. If I couldn't have her love, I wanted her hate, because at least it was something. And now... now she wouldn't even look at me. It was as if I didn't exist, as if *we* didn't exist.

"It's hunger." I nodded. "And sleep deprivation."

"You aren't smiling." Chase pointed out.

"Hunger should make me smile?"

"No." He shrugged. "But you always smile when you complain. You avert your eyes when you lie. So what gives?"

Damn him.

"Nothing." I smiled.

"Nicely played." Chase threw the ball back to me as we fell into a comfortable silence.

"Food is here!" Mil announced, walking into the hospital room with a bag of food that made my stomach grumble. She'd been sporting sweats all week, since she'd been staying with Chase every single damn night.

It pissed me off how easily they'd fallen for each other — how easy it seemed for them. Everyone had someone; everyone was blissfully happy. So yeah, I felt a bit like bawling black sheep. Sue me.

The smell of marinara floated through the air. Thank

God. I needed something to distract me from wanting to bang my head against the wall. Maybe I should be the one taking an extended vacation. I deserved it. But Luca had told me I needed to stay in the country while the rest of the families figured out what was going to happen to Campisi's empire — my empire. Was I the boss? Had I been reinstated as the son? Was my mother even alive? She'd fallen off the face of the planet since that fateful night.

I hated that, while the drama of Nixon, Chase, and Mil was all solved, my puzzle had just gotten more difficult. Scratch that. The pieces had been freaking mailed to the Seven Wonders of the World, and I'd been left trying to put together a puzzle without a stupid box to look at for guidance.

I froze, letting the ball drop to the floor. It bounced toward the door. Mo would be coming through that door any minute. I could feel it.

I knew she was following the food because the minute the smell of pasta dissipated, the smell of her apple perfume filled the air. I closed my eyes. I just had to smile. Smile and pretend like I'm careless. Play the part, be Tex — fun-loving, idiotic Tex — who doesn't have a care in the world.

Right.

I could play dumb.

I'd been doing it all my life.

I got off the floor and started helping Mil take the food out of the boxes. My hand touched a few paper plates and was instantly covered by one I'd memorized for hours.

Her hand.

I knew every crevice, the arch of her palm, the feminine curve of her thumb. Damn, I memorized things for a living, and I'd done a fair share of memorizing her. I could tell from the softness of her skin if she was out of lotion, or if she'd gotten less sleep by the darkness of circles under her eyes. I knew exactly how many eyelashes she had on any given day, give or take two.

Obsessed? I was a man living for one thing. Monroe Abandonato. And she hated me. She wasn't alone in that. I hated me.

"Tex?" Mo chewed her lower lip. She had purple circles under her eyes, and her hand was clammy.

"Are you sick?" It was out of my mouth before I could do anything about it. I felt her forehead. She didn't feel warm, but something about her was off. Her eyes looked glassy like she'd been crying, and her body looked frail. "Why aren't you eating?"

"Stop." She forced a smile. "Stop analyzing me."

I'd forgotten how much she hated that. "Sorry."

"Come with me for a second?"

"Sure." I followed her out of the hospital room. I told myself it was wrong to watch her hips as they swayed — it would be better if my memory wasn't so photographic. I'd be replaying images of her ass in those jeans all week long. Damn it.

Mo stopped at one of the abandoned waiting rooms and sat down, leaning forward so her elbows were on her thighs.

I knelt down so I was on eye level. "Mo? What's wrong?"

Tears streamed down her face; she wiped them away with shaking hands. "I just had to be sure. I mean, I had to... be sure, you know?"

"Sure of what?"

"Because it happens all the time to girls. They get stressed and—"

"Mo—" I took her face in my hands. "What are you trying to tell me?"

Her eyes closed. She wouldn't even look at me. "I'm pregnant."

My world stopped. Not what I expected. My stomach rolled, and my heart started hammering against my chest. We'd always, and I do mean always, used protection. I'd never put her in that position. Logically I couldn't explain it.

"I need you to pretend it's yours," she whispered, and then fell into full-on sobs against my chest.

"Pretend?" I choked out. "What do you mean *pretend?*"

"It was one guy!" She shook. "One guy, one night. I was mad at you, too drunk. I was so angry you'd left me. So, so angry—" She started trembling in my arms and I knew. I would protect her until my dying day. But first? I had a bastard to go kill.

I shouldn't have given in so easily. But love has a way of making you do crazy things. So in that hospital waiting room, with the love of my life in my arms, I said in a choked voice, "Okay."

EPILOGUE

Nixon

"Admit it." I kissed the top of Trace's forehead. "It was romantic."

She turned in my arms, her naked body sliding against mine as she straddled me, her hair falling in a current across her face. "Fine. I'll admit it."

"All you have to do is say the words." I put my hands behind my head and smirked.

"You suck."

"Say it."

"You're a romantic sex god with mafia mojo."

"And that…" I smacked her ass. "…is what you get for saying I lacked in the romance department when I hired Luca to marry us."

"He tried to kill you," she said through clenched teeth. "I apologize if I don't find your killer marrying us romantic."

"It's pretty bad ass when you think about it." I shrugged. "Like your husband."

"This marriage isn't big enough for you and your ego."

"Guess that means you'll have to go..." My voice died off.

Trace smacked me in the arm then reached for her gun on the nightstand.

"Have I ever told you how hot it is when you point a gun at me? No?"

She put the gun down and kissed me instead. Much better. We'd decided to honeymoon in Vegas for the next week and plan an escape vacation in another month, once things had settled a bit with Tex and his situation with the Campisi family. The way it looked was that one of us was going to have to go to Sicily for an extended stay.

At the sharp pounding on the door, I clenched my fists and yelled, "Go away!"

They knocked harder.

Grumbling, I got out of bed, threw on a bathrobe, and pulled open the door. Chase was standing there as if he'd just seen a ghost.

"What? What's wrong?"

"Tex and Mo." He shook his head. "They're gone."

ELICIT
Eagle Elite Book 4

Elicit: *To evoke or draw out (a response or an answer or fact) from someone in reaction to one's own actions or questions. Example: A corrupt heart elicits in an hour all that is bad in us.*

PROLOGUE

Tex

Rage consumed me as I looked around the building. A sea of familiar faces stared right through me. It was as if the past twenty-five years of my life meant nothing at all.

Had I been nothing to them?

Nothing but a joke.

The reality of my situation hit me full force as I fought to suck in even long breaths of the stale dusty air.

"It is your choice," the voice said in an even steady tone, piercing the air with its finality.

"Wrong." I stared at the cement floor, the muted color of

gray was stained with spots of blood, "If I'd had a choice, I would have chosen to die in the womb. I would have drowned myself when I was three. I would have shot myself when I had the chance. You've given me no damn choice, and you know it."

"You do not fear death?" the voice mocked.

Slowly, my head rose, I locked eyes with Mo and whispered, "It's life. Life scares the hell out of me."

A single tear fell from her chin and in that moment I knew what I had to do. After all, life was about choices. And I was about to make mine. Without hesitation. I grabbed the gun from my back pocket, pointed it at Mo and pulled the trigger.

With a gasp she fell to the ground. A bullet grazed my shoulder as I knelt taking time to reach for my semi-automatic from underneath my pant leg. When I stood, I let loose a string of ammo, the sound of it hitting cement, brick, bodies, chairs, filled me with more peace than I'd had in a lifetime of war.

I stalked toward him, the man I was going to kill, the man who had made me feel like my existence meant nothing. I held the gun to his chest and squeezed the trigger, and when he collapsed in front of me, it was with a smile on his face, his eyes still open in amusement.

Chaos reigned around me and then suddenly, everything stopped.

When I turned it was to see at least twenty dead, and Nixon staring at me like he didn't know me at all — but maybe he never had. And wasn't that a bitch.

He took a step forward his hand in the air, "Tex—"

"No." I smirked. "Not Tex. To you?" I pointed the gun and pulled the trigger. "I'm the Capo."

Part One: A Rise to Power
CHAPTER ONE

Two weeks before the incident...

Tex

"No! No! Stop!" Mo tossed and turned in her sleep, her arms flying around the bed as if she was trying to punch someone — though really she was only landing blows to the air.

With a sigh I grabbed her fists as gently as I could and woke her up. "Mo, you were dreaming."

Her long lashes blinked against her skin a few times, possibly clearing out the images that had just haunted her rest. "Sorry." Her glance fell to my hands as they held her wrists midair. Mo jerked away from me and moved to the side of the bed. "It was just a bad dream."

My touch used to comfort her. She used to crave it. At least I thought she did. It had always been about me and Mo. We were a team, a dysfunctional one, but a team's a team right?

"It's okay," I lied; it was absolutely not okay that she wanted nothing to do with me, that she was scared of me, that she was pregnant and I'd done everything within my power to make it easy on her — even when every day it was harder on me. "Just go back to sleep, things will look better in the morning."

But they wouldn't. She knew it. I knew it. Hell, everyone who knew us and our family knew it. Things never looked better in the morning.

Actually, I preferred night. Not because I actually enjoyed sleeping — hell, if I didn't need sleep I wouldn't do it. Too many images ran through my mind, pictures of death, blood, more death. But the real messed up part? I wasn't haunted by the dreams like Mo was — no, I was the exact opposite. It inspired me, it drove me, it motivated me. Hell, I was the one you'd least expect. Chase even had problems doing some of the dirty work.

But me?

I was the worst type of person.

Because I craved it like a drug.

I craved death. I craved war. I craved it like an addict. And I loathed the days of peace because they reminded me that I was basically an orphan. Unwanted, unloved, and now? Unloved by the girl I'd sworn to love for the rest of my life.

So sugarplums? Santa? Unicorns? Sheep? Nah, that shit didn't fit in my dreams.

It never did.

Mo moved next to me pulling the covers up around her frail body. She'd been losing so much weight it was ridiculous. Weren't you supposed to gain weight when you were pregnant? It stung that she didn't want me to go to her doctor's appointment with her. Apparently he'd said she was stressed. Right, like I could do anything to help that. I was doing everything within my power to fix things — to fix us — to fix her — to fix the family. Nothing worked.

Being with Mo wasn't just my peace, it was like I'd finally found someone that got me, someone who understood who I was, even when I chose not to reveal my whole self to her, one look, and I knew she knew. All the shit that went on in my head, but she didn't pester me, didn't make me explain anything, just loved me as I was. And now, it was gone. I was gone. There was literally nothing left.

My role was no longer fulfilling its purpose. I'd known it for a while now, but I hadn't wanted to admit it. But the signs were clear.

It was time to take my place. Time to bring the nightmare to life, to wake the beast, to be what I was born to be.

Vito Campisi's son.

RACHEL VAN DYKEN
Books

Made in the USA
Charleston, SC
05 June 2014